The Shopping Cart Man

A Yuletide Journey

By
Douglas V. Nufer

While some events in this book are inspired by actual observations of events in the real world, those events have been altered so as to make this book a complete work of fiction. Likewise, no character in this book is based on any one, specific person.

Doug Nufer is the author of several novels and short stories, including the published novel, "The Title of Liberty." He enjoys speaking on his works, and the topics they address, and can be reached via Peepsock Press, e-mail (info@peepsockpress.com), or at the following website: www.PeepsockPress.com

**PEEPSOCK
PRESS**
P.O. Box 51082
Provo, UT 84605

The cover art of "Old Bessie" was created for "The Shopping Cart Man" by Ken Corbett. See more of Ken's works on the Web and wherever fine art is sold.
Cover art photographed by Scott Hancock.
Cover layout by Scott Corfield.
Peepsock Press logo by Todd Purser.

Printed in the United States of America.

10 9 8 7 6 5 4 3

To the anonymous, homeless gentleman who unknowingly taught this author that not all those seeking money are trying to buy beer. May he and his unknown female companion find more generous and less critical benefactors in the future, and the means to purchase more substantial meals.

If this work prompts just one more person to seek after being a modern day Good Samaritan, then all of the efforts to bring it to print will have been worthwhile.

Acknowledgements

Many thanks to friends, family and countless others who do good deeds without recognition or reward. Keep it up, the world needs you!

This work could not have been completed without the contributions of several wonderful people who have contributed in the editing of text and story content for this novel. In particular, special thanks go to Richard May, Ken Nufer, Buck Gashler, Trish Blanchard, Jan Holman, Sandy Tuckett (who managed to get a character named after her), my parents, Harold and Marian Nufer, and my dear wife Teresa, who puts up with me on a daily basis and offers sound insights.

A round of thanks also goes to our kids, Jonathon, Holly, Merissa, Hannah and Josh, who have traveled thousands of miles, in seemingly endless road trips, to visit family and friends around the country. The trips just wouldn't be the same without them!

Special thanks go to Ken Corbett for the beautiful painting for the cover. I remain impressed and indebted to his talent and generosity.

Chapter 1
The Journey Begins

The load on top of their station wagon was a thing to behold. It was a mass of gray canvas bound together by length after length of thick nylon rope. Each length was carefully and securely wound around an edge or corner of the roof rack, and then pulled tightly – oh, so very tightly!

The brownish-gray '75 station wagon was already five years old, but kept in fine working order. Its proud owner, Frank, was a man who was just a year into his thirties. He would force the end of the rope between the rack and the tarp and then pull very hard on the rope, sometimes stepping on the length while pulling upward with his arms, using his foot as a sort of pulley to get the rope as tight as he possibly could. Then, holding the rope as taut and near to the rack as he could, he would do a double loop through the edge of the roof rack. With this in place, he would flick the loose end over the mass on the station wagon's roof and holler for his boy to "Catch hold of it!"

Luke, an amiable 11-year-old, stood with both hands raised high above his head, his fingers frantically outstretched, hoping to be helpful. Invariably, the rope would manage to fling past his hands and flop down across his head, draping itself unceremoniously down his front and back and lying uselessly on the driveway.

"Did you get it?" his dad, Frank, asked.

"Yeah, I got it!" Luke replied.

He grabbed at the rope with his right hand and pulled it off of his shoulder to free himself. It drooped limply in his palm like a massive strand of spaghetti. He let it flop to the ground and grabbed at the portion that was draped over the car.

"Pull it tight and then hold it," Frank said eagerly. "I'll come around and loop it through."

As soon as he felt the rope pulled taut, Frank hurried around to grab the loose end before his efforts to tighten the rope would be lost. He found his boy, Luke, holding the rope tightly in his left hand, while already tucking the loose end in between the tarp and the rack.

"Here, let me do that," Frank said.

"I can get it!" Luke insisted. "I can get it!" and he continued to tuck it in. Once the end was wedged through, he added to his father, "Here, take this and pull it."

Frank was proud to see his little man take the initiative. He realized he was breeding another generation of "roof rackers" as he so benevolently referred to "his kind of traveler."

"A couple more and we should be all set," Frank said, as he pulled the rope for the double loop through this side of the rack. "This extra loop keeps the rope from coming loose," he explained with a Mr. Wizard flare.

"I know, Dad, you've only told me a hundred times today," Luke replied as he turned to look around the garage. He walked from the driveway, where the production was taking place, into the opened garage. "Hey, Dad, isn't this Mom's makeup case?"

"What? What's that, Son?" Frank asked, as he busied himself with a knot.

The boy came out carrying a green American Tourister makeup case. Holding it up, he repeated, "Isn't this Mom's makeup case?"

"Oh, drat!" Dad managed.

He'd never been one to swear. He just had a certain way he liked things done and found surprises like this a tad frustrating. He looked over the tarp to see if there was somewhere he could sneak the little suitcase into it. However, every inch of it was secured. Actually, they were more than secured. Luke liked to say that the rope stretched back and forth across the tarp like Spiderman's web binding a criminal to a wall.

There must have been three times the amount of rope than was actually needed for the job. But, Frank always insisted on securing every loose flap, "Otherwise you spend your whole trip listening to the flap vibrating in the breeze," he'd point out expertly.

"I thought I told you to make sure we had everything loaded," Frank groaned to himself as much as to Luke.

"I did. I can't help it if Mom brings out stuff after we start!" Luke defended.

"Well, who? What?" Frank gave up. "Never mind, we'll put it in the wagon between the seats. We can fix it tonight when we stop. Tell your mother we're ready to go!"

It took another 15 minutes of people running in and out of the house, grabbing last-minute items and taking last-minute potty breaks before the whole family was sitting in the car ready for Dad to start the engine and get them on their way. Joyce, a woman in her late twenties, with a propensity for knitting, was up front sitting by her husband. She had a small sack at her feet with her yarn and needles ready to go.

Emma, the ten-year-old sister, had the entire middle seat to herself where she could stretch her little legs out just as much as she darn well pleased. She loved to read and had brought three books for the trip. Two of them were Nancy Drew mysteries. The third was C.S. Lewis' The Lion the Witch and the Wardrobe. Her mom had promised that if she finished these, she'd buy her a new book for the way home.

"Or, the way out!" Emma had added.

"All right," her mom had agreed. "If you really do finish them that soon."

The two boys, Luke and Kenny, were stashed in the third seat, which faced the rear, in the back. Surprisingly, they preferred it that way. Four years separated these two, but Luke was so pleased to have finally gotten a brother, that he was still eager to have him share in almost every one of his adventures. Almost.

There were times when a little brother could be a bother, but such was not the case on car trips. These two liked to sit far enough away from everyone that they could joke with each other without being overheard. Being in the very back, they had the added advantage of riding backwards, so they could face the cars behind them. They loved to stare at the other drivers and make them feel uncomfortable.

"Did you bring the cards?" Luke asked Kenny.

Kenny's eyes lit up as he reached in his pocket and produced a small, black plastic container with about a dozen cards inside. He didn't say anything, but a bright smile flashed over his face, revealing his pearly teeth. Kenny never spoke. At least he hadn't spoken in over two years. Not since "the incident". The family was so relieved to have him back, that they had learned to live with his silent behavior, and rarely noticed it these days.

"These should do the trick!" Luke laughed, as he took them from his brother.

Kenny's skinny body vibrated in a silent giggle, as he hit his older brother's shoulder.

"I know, I know, very punny," Luke grimaced. "Now we can entertain our rolling audience for hours on end!"

Luke looked at the box labeled "Professor Winder's Magic Cards" and started rummaging through them. Some of the cards were the same on both sides. Others had fake cards printed on them in a way that, when those were held in a hand with other cards, they looked like there were more cards in that hand than there really were. Their favorite part of the box was the thin sheet of black plastic which formed a false bottom by covering up the cards when the box was flipped.

"This is gonna be the BEST trick!" Luke said, holding up the plastic strip. "They might not be able to see the other tricks, but they'll definitely notice cards disappearing!"

Kenny's head bobbed up and down with excitement.

"Everyone all set?" Dad bellowed from the front.

"All set!" everyone screamed back.

"Let's have our prayer!" Joyce replied.

"Who wants to say it?" Frank asked.

"I'll say it!" Emma said, as she closed her book and set it on her lap. The family all bowed their heads and folded their arms. Emma then said, "Heavenly Father, thank you so much for letting us go see Grandma. Pray that we'll all be nice to each other and not argue. Pray that we'll drive safely and no one will crash into us. Pray that we can make new friends. Amen."

"Thank you, Emma," her mom said, turning back to give her a smile. "That was very nice."

"OK, here we go," Frank said, turning over the engine and pulling out of the driveway.

The back seat erupted in song as Luke began the family's traveling song. Soon the whole family joined in as they sang, "We're on our way! Pack up your pack! And if we stay, we won't come back! How can we go? We haven't got a dime, but we're going. And, we're gonna have a happy time!"

This was followed by a round of cheers.

"What a bunch of cornballs!" Dad smiled, as he made his way through Modesto and to the Interstate. They headed north on I-5 for a little over an hour. When they neared Sacramento, Dad hollered out, "Hey, kids! Who can find the Tower Bridge?"

Three heads suddenly popped up and bobbed around the windows, frantically trying to be the first. Luke pushed down on Kenny's head, trying to cut down on the competition. This led to some thrashing from Kenny, followed by a shout from Mom and a groan from Dad, as two high-pitched voices and Kenny's thumping on the window simultaneously declared that they were each the first and that the others really weren't. This was followed by accusations of cheating and other unfair practices.

"Last time I try to make this drive fun," Frank muttered as Joyce gave him one of her looks.

They turned East on I-80. As they passed a road sign, Dad called out, "Hey! It's only another 130 miles to Reno!"

"We should be able to eat lunch there," Joyce replied.

"But, I'm hungry now!" a voice from the back bellowed.

"For Heaven's sake!" Frank responded. "We just BARELY got started. Eat some grapes or something!"

Mom turned around and kindly asked Emma to open the food chest at her feet and get out some grapes for her brother. Emma rolled her eyes until she saw the little, red boxes of raisins. Within moments, all of the kids were chewing on their favorite snacks. None of them even bothered to ask why Mom didn't pack Lifesavers or candy bars. They were tired of being told how the sugar made them bounce off the walls, and even more tired of hearing dad's follow up lecture on how small the car was for any wall bouncing.

"I just hope Donner Pass is clear," Frank said to his wife.

"Did you bring the chains?" Joyce asked.

"Yes, but I hope I don't have to use them," he replied. "It's such a bother and we lose good time."

"I'd rather lose time than our lives," Joyce observed.

As they reached a steep incline, Frank's face brightened, "20th of December and not a flake of snow to be seen! This should be very good. We'll make great time!"

"Great time?" Luke whispered to Kenny. "We're barely moving!"

Kenny's body shook with laughter, which made Luke laugh until he snorted. This resulted in the backseat taking on the sounds of a pig farm until Mom said, "Boys!" followed by Dad pointing out, "That's enough!" and Emma rolling her eyes again in accompaniment to the word, "Brothers!"

"At least we're staying in front of THEM!" Luke said, pointing to a large RV that they had just passed.

The driver, a balding man in his late sixties, was behind the wheel. His purple-haired wife sat in the seat beside him. She saw the boys and waved. They smiled and waved back.

"Let's put on a show for 'em!" Luke suggested.

Kenny smiled and nodded, as he looked for the cards.

"Hey, my turn first," Luke said, snatching the cards from his brother. "You can do the next one."

For the next few minutes, the boys tried to amaze the couple behind them with their card prowess. They held up hands that suddenly grew or shrank, depending on their whims. Luke actually let Kenny do the piece de resistance of making a card disappear in the little plastic box whenever he'd flip it over and give it a tap.

For the first few tricks, the couple would clap, or give cute surprised looks, or an OK sign with their hands. It didn't take long, however, for them to be visibly tired of the boys' tricks. The old man did his best to look away, farther down the road. But, try as he might, he was stuck behind what seemed to be an endless parade of card tricks done with cards that – at his distance – were too small to really see.

Just as the old timer was getting distressed, things got worse. The boys themselves became bored with the game. They started making funny faces and slapping their heads with their hands in a taunting way, or pulling at their ears until the grandmother became visibly disturbed and the grandfatherly man had had enough. He honked his horn.

It wasn't one of those quick toots that elicits attention, or a series of quick notes of greeting. It was a long, low blast of annoyance that lingered in memory long after the man finally removed his palm from the center of his steering wheel, which caused Dad to sit up alertly.

"What the heck did he honk for?" he demanded.

Frank looked back in his side mirror to see the old man gesturing wildly with his hands and mouthing indecipherable words. He watched the man with agitated confusion, oblivious to his own boys, who were slinking down out of sight in the back seat.

"What IS his problem?" Frank demanded, clearly irritated. "He's going ballistic! I think he's going to pop a vein!"

"Maybe you're going too slowly?" Joyce suggested.

"I'm going 60!" Frank said. "I'm not going to go any faster than that! It's only 55, thanks to Nixon!"

"Well, maybe he's just in a hurry," she added. "Why don't you let him pass?"

"Because then I'd be stuck behind him and I'd spend the rest of the day looking at a rolling wall in front of me!" Dad answered. "I'll just pick it up a little and see if I can lose this idiot."

As their car slowly pulled away from the RV, the boys tentatively poked their heads up and looked out the rear window. In spite of the gulf between them and their former audience, turned adversary, they were still intimidated – at first. This wore off in fractions of a second and they smiled at each other and then waved a fond, final, taunting farewell. The older couple tried their best to ignore them and slowed a little to let the boys get even farther away.

The boys snickered and gave each other the thumb's up and took turns holding out a palm to let the other to give him "five," trying to keep it quiet enough that Dad wouldn't overhear them. They weren't able to contain themselves, however. When Dad heard the commotion, he looked at his boys in the rearview mirror. He saw them smiling and bouncing around and asked what they were up to.

Luke wisely shifted the topic and said with a loud, proud voice, "Boy, Dad, you sure showed them! What was that all about anyhow?"

"I don't know, Son," Frank replied, sighing and shaking his head. "There are idiots everywhere, though. Just remember that!"

"Frank!" his wife chided him, trying not to smirk with agreement.

"Well, it sure seems that way," Frank said in a sullen, subdued tone as he looked at the road stretched out in front of him. "Who knows what type of people we're going to come across on a trip like this?"

Chapter 2
A Parable for Our Time

They continued on their way, passing cars and being passed. It wasn't long before they came to another steep incline and Dad saw something rambling in front of him at a considerably lesser speed than his own.

"Oh, great," he groaned. "Another one."

His groan caught everyone's attention.

"Another what?" Luke asked with keen interest.

"Another of those mobile homes," Dad said. He emphasized the words "mobile homes" with a derision that made his newfound prejudice painfully clear.

"That's not a mobile home," Emma corrected. "It's an RV."

She was sitting behind her mother and was as curious as the rest of them to see what sort of driver inhabited this vehicle. She peered out her window as they approached, inspecting every detail of the rolling home away from home.

"Thanks for the clarification," Dad said. "I just hope this one's better than the last one."

"Just be polite, Frank," Joyce reminded him. "He's already moving over for you. You should be fine."

The whole family looked out their windows as Frank continued to catch up to the large, silver vehicle. It had a back door with a ladder next to it that led to the roof.

"Neat!" Emma shouted. "What's the ladder for?"

"For climbing up on the roof," Luke said as he plopped himself into the seat behind his father. "What do you think?"

Kenny looked at his brother for clarification. Luke just smiled smugly, waiting for the next question.

"What do they need to climb on the roof for, anyway?" Emma asked.

"To scrape off leaves, of course!" Luke said, rolling his eyes. "Sheese! What a nimrod!"

"Luke!" Mom said. "That isn't nice!"

"Yeah," Dad added. "Emma's never even been hunting before!"

"Huh?" the kids said in unison.

Frank laughed to himself while his wife glared at him and said, "Frank! That doesn't help."

"Oh, all right," Dad looked at his kids in his rearview mirror and explained, "Nimrod was the name of a mighty hunter in the book of Genesis."

"Huh?" Luke repeated, while Kenny shrugged, confused.

"Nimrod was the great-grandson of Noah, in the Bible..." Dad began to explain, but was interrupted.

"Hey!" Emma said rather suddenly. She had spied a round, red sticker pasted to the back left-hand corner of the RV that they were now passing. It had a smiling face of a man with a halo and three words, which Emma read.

"What's the 'Good Sam Club'?" she asked.

"The what?" Luke asked crowding up to Emma's window and forcing her to sit back in her seat.

"Stop pushing!" she responded. "It's my window!"

"What was that?" her mom coaxed.

"I asked, 'What's the Good Sam Club?'" she repeated.

"Why do you ask?" her mom continued.

"Because that RV has a sticker on the back that has a smiling face and it says, 'Good Sam Club' on it," Emma explained. "And, the face has a halo over it."

"Oh, that," Frank said. "That's a club that people who own RVs can join."

"Fraank!" Joyce began to interrupt again, wanting to cut off another of his sarcastic tales.

"It is!" Frank defended himself. "It's a club that's been around for ten years or so. Anyone who has that sticker on their RV is a member of the club. If they see someone with that sticker on an RV pulled over to the side of the road with some sort of problem, someone else with a sticker like that is supposed to pull over and help them. That way everyone in the club watches out for everyone else."

"Really?" Joyce asked cautiously, sensing that his story actually seemed plausible.

"Really!" Frank said.

"How do you know so much about RVs?" Luke asked.

"Oh," Frank replied with the beginnings of a grin, "you have to know these things when you're a dad!"

Joyce rolled her eyes at this one.

"But, why do they call it the 'Good Sam Club'?" Emma continued.

They were slowly pulling past the RV and Emma looked up at the driver's window. A very friendly looking old man was behind the wheel. She waved at him and he smiled and waved back. Kenny saw him too and pumped his right arm the way he loved to do for truckers. The RV driver obliged him and gave two quick toots on his horn.

"Good gravy!" Frank said with a start. "Now, what's HIS problem? What IS it with RVs?"

"He was just being nice," Emma blurted out quickly. "Kenny asked him to honk, so he did!"

"Huh? Oh," Frank said, calming down. Speaking into the rearview mirror he added, "Well, don't do that on RVs, Kenny. Just trucks."

Kenny nodded sheepishly and then looked out the rear window. He waved to the old couple who were slowly falling behind them. They smiled and waved back.

"You haven't said why it's called the 'Good Sam Club'," Emma reminded her self-proclaimed omniscient father.

"I believe that stands for 'Good Samaritan'," her mother pointed out before her dad had a chance.

"Why would they call it a 'Good Samaritan Club'?" the confused girl asked.

It seemed that the more her questions were being answered, the more confused she was becoming.

"Well, it's taken after the Good Samaritan from the Bible story," Frank put in. "You remember the story, don't you?"

"Yeah, I think so," Emma said.

"You think so?" Dad asked.

"It was like this," Mom said. "Jesus was asked by some men what the greatest commandment was. Jesus told them that the first great commandment was to love God, and the second great commandment was to love your neighbor. When someone asked who their neighbor was, Jesus told them the story of the Good Samaritan."

"Back in those days," Dad added, "the Jews and the Samaritans hated each other. They didn't trust each other and they couldn't get along."

"Like the Americans and the Russians?" Luke asked.

"Something like that," Frank acknowledged. "Go on, Joyce."

"Well," she continued, "one day there was a Jewish man walking along a road in the middle of nowhere. Some robbers caught him, beat him up and stole everything he had. Then they left him in the roadside to die. A Jewish Rabbi came along and saw him, and passed by on the other side of the road, so he wouldn't have to help him. Then someone else came by and did the same. Finally, a Samaritan – someone who was supposed to hate Jews, and was hated by the Jews – came by and saw the man.

"He knelt down and gave him water to drink. He bound up his wounds and put him on his donkey. Then he took him into town and found an inn. He gave the innkeeper money for the man to stay there and told the innkeeper that if the man spent more, he would come the next week and pay it for him."

"Wow!" Luke said from the back. "Free money!"

"That's not the point of the story!" Frank corrected.

"Yes," Joyce said. "The point is that we are all everyone's neighbor and when we see someone in need, we should stop and help them."

"Gee!" Emma said with wide eyes. "Are there still Good Samaritans around?"

"No, silly!" Luke said, pushing on her shoulder. "That's just something in the Bible!"

"We can ALL be Good Samaritans," Dad said, trying not to let the lesson be lost.

"Yes," Joyce added. "Anyone who does a good deed can be a Good Samaritan."

"And, you don't even need a sticker," Emma said with a contemplative smile.

* * * * *

The trip wore on. Every 30 minutes or so, Luke would hop from the back seat into the middle seat with Emma. She, in turn, would complain about his feet kicking her book. He would point out that he had every right to be there. His mother would back up the claim, but then add the warning that he needed to be considerate. He'd stay for a while and then, getting bored, pile back into the rear seat just in time to wake up Kenny.

It was nearly half past noon as they approached a sign welcoming them to Reno. Frank looked through his mirror and was both pleased and relieved to see that all three kids had fallen fast asleep. Emma was stretched out in the middle seat, with her book dropped to the floor.

Kenny was lying in the space between the middle and rear seats. Thankfully, he had finally fallen asleep there. It was that odd, small opening that was formed when the two seats were pulled up into their sitting positions. It was never meant to be a seat, but Kenny liked to climb into it. His little rib cage was just small enough to fit between the two sides, as long as he didn't breathe in too deeply. He had a pillow behind his head and his feet were propped up on his mother's makeup case.

Frank concluded Luke was sleeping, laid out on the rear seat, by the mere fact that he couldn't see him, or, even better, hear him. He was certain that if Luke was awake, he would have either been bounding over the seats again, been in the process of telling more corny jokes, or simply be poking his brother. Even Joyce's head was nodding.

As glad as he was for this peaceful moment, he knew it couldn't last. He needed gas, and they all needed food. If they didn't stop in Reno, who knew how far they'd have to go?

"We're entering Reno," he said softly to Joyce.

"Oh, good," she replied, trying not to sound too sleepy.

She looked outside, blinking her eyes as she tried to get her bearings.

"Should we let the kids sleep, or wake them up?" he asked.

Looking back and then turning to her husband, she said, "Oh, let's let them slee- "

She was cut off by a loud voice in the back shouting, "Hey! We're in Reno! This is Reno, isn't it?"

At this, two other sleepy heads slowly bobbed to the surface. Emma asked if what she'd heard was true.

"So much for sleeping," Frank smiled to his wife.

Kenny nudged Luke and nodded his head with a determined, questioning look. Luke always seemed to know what was on Kenny's mind. Because of this, he was his self-designated interpreter. It helped them form a bond that was even closer than most brothers.

"How much farther to Grandma's house?" Luke asked.

"Oh, for good grief," Dad fumbled. "We just barely got started!"

"Grandma lives in Oklahoma, Kenny," Mom replied more soothingly. "Reno is in Nevada. We've only gone to one state so far. Oklahoma is still three more states away. It will take a couple of days still."

"Oh," Luke said uncomprehendingly. "Well, tell me when we get there!"

"I will!" Joyce promised.

Shifting the topic to more current events, Frank asked, "Food or gas first?"

"FOOD!" was the enthusiastic reply by the hungriest voices in the car.

"Gas?" Frank mocked. "OK, but I thought you were hungry."

"We said 'FOOD!'" the kids vigorously countermanded.

"Frank," Joyce said, "don't taunt them!"

"OK, food it is," he laughed.

Chapter 3
Food for the Soul

They slowed down as they drove into town. All of the kids had their faces up to the windows, looking for food. Dad kept heading down the main street, looking straight ahead. Joyce looked for a nice restaurant.

"I'd like to just drive through town," Frank said. "And, find something on the other end."

"Why?" Joyce asked.

"Because when we're done, we can hop back on the highway and get going again," he said. "We'll lose less time that way."

"What does it matter if we drive through town before eating than if we drive through town after eating?" Joyce asked, confused. "Don't we end up driving through town either way?"

"We have momentum right now," Frank explained. "And, if we wait until after we eat, and then drive through town, we won't have that same momentum. Not until we get back on the Interstate. This way we don't lose time in town getting back that momentum. We just hop on the Interstate and go."

"But– " Joyce was about to question his logic, and then thought the better of it. Frank was pacified with having explained his reasoning. She figured that, since he did most of the driving, it was probably best to just let him drive however he liked.

"Besides," Frank added, "this way we can see if there's any place good to eat that's near a gas station. If we don't find anything we like on the other side of town, we can always double back."

"That's true," Joyce acknowledged, although she knew that the likelihood of actually doubling back was slimmer than the chance of the kids all falling back to sleep after lunch.

On the far side of town, they found a McDonald's near a Phillips 66 gas station. They were actually right next to each other, which, for the day, was a fortunate and rare find.

"Hey!" Frank said, pointing. "Check it out! Right next to each other! What a deal! Let's go there!"

"But – " Joyce started to say.

She had just seen a nice diner on the other side of the street. Her intended recommendation was drowned out by the cheering of the hungry travelers. Frank pulled into the parking lot and the boys beat on the back window, pleading to be let out quickly.

Frank got out and walked around and pulled the tailgate open and the boys lunged out. They staggered about momentarily in their newfound freedom, then made a beeline toward the McDonald's. Emma was prepping to race around and join the boys, when she suddenly stopped still in her tracks.

Her mother saw her strange behavior and was concerned. She walked up to her daughter and put her hand on her shoulder.

"What's the matter, Emma?" she asked.

Emma didn't speak. She was very quiet and leaned into her mother. She pointed slowly. Joyce followed with her eyes to see where her daughter was pointing.

Coming from behind the back of the restaurant, making his way around a stained and smelly garbage bin, was a man. He looked to be in his late 50's or early 60's. It was hard to say. His clothes were old and unkempt. There were holes and patches with holes in his ancient pants and faded coat. Bare fingers poked through his tattered, knitted gloves. His hat was pulled down tightly over his ragged, greasy hair. It was an old hat that looked like it had hit its heyday in the '50's.

Surely, Emma thought, such a hat could not keep a man warm. She could see that his bare ears were red, testifying to that fact. Her eyes quickly shifted to scanning his beleaguered face. His beard was scraggly and uneven. The whiskers had more salt than pepper to them. He had wrinkles that spread across his sunworn face. As he approached, she noticed his eyes.

They were a brilliant blue. They seemed wholly out of place for this unwelcome vagabond. While his clothes cried out in decrepit desperation, his eyes seemed to have a calm serenity about them. There was a flicker of majesty in them that she could behold even from a distance. It gave Emma the sudden feeling of dignity and self-respect that was well deserved. It contradicted every other facet of this man she had never seen before.

Just as quickly as it had manifested itself, it was gone. The eyes were still as blue, but they lacked the magic she had glimpsed so briefly. She wondered what had caused the change. What she couldn't know was that it was at this moment that the man had seen her father.

Whatever dignity or majesty he may have held within himself, fled as he once again became a beggar. With a feeble hand extended, the man began to slowly, meekly approach her father. It was clear he was begging for money, in spite of the inarticulate, barely audible mumblings that he uttered with what seemed like sincere humility.

Frank made out the words "just a quarter," but smiled apologetically as he slowly shook his head and prepared to continue toward the restaurant's door. Emma was moved and shocked. Then an idea flashed into her mind. It was more than an idea. It seemed to her to be not only the right course of action for this man, but for them and their own core beliefs. As Emma watched her father turn away from the man, she became nearly frantic. She turned toward her mother and looked searchingly into her eyes with a mature look of concern that startled her mother.

"What is it, Emma?" her mother repeated.

"That man!" Emma said.

"Don't worry, Sweetheart, he won't hurt us," Joyce comforted her and began to guide her with her arms away from the intruder.

"No, no," Emma protested. "That's not what I meant!" She pulled free of her mother and looked up at her. "The Good Samaritan!" she said enthusiastically.

"The what?" Joyce asked, confused.

"The Good Samaritan!" she repeated. "You know, that story from the Bible!"

"Yes, I remember the story," her mother replied, still confused. "But, what – "

"We need to be the Good Samaritan!" Emma interrupted. "He's the man in need, and we need to be Good Samaritans!"

Joyce saw that her daughter's eyes were sparkling with excitement. Emma was bouncing up and down. She called out to her father before Joyce had a chance to say anything.

"Dad! Dad! Come here!" she called out.

Puzzled, he came back toward the car.

"What is it, Emma?" he asked.

"That man!" she said. "We need to help that man!"

"What?" he asked. "Why?'

"Because we're Good Samaritans," Emma answered. "We have to give that man some money, so he can get some food."

"We're what?" Frank asked.

"Good Samaritans," Joyce put in, realizing that they had entered not only a teaching moment for their daughter, but the opportunity to show how well they actually believed the principles they taught their children in the lessons and stories that they shared so routinely. "You remember, we were just talking about how the Good Samaritan helped a man in need when no one else would."

"And, this man is in need!" Emma said in earnest.

"But, he just wants money to buy beer!" Frank said under his breath to Joyce.

"We don't know that!" Joyce rebuked him mildly. "This means a lot to Emma," she added.

Frank looked at Emma and saw that it was true. Emma was looking at him with puppy-dog eyes full of expectation and hope. She had that pleading look that let him know that this was something from which she would not back down, without severe disappointment.

"As I said," Frank reiterated, "he'll just use our money to buy beer!"

"Frank!" Joyce interjected.

"I'm telling you," Frank defended himself, "that's all these people want: money to buy beer!"

"Daddy!" Emma persisted, "he looks hungry!"

They looked back over at him. He had shuffled away from the doorway and back toward the garbage bin, but not out of view. He was coyly keeping an eye out for other newcomers whom he could approach with his plea for assistance. He did look hungry to Joyce. Frank still felt he looked more thirsty than hungry.

"I'm trying to tell you, Sweetheart," Frank said imploringly, "he may be hungry, but he's probably just going to take the money and do something bad with it, like buy beer."

"Daddy!" Emma responded, "Should we really judge a man we don't even know? I think he's hungry and I think we should help him if we can."

Not wanting to belabor the issue any more than they already had, Frank gave in. "All right, Emma. I'll give the man some money."

He reached into his pocket, pulled out his wallet and fingered out a dollar. As he pulled it free, he began to walk to the man, passing Joyce as he did so. When he did, he leaned toward her and said under his breath, "But, I'm telling you, he's just going to buy beer."

"Frank!" Joyce hushed back at him.

Emma was all smiles as Frank walked right up to the man and nodded his head, excused himself and handed the man a crisp, new dollar bill. The man's eyes lit up. He stuttered an excited thank you, bowed his head several times and then quickly turned and hurried to the back area. He disappeared from view behind the garbage bin, leaving Frank standing without a companion.

Turning back to his wife and daughter, he shrugged and mouthed, "See, I told you!"

Kenny and Luke, who had entered the restaurant before the incident, came to the door and pushed it open from within.

"Come on everybody!" Luke shouted as he poked his head through the doorway. "What's the hold up?"

"That's just it," Frank said with a rude leer, "I've just been held up!"

"Frank, please!" Joyce rolled her eyes.

"What's that mean?" Luke asked.

"Nothing," Frank said. "Let's go eat."

"We've been Good Samaritans!" Emma said to Luke as she proudly walked passed him and inside.

"You've been what?" Luke asked, looking at his mother.

"Good Samaritans," she responded with a smile. "Come on, let's go eat."

The family went in, ordered, and were soon enjoying some burgers and fries at a table. Emma suddenly stopped mid bite and sat up straight.

"He's here!" she said, pointing.

"Who's here?" her mother asked, then followed her excited gaze and turned to look toward the door. "Well, I'll be."

"You'll be what?" Frank asked his wife.

"Turn around and look," she nodded clandestinely.

Frank turned just in time to see the man standing in the doorway. He had stopped and propped the door open with his back. A lady, dressed as poorly as he, stumbled in. She blinked and looked around briefly. When her eyes caught hold of the menu above the counter, they stayed fastened upon it. She inadvertently licked her lips, and caught herself in the act. She stopped quickly and tried to hide her hunger.

She turned back to the man. He motioned with his arm toward the counter and nodded with a smile. He let her know that this special treat was real and would be for her. He walked with her to the counter and stood by her side. He ordered one of the children's meals and waited patiently for it to be prepared and delivered.

The sack of food was soon handed over and graciously received. The man, proving himself to be a gentleman in spite of his appearance, escorted his lady to a table for two. He motioned for her to sit, which she did, and then he joined her. He pulled their meal out of the sack as if he were Santa pulling out the contents of a large stocking. He unwrapped the tiny burger and gingerly tore it in two. He handed the larger half to the woman and gave her a smile.

Her eyes grew as the food neared her. She brought it up to her mouth with both hands. The dreamy look in her eyes seemed to cast aside her disbelief at her good fortune. He watched her bite into the bounty and smiled satisfactorily, then bit into his own. He closed his eyes and let the flavor and substance melt and swirl within him. They continued to eat with the gratitude and enthusiasm of a family enjoying a Thanksgiving feast.

All the while, Frank, Emma, and Joyce continued to give furtive looks at the couple. Oblivious to the goings on, Kenny and Luke simply ate. Emma smiled with delight as she saw the man eat. She was thrilled to have done something kind for him. Joyce looked from Emma to Frank. Frank was clearly feeling guilty. He looked at the monstrous burger in his own hands and then over at the meager portions the couple were eating and felt very guilty.

"See, Daddy!" Emma said with a mouthful of fries. "They didn't buy beer!"

"Honey!" Joyce reminded her softly. "Not so loud, please!"

"No, Sweetheart," Frank admitted, "they didn't."

"He really WAS hungry," Emma added, "and he's sharing his meal with his girlfriend! We really ARE Good Samaritans!"

"Yes, we really are," Joyce replied and then gave Frank a look that showed she shared his misgivings.

"Oh, yes," Frank said with a dismal lilt. "We're GREAT Samaritans."

Frank looked over at the man and saw him cross his legs under the table. Frank could see large holes in the man's socks. He looked up at the man's face. He had a contented look as he gestured to the small bag of fries and offered it to the tattered lady next to him, who smiled and took one that she dipped with a generous helping of ketchup. Frank slowly put his burger to his own mouth and nearly gagged on the bite.

Chapter 4
After Thoughts

Frank and Joyce hadn't said much as they moved the car next door for gas. They didn't need to. They both knew that they each felt the same way.

The boys hadn't bothered to ride to the gas station. They just ran across the parking lot and inside the station to find the bathrooms and then look at the souvenirs and candy. Emma had walked the distance with a satisfied look on her face.

Joyce excused herself to go keep an eye on the children while Frank pumped the gas. He got the gas started and stepped away to wipe the front window clean. He was nearly done before he noticed that the gas wasn't pumping. In checking it, he found that the tank was far from full. He set the latch on the nozzle again and stepped away to finish cleaning the windows.

He only took a couple of steps, however, when he heard the nozzle click. The latch had slipped. He worked it again and found that it wouldn't stay.

"Darn nozzle," he mumbled and stayed put holding the nozzle open to fill the rest of the tank.

He was still holding it, lost in thought about the man and his missed opportunity to do a genuinely good deed, when his thoughts were disrupted by movement at the restaurant. The door had opened and two familiar figures were coming out. It was the man and his lady friend.

Frank watched them both pull their collars tightly to them. They turned toward each other speaking words that Frank could not hear. She reached over and lightly placed her fingertips to the man's chest for a moment, obviously thanking him. He nodded in reply, and to Frank's surprise, they parted.

The unknown lady walked behind the restaurant and disappeared beyond the garbage bin. The man stood a moment, then turned away and began walking toward the gas station. Frank thought the man would come and thank him for the meal. He prepared himself by quickly digging into his wallet for a few more dollars. He held them in his pocket, ready to retrieve them, while his other hand held the gas nozzle.

Frank was tensing up, trying to think of the best way to let the man know that the gift of the meal was no great thing, that the man really didn't need to thank him, and that, in fact, he'd like to give the man a few more dollars. He was still trying to put all this into words as the man turned toward the station. He didn't even seem to notice Frank.

Frank's mind began to buzz. He felt that his chance to do right might disappear. He wanted to catch the man before he was gone. He wasn't sure what he was going to do, but he wanted to do something. He started to walk over to him, but the nozzle clicked and stopped pumping. He quickly stepped back to it and squeezed it to start the flow again.

Meanwhile, the man continued to walk and Frank was afraid he was going to lose him. He had to get his attention somehow, but he could hardly call out to him, as he had no idea what the man's name was. He certainly wasn't on familiar enough terms with the man to simply call out to him. He was nearly panicking as he tried to think of words to say.

His tension was eased somewhat when he saw the man sit down on the walkway's edge, near the station's front door. The pump clicked off again and jostled Frank's attention. He realized that he had been staring at the man. He turned and squeezed the nozzle again. It switched off almost immediately.

He squeezed it again and again it switched off.

"What the hey?" he asked himself and then looking at the pump's meter, he realized the tank was finally full.

He was surprised that so much time had passed. He still hadn't come up with a plan for approaching the man, but now seemed to be the time. He replaced the nozzle, screwed the gas cap back in place and walked toward the station to pay.

He figured his best chance would be to say something as he passed the man. He walked toward him, or rather the door. A thousand words pummeled his mind, screaming to come out, none of them seemed to make much sense, though. He was nearly to the man. He had only a step or two to go. He licked his lips, preparing to say something.

"Hi," he said to the man.

The man hardly noticed.

"Hello," Frank followed up, trying to make sure he had gotten the man's attention.

The man was sitting on the curb, looking down. Upon hearing Frank, he slowly looked up and their eyes met. There was no distinct sign of recognition in the man's eyes. Frank waved awkwardly to the man and repeated his greeting. The man gave a pleasant, little smile and returned the greeting.

Frank was on the verge of following up with something more when the station door flung open and his two boys rushed out between him and the man. The moment was gone. Frank walked into the station to pay. Joyce met him in there and, seeing he looked troubled, asked if everything was all right.

"Oh, uh, yes certainly," he fumbled. "It's just that, uh, I saw that man again."

"'That man'?" she asked, a bit puzzled. Then, realizing who he must have been referring to, she asked, "Do you mean the man from lunch?"

"Yes, he's right outside."

Frank nodded with his head. Joyce looked toward the door. It was just pulling closed. She could just see a pair of shoes through it. Most of the view through the door was obstructed by a hand painted portrait of Santa greeting customers as they entered the station. She could see better through the window to the right of the door, between a stack of Pennzoil canisters and a "Seasons Greetings!" window painting.

There, with his back against the glass, was the now familiar shape of the man. His brown coat was pulled tightly against his skin. Joyce could seemingly see his backbone protruding against the back of the tattered fabric. His hat was pulled down tightly, close to his red ears. She could see wisps of steam float away in the cold air with each breath he took.

Joyce couldn't help observing that the old man seemed chillingly content with his life. No, that wasn't right, she corrected herself. It was more a matter of him being complacent with it. Surely he wasn't content. She wondered where he lived, or at least where he spent his nights. She assumed it must be out in the cold, and wondered what - if any - covering he would enjoy. She thought that perhaps his only protection from the cold would be a bunch of discarded newspapers or, if he was really fortunate, perhaps an old, smelly blanket. She shivered involuntarily at the thought.

Now that she knew he was sincere when he asked for money, she felt terribly guilty for not having done something more for him. It wasn't because she wanted to look good in the eyes of her daughter, at least not now. It was because she felt a sincere feeling of pity for him. Not really pity, so much, but an odd sense of obligation. It was as if fate had given her and her family the opportunity to help a fellow sojourner and she and her husband had merely looked the other way.

How could they have done such a thing when they themselves were so richly blessed? How could they look at another of God's children, whose head hung down in despair and have not helped to raise it up again? A child of God? No. Well, yes. Surely. Yes, this was another of God's divine children, yet, he had seemingly lost his way somehow, she concluded. From the looks of the man, she surmised that he must have wandered into some of the lonely, foreboding paths of life.

Joyce wondered how long the man had been in such an abysmal state. She wondered at the life the man had lived. She wondered why it was that she had not been more willing to trust a hungry man who had simply asked for lunch money. What kind of world was it where people looked at each other as strangers who quickly categorized each other, and once that categorization was completed - without a lick of factual data - proceeded to base their entire, brief interactions with each other on that fast paced series of assumptions? She was ashamed to have fallen in step with such cruel prejudices.

"I wish we had done something more for the dear, old man," she said to Frank.

"So do I," Frank agreed. "I just don't know what to d– "

"Hey!" A gruff voice from behind them interrupted their thoughts. The attendant stepped out from behind the counter and made a beeline for the door. "'Scuse me!" he said, as he stepped between Frank and Joyce.

He pushed the door open and shouted, "Hey, you!" motioning to the man.

"I told you to stop hangin' around here!" the attendant shouted roughly. He waved his hand at the man, as if he were waving off a pesky fly that didn't know better than to continue to buzz around his face. "It bothers my customers! Now, get out of here!"

The man turned his head and saw the attendant. He moved slowly, like a bear being moved from a riverbank. He knew the message without needing to hear the words. He turned away and started to stand. It took him longer than it seemed it should. His old bones just weren't what they used to be.

"Quit stalling, and git!" the attendant shouted. "Don't make me call the cops!"

The man stood and started to wander off, back in the direction of the McDonald's. The attendant watched to make sure he would leave. He would have stayed there the entire time it would have taken the man to leave his property, if Frank hadn't interrupted him.

"Sir, can I pay now?" Frank asked.

"Eh? What?" the attendant said, stepping back into the warmth of his station.

"I'd like to pay now," Frank repeated.

"Oh, yes, certainly," the attendant replied, stepping behind the register and offering a settling smile. "Sorry about that. I keep telling him to take a hike, but he keeps coming back." As he said this, he glanced out through the words "Peace on Earth!" painted on the station's door, to verify that the man had indeed left.

"He comes often, then?" Joyce asked.

"Yeah. Too often, if you ask me," the attendant said. "He just comes and sits and waits. He'd sit there all day if I let him."

"Waits?" Frank asked. "What's he waiting for?"

"Who knows? Who cares?" the attendant said, as he rang up their bill. "I just don't want him waiting around here, see? It bothers people." He looked them in the eye with a knowing look and added, "He's probably just waiting for someone to give him money to buy beer! You know what I mean?" He then laughed until he snorted.

"Yeah, I know," Frank said dismally as he received his change. He tried to laugh, but only managed an awkward, crooked smile. He looked sideways and saw Joyce feeling equally uncomfortable.

"Thanks, mister," the attendant said. "See ya. Oh, and, have a merry Christmas!"

Frank and Joyce returned the greeting and then turned to leave together. They were both concerned about the man and what they could or should do for him. It could be argued that they simply wanted somehow to appease their guilty consciences. More than that, though, they knew they genuinely wanted to help him.

Joyce was just turning to Frank to ask what he felt they ought to do when the station door was again pulled open. This time it was Emma. She burst in with a mile-wide smile and an eager look.

"He's here!" she said in an excited tone. "He's here!"

"Yes, we know," Joyce acknowledged.

"We were just going to talk to him," Frank added.

"You were?" Emma said with anxious surprise. "What were you going to say? Were you going to give him more money? Because I really think you should. That hamburger wasn't very big and it was awfully nice of him to share it with that lady. Do you think that was his wife? Who do you think she was? I bet they're still hungry. Don't you?"

"Hold on, young lady," Frank said, overwhelmed. "Take a breath!"

"We don't know," Joyce said. "We were just going to talk to him and say hello."

Frank sensed someone looking at him and turned his head to see the attendant. He couldn't decide if the attendant was surprised, curious, amused, distrustful of their motives, or simply could not hear all that was going on. At any rate, he felt uncomfortable. He turned back to his family and ushered them to the door.

"Let's go," he said.

Chapter 5
A Kind Offer

They stepped out and let the door close behind them. Joyce and Frank stood in the doorway a moment, trying to strategize. Meanwhile, Emma walked right up to the man. Like picnic flies, he had returned. He was sitting on the curb of the walkway that surrounded the station, just out of the attendant's sight. His feet were clad in faded boots that rested in the gutter. His knees poked up and he was resting his forearms on them. He was hunched forward and had a blank expression. He did indeed have the appearance of one who was waiting.

"Hey, mister!" Emma said, standing in front of him.

He didn't move. He just sat with a blank stare. Had they not known better, they would have thought that he had been sitting there all day.

"Mister!" Emma repeated. This time she reached out her tiny fingers and lightly touched his knee.

At this, the man startled from his daze and slowly turned his gaze upward and met Emma's.

"Mister," Emma smiled and continued to talk, but the man heard none of it.

He was marveling at her smile. His eyes took on a dreamy look. He couldn't remember the last time that someone had smiled at him. He certainly couldn't remember when a child had last smiled at him. Most kids shunned him. This shunning, he knew, was encouraged by their parents.

When they'd see him approach, they would quickly put an arm around their child and whisk them away. What hurt most of all was when he'd catch them telling the child not to look at him and to just keep moving.

Not to look at him? Why, he wondered. Was he some sort of leper? Would looking at him really hurt the child so much? Was he so inhuman that he was unbefitting of the mere kindness of a look, a smile, a friendly nod, perhaps even a gentle "Hello"?

And yet, here before him seemed to be a tiny angel of life. She was standing before him without quivering, without shrinking, without being pulled away. Where were her parents? Why had they not come to rescue their daughter from contact with him? He turned his head reluctantly, not wishing for this friendly apparition to disappear, but irresistibly curious.

There they were, coming out of the doorway. They were approaching the girl. He knew what would happen next. They would see their daughter talking to him, and hurriedly grab the girl and pull her to safety while giving him a look of disgust. Perhaps he would become the unwilling recipient of several well-placed words of derision. He had experienced such scenes all too often, and braced himself for another insulting encounter. It didn't matter that he had done nothing more to provoke it than to be guilty of sitting there. Still, he knew it would come.

He saw the parents' awkward movements and knew that they were seeking fitting words of ridicule. As he braced himself, he wished he were as numb to the words as he tried to show. But, the truth was, that in spite of his calm, blank exterior, the words would still sting and hurt.

The pair approached. As they did so, the man noted two things which surprised him. The first was that they did not come quickly. Usually, the parents would dash as fast as they could and snatch their youngster away from him as if too much exposure to him might somehow be harmful. The second was that they did not approach the girl. If anything, they seemed to ignore the girl and be more intent on coming to him. Were they that abrasive? Did they want to vent on him before bothering to rescue their darling?

He simply sat and waited.

The father was the first to speak. The man found that he had to listen carefully to catch the words. Rather than shouting harsh words in rapid succession, these came slowly, awkwardly, softly, almost apologetically.

"Hi," the father began. "Uh, I hope we're not intruding..."

The words continued to stumble out haphazardly. The old man was confused by what seemed like an awkwardly respectful tone and submissive way in which this man stood before him. He tried, but failed to remember the last time someone had spoken to him in such a manner. He was so distracted by this that he forgot to actually listen to the meaning of the words themselves until the parent had already slowly rambled on for several sentences.

He became aware that the noise of speech had ended. He saw that the father was still standing before him, looking very uncomfortable. He sensed he had been asked something, but for the life of him, he had no idea what it was. He stared up at the stranger with unblinking eyes.

The father shifted his feet and cast sideways looks at his wife. He whispered to her through the side of his mouth, "I don't even know if he heard me, Joyce."

The old man saw the lady step forward. He noticed the sun hit her hair and make it glisten. It produced a sort of halo around her angelic face. She was bending down toward him, preparing to speak. He decided he wanted to hear her words and bent his full attention on her, watching as her lips began to move.

"Could we?" she asked in a kind, almost pleading voice.

His head was swimming. He had no idea what she was asking, but sensed that he wanted to agree to whatever it was.

"Could you what?" he said at last.

"Could we give you a ride anywhere?" Joyce continued.

"A ride?" the man said, taken aback. A dreamy look melted into his eyes. He seemed to slide into another world. He went silent as a serene look eased its way across his face.

"He doesn't seem to be all here," Frank whispered to Joyce.

"Hush!" she whispered quickly, but softly.

"Well?" Frank shrugged as he tilted his head toward the man a couple of times.

"We'd love to give you a lift to wherever you need to go," Joyce added to the man.

The dreamy, contemplative look had not left his face. His lips parted, but no words escaped them. He licked them, preparing to speak. The couple – and their girl – watched with anticipation.

"I've always wanted to see Oklahoma," he said at last. It came out more as a statement of a lifelong goal, than as a request.

"Oklahoma?" Frank straightened suddenly and repeated incredulously. "The musical?"

"No," the man corrected in a surprisingly rational manner, "the state."

"Oklahoma?" Frank repeated screwing up his face in puzzlement.

"Hey!" Emma shouted, jumping with excitement. "That's right where we're going! He can come along! Can't he?"

"Well, no, I was thinking more of taking him to a park or something," Frank corrected.

"But, you said you wanted to help him!" Emma pleaded.

"Yes, but Oklahoma!" Frank protested.

"Frank, you did say you wanted to help him," Joyce reminded him with a coaxing tone.

"I know, but Oklahoma!" Frank repeated giving his wife a surprised look.

"What would the Good Samaritan do?" Emma continued.

"He'd probably just –"

"Frank!" Joyce cut in, stopping what she feared would be a sarcastic reply. "It doesn't sound like it would be out of our way. It would mean a lot to Emma. What could it hurt? He seems like a nice enough man."

"I can't believe you're really saying this," Frank replied, looking into his wife's eyes.

"I know," she agreed. "It's really strange, isn't it? But," she looked over at the man who had a pleasant look as he sat patiently, "it somehow seems like the right thing to do. I don't know why, but it just feels right." Looking back to Frank she added, "Maybe we really were meant to be Good Samaritans."

"Maybe," Frank nodded, "because I can't seem to find a reason to argue against this. Not deep down, anyway. My head tells me this is craziness, but I can't explain to myself why I have to admit that something seems to be OK with it. I just don't get it," he conceded.

He stood pondering for a minute. He was unable to shake the feeling that was overpowering him. As crazy, dangerous, spontaneous, and insane as his mind told him it was, something deep inside of him comforted him – nearly pled with him – telling him it was the right thing to do. Finally, he turned back to the man who still sat on the curb and seemed to be in a world of his own.

"Mister," he said, "we can do that. We can take you as far as Oklahoma."

"Really?!" Emma shouted, "We will?" She was jumping with excitement.

"Really?" the man whispered. "I've always wanted to go to Oklahoma. God bless you! God bless you all!" he repeated as his face lit up with a shine that melted Joyce's heart and moved Frank as well.

"Well," Frank said rather sheepishly, "you better gather your things. We'll be heading out soon."

"I don't got much, but the clothes I'm wearin'," the man said. "But, I really would like to tell Bessie goodbye."

"Is that the lady you ate lunch with?" Emma asked, concerned and feeling suddenly sad that he might be parting with a good friend. She wondered how hard it would be for him.

"The lady?" he asked. He paused as his mind had to work to remember all the way back to lunch. When he did, a little grin of understanding crept across his face, "Oh, her! No, no that's not Bessie. I just happened to see her shortly before going in myself. She looked hungry, so I offered her a bite to eat. Come with me and I'll show you Bessie."

He put a hand down on the curb to brace himself for standing, and twisted to lean on it. Emma bent forward to help him and Frank did the same. Frank gingerly, but firmly, took hold of the inside of the man's elbow and helped pull him to his feet.

The man was surprised at Frank's strength. As he got to his feet, he straightened and turned to Frank and thanked him. Then he turned toward the side of the station.

"Bessie's just back here," he said. "Follow me."

They followed him as he walked to the side of the station and then kept going toward the back. They passed old oil drums and debris along the way. The man paused and pointed toward a large, blue trash bin with gray streaks of rust splattered across its face, particularly where streaks and scraps showed where the trash truck would grab hold of and lift the bin for emptying.

"Bessie is a trash bin?" Frank asked, not meaning to say it aloud.

"The trash bin?" the man asked surprised. Seeing the bin as if for the first time he laughed lightly and said with a smile, "No, no! Bessie's next to the bin!"

Frank's gaze shifted. He saw dirt, rocks, cardboard, and an old shopping cart full of stained blankets as well as a squeegee and rags in the bottom area. On the front of the cart, tethered with old bits of wire and twine, was a tattered Christmas Wreath complete with a big, red bow. The wreath looked strangely out of place on such a cart.

At the sight of the wreath, Frank realized that this was as close as this homeless man could come to decorating his "home" for the holidays.

Frank swallowed deeply and thought, "'Tis the season..."

He still wasn't sure about who "Bessie" was and certainly didn't want to offend the man, but he had to ask for clarification.

"Is 'Bessie' the shopping cart, then?" he asked with hesitation.

"Oh, yes, she started out that way," the man acknowledged as he reverently walked up to it and ran his hand along the cart, straightening the wreath as he did so. "But, over the years she's become something more."

"Something more?" Emma asked, looking at the cart with wide eyes and anticipation. "What?"

"A good friend," the man said, lightly caressing the worn handle.

"Um, Bessie never talks to you or anything, does she?" Frank asked awkwardly.

Joyce shot him a wary glare as she shushed him with, "Frank!"

"I just want to know what we're getting into," he whispered sideways to his wife.

"No, no, no!" the man reassured them. "Bessie never talks. I'm not crazy, you know. It's just that," he paused a moment then added, "It's just that, well a man grows used to something he uses a lot. He gets familiar with it. He sort of learns to depend on it. And, in some ways he finds some comfort and support from it. Especially during the long, cold days of winter." He shook his head and concluded, "It's silly. I don't expect you to understand."

"No, I think I do," Frank acknowledged. "I sometimes get that way about my car."

"You hate that car," Joyce pointed out.

"Well, it's kind of a love/hate thing," Frank corrected. "At any rate, I see what he's saying."

The man's comment about long, cold wintry days moved Frank. He wondered just how many long, cold days the man had seen. And, he thought of the even longer, colder, black nights. He knew that the temperature must only be a portion of the coldness the man referred to. The bitterest cold probably came from people such as himself. He began to gather a resolve that what they were proposing to do truly was worthwhile and right.

"You - uh - you just say your goodbyes," Frank said. "I'll get the boys into the car. We'll be out front waiting for you."

He motioned for Joyce and Emma to follow. Joyce did, but Emma lingered a moment longer and stepped closer to the man.

"I'm so glad you're going to come with us," she said with a smile. "You're going to be the best part about this trip!"

She turned away quickly, causing her hair to flare up and then fall about her shoulders and then bounce as she skipped to the front of the building. The man watched her disappear around the corner and then turned back to Bessie. He patted her handle again as he spoke.

"Well, Bessie," he said, "you've served me well. I guess it's finally time for us to say goodbye. Thanks for all you've done. I'm sure someone else will find comfort in you."

He glanced at the belongings she contained. Most of them were simply to keep him warm. Others, like the squeegee and rags, were used to drum up small change for meals. He wouldn't need them in a car, and didn't believe he'd need them in Oklahoma.

He eyed the contents of the cart a moment longer. His eye lingered on one object in particular. It was a colorful blanket, with red, blue and purple squares. He had used it to cover himself on many cold nights. He knew that it could grow stiff with sweat and grime. But, he also knew that after the cleaning of a good rainstorm it would become soft and inviting again. He stroked it lightly with his fingertips while his mind pondered his choice.

Of the many things he had collected over the years, it was the one item he was most tempted to take with him. As much as he knew he wanted to keep it, because of the warmth it had provided, he knew, too, that some other poor soul could certainly benefit from the comfort it could offer. When he realized this, it became a quick decision.

"I'll leave it all for someone else," he said to himself, as he turned away from the cart.

Another man would have been embarrassed at the thought of the tear that glinted in the corner of his eye - over a shopping cart - but, another man could not appreciate the bond he had felt and was now breaking. He turned away, and never looked back.

The cart, its contents, and the wreath remained behind, perhaps to be discovered by another homeless person looking for what little solace they could offer. Or, perhaps to be tossed inside the dumpster and permanently removed from public view. His heart hoped it would be the former.

Frank and his family were sitting in the car ready to go. Joyce had just explained to the boys that they'd be taking on another passenger: a guest. Emma had touted the fact that they were all going to be Good Samaritans. Dozens of questions and quick answers were flying around the car as they saw the man round the corner. Suddenly, a thick silence filled the air.

They all sat there frozen in place as the man approached. He sensed an awkwardness as he neared the vehicle and stopped. Emma pushed her door open and leapt out.

"You'll sit in here with me!" she declared and nearly pushed the man into the car.

He sat down and Emma pushed the door closed then ran around to climb in from the other side.

"Welcome to our car," Joyce said, as she turned and gave him a smile.

"Yes, welcome," Frank repeated, looking through the rearview mirror.

Turning to Joyce, he whispered, "'Welcome to our car'?"

"It seemed like a nice thing to say," Joyce replied lightly pushing his arm and smiling.

"I'm Emma," Emma said proudly. "And, those are my brothers in the back."

"I'm Luke," the older one said, "and, this is Kenny," he said, teasingly pushing on the back of Kenny's head.

"How do you do?" the man asked Kenny.

"He don't talk," Luke said with a serious, brotherly look. "There's nothing wrong with him. He just don't talk."

"Doesn't," Joyce corrected.

"Doesn't," Luke repeated.

"Why not?" the man began to ask, but the words died on his lips. He sensed he shouldn't ask. He changed subjects and as Frank pulled out of the station and onto the road, he said, "I can't tell you how wonderful this all is. Thank you so much for letting me join your family on this trip."

"We're happy to do it," Frank said, surprised at how sincerely he felt.

They were nearing the edge of town in silence when Frank said, "Say mister, uh, what is your name? We can't very well call you mister, now can we?"

"My name," the man said, a bit taken aback. "My name is -" his voice trailed off. He was obviously going into deep thought. "No one has asked me that in so long, that I don't rightly remember it. What would you like to call me?"

"Huh?" Luke asked. He and Kenny exchanged puzzled looks.

"Yes, what would you like to call me?" he repeated.

"But usually, people tell other people what they want to be called," Emma said.

"Well, you people are doing so much for me, I think it would only be fair to let you pick a name that you want to hear and say."

"What an interesting offer," Joyce pondered.

"A weird one," Frank mumbled.

"How about 'Sam'?" Emma suggested.

"Sam?" Frank asked. "Why Sam?"

"Because it's short for 'Samaritan'," she explained. "And, that's what we're being."

"That's what WE'RE being," Frank said. "Not what HE is."

"Yeah but, –" Emma began to defend herself when she was kindly interrupted.

"I think 'Sam' would be fine," the man, now known as "Sam", commented.

"Great! Sam!" Emma smiled. "He's got a brand new name, now!"

"Now, if we could only get him some new clothes," Luke muttered.

"Luke!" his mother cautioned, "that's unkind!"

"Sorry, but you're not back here," Luke said, trying VERY hard not to specifically mention the smell.

Joyce was trying to find a polite way to chastise him in front of their new guest, but Frank interrupted.

"No. No, Luke's right," Frank said. "We should get some nice clothes on him. At least, I think that's what the Good Samaritan would have done."

Chapter 6
New Duds

"Really, you shouldn't," Sam mildly protested as Frank pulled the car to a stop in the KMart parking lot.

He was embarrassed by the attention, but even more embarrassed at the thought of offending his newfound friends. He wanted to pull back and turn down the generous offer, but at the same time, he couldn't. He knew he needed clothes, and that he had no other means to get them. He had to relent to Emma's and Joyce's urging and coaxing.

Emma had already gotten out and run around to his side of the car and opened the door. She was now reaching in for his hand to pull him out. Her smile was breathtaking in its jubilance. She was nearly jumping with excitement. He reached out his hand and took hers.

The contrast between her soft, white hand, and his rugged, rough and dirty one shocked him. He suddenly withdrew it as a leper may have pulled back from the view of a passing queen.

"Come on!" Emma repeated. "It will be all right! It'll be fun!"

"I doubt that," Sam managed to say under his breath.

All the while, his thoughts were awash with surprise at how his uncomely appearance and texture did not seem to deter the little angel. He knew that the touch of his hand must have been a disgusting shock for the girl, but here she was holding out her hand to him again, daring to be touched once more by the foul being that he was.

He looked into her eyes and saw pure innocence, devoid of human ills. He was touched and moved within. It slowly dawned on him that the thing that would make this sweet person happiest would be to try to care for him. He knew that he did not want to deny her that happiness, and resolved to do whatever it took.

"I'll come," he said at length, and climbed out of the station wagon.

As they approached the store entrance, Sam stayed in between the kids. He would have looked like a grandfather flanked by his family, if it weren't for his ragged, decrepit appearance. He could suddenly feel the dirt on his face, and the sweat matted into his hair. He felt like he didn't belong and hesitated.

Frank was nearby, and also felt the awkwardness of the situation. He stepped closer to Sam and said, "It's alright Sam, we're all with you."

"Yes, please don't feel bad. We're happy to have you with us," Joyce added in a sweet way that made Sam believe her.

Their reassurances made him feel much better. He looked down and saw Emma smile up at him. He smiled in reply and felt a weight lift from him. Sam was suddenly shocked by the sensation of the little girl's fingers wrapping tightly around half of his own. He looked down and saw her holding his hand. He felt a lump grow in his throat but only managed to smile.

"Come on!" Emma urged. "Let's go get you some clothes!"

She started through the door and pulled on his hand. He followed. His feet hesitated a moment, but his heart pushed him forward.

Once through the entryway, Sam looked around at the shelves of clothes, food, pharmaceuticals and other items he could see. He saw the customer service desk and the young woman staffing it. He paused a moment, and raised his right hand to his chin and rubbed his fingers against his ragged beard, looking contemplative and nervous.

The whole family saw his hesitation and wanted to help ease him into feeling more at home.

"Frank, do something," Joyce coaxed.

"What should I do?" Frank asked.

"I don't know," Joyce confessed. "Just talk to him or something. I think he's about to run out or something."

Frank stepped over to him and asked if he was all right.

"I, uh," Sam stammered. "I, uh, I need to use the bathroom."

"The restroom?" Frank asked. "Oh, uh certainly. I think it's over that way." He pointed beyond the customer service desk.

"Oh, yes," Sam replied, reading the large, red sign that spelled "RESTROOMS".

Sam still didn't move.

"Is there something else?" Frank ventured, doubtful on what to do, and a little fearful that Sam would want him to follow him inside.

Sam leaned close to Frank. Frank was nearly overwhelmed by the good man's breath and odor, but tried desperately not to flinch. He could see that Sam wanted to say something private to him. His mind was racing with guesses as to what that might be. He was a little fearful at some of the possibilities.

"It's just that," Sam paused. Frank's heart was pounding so hard he thought it could be seen through his coat.

"It's, uh," Sam stammered again.

"It's just what?" Frank asked patiently.

"It's just, uh –" Sam paused and then in an even lower voice, with his mouth right up to Frank, he finished, "It's – uh – do you have a comb?"

"A what?" Frank asked. Then, realizing what the request was – and feeling extremely relieved – he said, "A comb? Oh, yes, certainly!"

Seeing that Sam felt self conscious about his appearance and his quest to remedy it, he decided to maintain the low profile of the transaction and slyly reached into his back pocket and produced the wanted item. He slipped it into Sam's palm like an uncle slipping a twenty to his nephew after high school graduation.

"Thank you, so much!" Sam said, with a great deal of relief in his eyes. "I really appreciate it!"

"Not at all," Frank said. Then adding as Sam hustled over to the restrooms. "Keep it!" Under his breath he added, "and I really mean it."

Frank stepped back over to Joyce who asked what that was all about. She had not been able to hear the hushed conversation. Like Frank, she had also wondered what on earth Sam was asking.

"Oh," Frank said calmly, "that? He just wanted to borrow my comb."

"Oh, that's sweet," she said with a motherly smile.

"Sweet?" Frank questioned. "I guess that's what you call it. I think he just feels very self conscious about being here in his current condition."

"Who wouldn't?" Luke asked.

"Now, Son," Frank replied, "no rudeness. Sam seems like a very nice man. We should make him feel like a member of the family."

"Oh, I know, Dad, I know," Luke replied. "I kinda like the old guy. But, I'll sure be glad when he gets a shower!"

Kenny nodded his head and smiled. He bobbed up and down so enthusiastically, it reminded them of Dopey in Disney's "Snow White". "Only in the cute way, not the dopey way," Luke would have pointed out. It made them all laugh and eased their tension.

They were still giggling as Sam emerged from the restroom. He had tossed his tattered hat into the trash with the paper towels. His long, gray hair was wet and combed straight back. He had obviously spent considerable effort at the sink scrubbing his hands, face and head. Even his scraggly beard was somewhat combed. He had done his best, but the long whiskers curled and looped in awkward ways. He was still tugging at it, trying to get it to behave.

"Now I know why those fancy hairdressers talk about 'taming' hair," he said, as he approached his new benefactors.

This put them all at ease and they burst out in a full chorus of laughter. The clerk at the customer service desk looked over to see what the commotion was all about. All she saw was a group of happy people sharing a moment that she could not possibly interpret, and returned to her work.

* * * * *

It seemed like only a few minutes had passed, but it was well over an hour. The family had coaxed, encouraged, and at times applauded Sam as he shopped for clothes. Joyce had stepped up and taken charge. She marched him into the shirt section, then the pants section. She even got him socks. And, to his embarrassment, but great thanks, underwear. She made sure to pick out two or three of each item so that he would have changes of clothes.

He didn't dare try on clothes, lest he stain something that did not fit. The shirts didn't worry her so much, but Joyce had to finally convince him to try on a "best guess" pair of pants, so that they could be relatively certain of his size. To everyone's relief, that first pair was a good fit, and Sam said he'd take them. Luke had muttered that that was good because no one else would ever want to wear them now, to which he got a nudge from Frank, who couldn't help but smile and repress a bit of a laugh.

After a stop for shoes and a decent coat, they headed over to the toiletries department, while Frank went in search of a duffle bag for Sam to store his new belongings. Sam was soon outfitted with a new comb, razor and scissors for his beard, shampoo, and – unbeknownst to each of them – the three kids separately, but simultaneously, handed him a stick of deodorant. He smiled self-consciously, but then they all laughed.

"I'll use them all!" Sam promised.

"Why wait?" Emma suggested inadvertently.

As they were heading to the checkout stand with a basket full of goodies, Joyce paused.

"You know," she said, "there's really nothing wrong with him putting some of these things on in the dressing room."

"You can do that?" Luke asked with cautious surprise. "Isn't that stealing?"

"No, no," Joyce calmed her wide-eyed youth. "It's OK so long as you keep the tags and show them to the checkout girl." As Frank rejoined his family, she tossed a toothbrush and toothpaste into their basket.

"I don't know," Luke fretted uncomfortably. "Putting on stuff that isn't paid for doesn't seem right."

"It's just like when Mom gets you shoes," Emma put in. "You always put them on and wear them out of the store."

"Yeah, but that's just shoes," Luke clarified, "not a whole wardrobe."

"It'll be fine," Frank confirmed. "Come on, Sam, let's get you dressed up."

As Sam stepped toward the door to the dressing room, Frank handed him a little, plastic cylinder he had picked up from the hygiene area.

"While you're in there, you may as well put some of this on," he suggested. "No offense intended, Sam."

Sam looked at the cylinder and immediately recognized the white sailing ship on the red background of the Old Spice bottle. He smiled and blushed at the same time.

"Certainly!" he said. "Thanks, I'll put on an extra dose."

"What was that?" Luke asked his dad.

"Just some deodorant," Frank replied offhandedly, as he turned his gaze back from the door Sam had used.

"Deodorant?" Luke exclaimed with a concerned expression. He looked panicky. "But, we haven't paid for it!"

He looked imploringly at his mother. She tried very hard not to roll her eyes. Frank used no such restraint and simply waved to her to take over the conversation.

"It will be all right!" she explained. "We'll just pay for it along with everything else."

"But, he's using it NOW!" Luke restated his position. "And, we haven't paid yet!"

"But, we know we WILL pay for it," Joyce continued.

"Jeepers, lighten up already," Emma said.

Even Kenny was nodding in agreement.

None of this helped Luke. He still felt violently dishonest, and paced back and forth while they waited. He was certain the whole transaction had been caught by some sort of security guard and at this very moment store management was planning on sweeping in to arrest the whole lot of them. He decided then and there to keep aloof of the whole situation and physically keep his distance. When they would go to the checkout counter, he'd simply stand back a few feet so that he could claim he had nothing to do with anything once the checkout girl caught them with the stolen goods.

What seemed to Luke as an eternity, passed. Finally, Sam emerged looking much better than he had before. His beard was still behaving wickedly, but he looked much better in the new clothes and shiny shoes. He carried his old threadbare clothes draped over one arm (carefully concealing his underclothes).

"Well, I guess I'm ready," he said.

"Yes, let's go pay for this booty," Frank said, while Luke vigorously nodded his head in frantic agreement.

At the word "pay" the reality and charity of the situation struck Sam again.

"I really do deeply appreciate this," he said meekly.

"Don't think about it," Frank said with a smile. "We're happy to do it!"

Frank put his hand firmly on Sam's shoulder. It sent a warm, calming sensation through Sam, the magnitude of which Frank could never fully understand.

"Say, you even smell better!" Frank added with a wink. He walked over and patted Luke on the head, tousling his hair. Luke stopped and backed away, still concerned.

*****

They paid without incident. Once outside, Sam unceremoniously and unequivocally dumped his old clothes into the trash bin out front. He couldn't help allowing a satisfied, grateful grin to spread across his face. It was accompanied by a warm feeling deep within his chest.

Chapter 7
The Drive

"You see, Luke," Dad said, while looking in his rearview mirror at his somber boy. Luke was sitting in the far back with his back to his father. "We didn't get arrested after all. We paid for everything and everyone's happy."

"Arrested?" Sam asked with concern. "Why would we have been arrested?"

"Oh, that's just Luke," Emma burst in from beside him. "He's always afraid that if you do something illegal, you'll get arrested."

"Well, you do, don't you?" Sam asked. "What was illegal? I saw you pay for these clothes..."

"Yeah, we paid," Emma continued, "but Luke was all worried about you putting them on BEFORE we paid. He thought that was illegal and they'd arrest us."

"Well," Sam said, turning slightly toward Luke behind him, and speaking up so Luke would be sure to hear, "I think that's admirable. Any boy with that much consideration for the law will make a fine man someday."

Luke didn't say anything. He didn't even turn around. But, as the car continued down I-80, toward Oklahoma, he decided he kind of liked this man, Sam.

* * * * *

They drove on and on. Hour after hour. Anyone who has driven across country has become familiar with the tedium of endless days of driving. Sitting in the car, keeping eyes on the road, letting trees and signs fly by. Seeking for small things to keep the mind occupied. Estimating distances from one turn in the road to the next horizon. Watching passing cars for interesting license plates. Searching passing signs for letters of the alphabet. Listening to radio stations fade into and out of range. Tedious, endless driving.

Even on the best of drives, the days seem to wear on for weeks. Pile in a few kids, and the drive can take on a life of its own. It was fortunate for everyone that Sam's presence put a bit of a neutral plug into the normally enthusiastic – and equally endless – chatter and antics from Luke and Kenny.

* * * * *

Joyce turned her head, trying to look casual. She saw the man – Sam – sitting behind her husband. He had a pleasant look on his face, from what she

could see. His head was turned toward the window. He was staring out at the
landscape as it raced passed. His clothes looked good on him. His hair was
still a matted, greasy mess, but it was combed as best as he could. She could
tell that he had really tried.

She thought his efforts with his beard were cute and almost laughed, in
spite of herself, as she looked at the gnarled and curled whiskers. He had
really tried here, too. She wanted to grant him that dignity.

She turned farther and could see that Emma was smiling with her book on
her lap beside the man - beside Sam. She had to keep reminding herself that
this stranger, this man, had a name that he had given them the opportunity to
give to him. Or, what was that again? It all seemed so surreal. They had
actually named this man? He was in their car now? They were taking him to
Oklahoma? They barely even knew the man. In fact, they DIDN'T know
him. That was the whole point, or was it? She was beginning to confuse
herself and her eyes slid toward her husband.

She looked at the puzzled look on his face. He seemed to be running
through a conversation in his own mind. She saw his eyebrows twitch, furrow
and relax multiple times. She guessed that he was rehearsing the events over
in his own mind, probably asking the same questions of himself. She watched
him for a moment. He was oblivious of her stare. She reached her hand over
and brushed his arm.

"Frank?" she asked quietly.

"Huh?" was all that he managed to reply. He was rattled for a moment as
he shook his thoughts free and brought himself back to the present. He
turned his head and saw her attempt at a smile. "Oh, uh, what is it?"

"I was just wondering -" she began, but he finished.

"If we did the right thing?" he asked very softly.

She nodded.

"I've been wondering that myself," he admitted. "It's strange, but the more
I think about it, the more it seems right. I think we're going to be OK here."

"That's what doesn't make any sense," she agreed. "It shouldn't be OK. It
should be a terribly frightening thing. As much as I'm concerned about what
we're doing, the more at peace I feel about it. He really does seem like a nice
man."

"They all seem nice before they flip," Frank added.

"Frank!" Joyce exclaimed.

"I know," he said. "Just kidding."

"It's not funny!"

"I know. He does seem like a good man, though. And, I can only imagine
what must be going through HIS mind. Here he is going across country just to

see Oklahoma! Couldn't he just go to the library and check out some picture books?"

"I really don't think he has a library card," Joyce grimaced.

"I suppose not," Frank agreed. "I'm afraid they probably wouldn't have let him in either."

"I can only imagine the kind of life he's led," Joyce sighed wistfully, stealing another look at their guest. "How many people do you think he sees in a day? Asking for help. Getting none. How can anyone live like that?"

"Yeah, I know. I know it all too well," Frank said. "I was one of the ones who snubbed him, remember?"

"But, you're not snubbing him now!" she added hopefully. "This could be the start of a whole new life for him."

"A whole new life?" Frank asked. "In Oklahoma?"

His mind drifted a moment or two as he tried to picture Sam panhandling in the panhandle state.

"Say," he said at last, "do you think he'll want a ride home?"

"A ride home? What do you mean?"

"You know, when we head back home," Frank explained. "Do you think he's going to want us to take him back with us?"

"I don't know. I hadn't even thought about that!" she admitted.

"I guess we'll just take it one day at a time."

* * * * *

Sam sat staring idly out his window. To the casual observer, the flat desert terrain offered little of interest, but Sam's eyes were pulled toward it as if in a trance. Emma continued to steal furtive looks at him, and kept smiling from ear to ear, very pleased with herself. Sam hadn't said a word in hours. He just sat and stared out the window for mile upon mile.

Joyce had thought he had fallen asleep, but when she saw his head turn to view some passing feature, she nudged Frank and nodded toward the man. Frank nodded knowingly. He had been able to see in the mirror that Sam's eyes were wide open in some state of wonder, he had supposed. Joyce considered beginning a conversation with him, but thought the better of it, deciding to not disturb him.

"You know," Sam said out of the blue, "if you keep your eyes fixed on the wires, it looks like you're sliding up and down as they pass."

"Huh?" Emma asked alertly. "What slides up and down? What's passing?"

Sam's eyes never left his window. He reached his hand up and pointed to where he was staring.

"Out there," he said. "See those telephone lines?"

Emma moved beside him, and leaned forward in front of him so she could look out his window. Having overheard them, Luke was intrigued. He leaned over to his own window in the back.

"Yeah, what about them?" Luke asked.

"Well, they're supported by those poles we keep passing," Sam explained.

"So?" Luke asked.

"Put your eyes in one place," Sam continued. "Focus on one spot on the wires. Pretend that spot is traveling with you, moving along the wires. Each time the line comes to a pole, it shoots up to a point and then rushes down again until it gets halfway between poles. Then it goes up again."

"What do you mean one spot?" Luke asked.

"I think I know what you mean," Emma said, getting excited. "It's not really one spot on the wire, but a sliding spot. Like if you were able to stick your hand out the window and hold your finger out touching the wires. If you kept your finger steady, and let it slide, you'd be looking at that 'one spot' but the spot would slide along the wires, right?"

"Precisely!" Sam said, pulling his gaze away long enough to give her a smile.

Joyce paused in her knitting momentarily as she and Frank listened intently to this odd conversation, while Kenny slept in his little compartment between the seats.

"Do you see it, Luke?" Sam asked.

"No, you mean - wait! I do see it!" he responded with excitement. "Yeah, the wires go up and down and just keep sliding! Weird!"

"Now," Sam added, "don't imagine you're sticking your finger out the window, but pretend YOU'RE out the window. Imagine you're some sort of skater up there on the wires, sliding along on the top of them."

"Hey, I see what you mean!" Luke said. "Hey, this is fun. Here I go - UP! And back down. UP! And back down. Sheesh, I'm gonna get dizzy!"

"Aah!" Emma screamed with a laugh. "I fell off! I didn't see that turn coming!"

Joyce looked over and saw that the telephone poles had taken a turn away from the road to make way for a ravine. She smiled and had to suppress a little giggle.

"Hey, here we come back again!" Luke shouted. "Get ready! Hop up there! NOW!"

In their minds, three skaters were now up on the wires doing an impressive balancing act at breakneck speeds. They must have kept this up for over an hour.

Just as they were ready to move onto other diversions, little Kenny woke up. Luke explained the game to him and they all joined in anew, laying claims of passing each other on the wires. Emma suggested they try a relay in which their imaginary skaters passed a baton between each other as they took different wires and occasionally managed to slip over to cross wires and climb higher or farther out, depending on what the lines provided. Then they'd come slamming back together again.

"They're really getting into that, aren't they?" Frank commented to his wife.

Joyce's knitting stopped for a moment again as she looked back and saw the four of them eagerly looking out the window toward the wires. Sam was pointing and smiling as he warned Luke about an upcoming transformer. They all shouted with delight as Luke pretended to hit the pole and fall "dead" in his seat.

"Yes, they are," Joyce said, smiling. "They certainly are. It looks like the kids are really taking to Sam, too." She smiled broadly as she looked back at her knitting and busied herself again.

"Maybe it wasn't such a bad idea after all," Frank said, giving a look in his rearview mirror at their antics.

"He seems like a very nice man," Joyce added. "I wonder how he came to be so down. Do you think he's always been a –" Joyce hesitated. She tried to finish it, but didn't dare say the word.

"A 'bum'?" Frank whispered.

Joyce nodded, keeping her face turned away from the back and trying to hide her dejected look from Sam.

"I don't think so," Frank surmised. "I have a feeling there's quite a story behind our new friend."

* * * * *

They continued driving for several hours. They played the wire-skating game during much of it, but also the standards of the alphabet game and others. At one point, Emma suggested playing "I Spy with My Little Eye," but Luke nixed it. He said he really didn't like that one. Emma and Sam played without him, while he and Kenny entertained motorists with their magic card tricks.

Around 5 pm they pulled into Elko. Frank smiled when he saw a sign advertising the annual "Cowboy Poetry Reading" that would be held in January. Elko was one of those quaint Nevada towns that was steeped in its own traditions.

"It's good to have traditions," Frank thought silently. "Do you want to stop for dinner?" he asked Joyce quietly, trying carefully to not be overheard. He didn't want the kids to hear the question, in case she didn't want to stop, but they did.

"What's the next city?" she asked.

"It's Wendover," he replied. "Another two hours or so."

"We better stop then," she surmised. "I don't think anyone's starved, but I don't think we can hold out that long."

"There's a handful of tiny towns in between," he suggested.

"Yes, but who knows what they have?" she added.

"Good point," he agreed. "Let's stop." Looking in the rearview mirror he loudly asked, "Who's hungry?"

Sam was taken aback by the thundering reply. He'd never experienced anything like the chiming chorus of "I am!" that suddenly rang through the car. They chanted it over and over with increasing decibels. He covered his ears and looked around in startled amazement. The kids suddenly noticed their new friend's reaction and were just as suddenly concerned when they realized they may have harmed the old man in some way. Joyce gave them a warning glare. Everyone sat in tense anticipation for a moment, like a rock teetering on the edge of a cliff, wondering how Sam would react to this outburst.

His head was scrunched down into his shoulders. His eyes were clenched shut. He had shifted and propped his fingers into his ears, causing his elbows to stick out to either side.

First one eye relented and cautiously opened, looking around timidly, then the other did the same. He kept his fingers in his ears as he slowly peered around. Seeing no hint of further abrasions, he slowly let his hands drop, with his fingers still primed for reentry. The family continued to fret and stare, waiting for his response to the onslaught.

"Well, I'll be!" he said slowly. Then he added, as he still looked about him, "I'd have to say these fine children are hungry!"

The smile lines that quickly grew across his weathered face relieved the tension and everyone smiled back and then burst out in infectious laughter.

"Sorry, Sam," Emma apologized with a sheepish shrug. "We'll be better!"

Everyone agreed and laughed some more, as Dad pulled into a service station for gas.

Chapter 8

Dinner

"It'll be all right," Joyce reassured Sam.

He had stopped in the doorway of the Denny's restaurant. Frank and the boys had already entered. Emma was standing by Sam's side, trying to be supportive.

"I don't know," Sam stalled. "They just don't like my kind coming into nice places like this."

"They don't like nice grandfatherly men coming in to eat with their family or friends?" Joyce asked with a smile, trying to put him at ease. "I think you're mistaken. Come with us."

She reached out and took hold of his hand. As with Emma's earlier, he couldn't help but notice that her soft, smooth skin was a stark contrast to the dry scratchiness of his own. Emma grabbed his other hand and started to pull as she reached out to open the door.

"Yeah, come on, Sam!" she said, looking back at him with a smile. "You don't want to make us late! Dad hates it when we take too long. 'Got to get back on the road!'" she mimicked her father by gritting her teeth and trying to speak in a voice much deeper than her own.

"OK. All right. I'm coming," Sam said. "Just don't scold me, sir." He gave Emma a wink as the three walked through the door and foyer and into the restaurant proper.

Sam felt conspicuous and uneasy, as if all eyes were on him. He was particularly paranoid when a pleasant young woman with a nametag approached them. He was certain she was going to send him back the way he had come. He was so disturbed he couldn't even hear her question, and was relieved when Joyce responded.

The waitress was saying something and pointing. Before Sam realized what was happening, he found himself walking with Joyce and Emma in the direction she had pointed. They walked halfway across the room before Sam saw Frank and the boys sitting at a large table. They were waving and smiling. In the back of his mind, Sam played back the hostess' and Joyce's conversation and realized that they had been asked if they could be helped and Joyce had said she was with "them" and had pointed to the other part of her family.

Sam was now sitting. He was mulling over the ordeal, coming to grips with the thought of his actually sitting INSIDE a restaurant with a menu in his hands. His head was swimming. He was trying to convince himself that he was

NOT about to get kicked out at any moment. He remained paranoid and skittish, jerking and jumping at the sounds around him.

Someone laughed and he was certain it was about him. He turned his head cautiously, but saw that it was just a group of men sitting together telling jokes after a long day on the job. He looked at them curiously, wondering what sort of work they had done, what it was like to work for a full day, to receive a paycheck at the end of the week, to have friends his own age, to –

He jumped suddenly, startled by movement and a voice on his right. He looked and saw a well-built man standing there, leaning toward him. He had obviously just spoken, but Sam had no idea what it was he had said. He could certainly guess it well enough. The jig was up. He knew he had been found out and may as well go quickly without making a scene and embarrassing this nice family, who had already done so much for him.

"I'll go," he said, as he started to rise sheepishly.

"Pardon?" the lad asked.

Frank and Joyce were both looking at Sam and saying something or other to him, with quick concern.

"I'll go quietly," Sam repeated.

"I'm sorry, I don't understand," the waiter repeated. "I just wanted to know if you'd like something to drink. Perhaps a glass of water?"

Sam had risen halfway. His hands were clenched on the arms of his chair. He paused in that position and looked around the table in bewilderment.

"Water?" he asked, amazed.

"Yes," the waiter confirmed. "Would you like some water?"

"Uh, yes, please, certainly," Sam said slowly. "Certainly. I'd love some water. A nice, big glassful if that isn't too much trouble."

"Not at all, sir," came the reply, followed by the appearance of a large clear-plastic pitcher which the waiter used to fill Sam's tall glass.

Sam sat back down slowly as the glass was filled. The ice made a tinkling sound as it slipped from the pitcher and tumbled into the glass. It sounded like the ringing of a bell. He watched the glass fill. His hopes and confidence filled along with it. He was coming to grips with the concept that he was going to be allowed to stay, and even eat, in this warm, inviting place. He decided he was beginning to appreciate what Heaven must be like.

With this thought, Sam caught a glimpse of his reflection in a window. He frowned and turned his head away quickly. Clearly, he felt there was nothing heavenly about his appearance.

"Frank, would you mind if I slipped into the restroom for a moment?" he asked.

"What? Uh, we haven't ordered yet," Frank stammered. Then, realizing he should be more gracious, he took on the role of host, smiled warmly and said, "Certainly. It looks like it's right over there," Frank pointed.

"Thank you," Sam said, ducking away uneasily. "I won't be long."

While Sam was away composing himself, Joyce turned to Frank and said, "It's sure nice of you to do this for him."

"Yeah, looks like he hasn't been in a restaurant for years," Frank observed. "I hope this doesn't turn out to be just too much for him."

"What do you mean?" Emma asked, eavesdropping.

"Well, too much of a good thing can be hard to take for some people," her mother explained.

"Like too much Christmas?" Luke piped in, also eavesdropping. "I don't think I could ever have too much Christmas."

"I thought you were coloring," Frank said.

"That just takes eyes and fingers," Luke explained, "not ears. I can still use them for other things."

"Such a clever boy," Frank said, as he gave a wry smile.

"We just don't want to push too much onto Sam too soon," Joyce said. "Just don't rush him. There's so much that we take for granted that he's just not used to."

"But, what about – ?" Emma stopped herself when she saw Sam coming back to the table.

Sam was still wiping his hands as he came to the table. It was obvious that he had just put in some concerted effort on his hair and beard. Both were damp. His beard continued to curl in some places and stick out awkwardly in others. Without speaking to each other, the family all knew to not say anything that might embarrass him. They just welcomed him back and let him sit.

"Luke, hand Sam a menu," Frank said, trying to prevent the topic of his appearance being brought up.

"But, he's got one right there at his place," Luke responded with confusion. He reached over and tilted the large, laminated menu for Sam, who had just sat down between him and Emma.

"Yes, thank you," Sam said. "Thank you very much."

He took the menu carefully in both hands and looked at the pictures on the front. His gaze lingered on the pictures of delicious meals. He opened it slowly and his eyes went wide. There was a two-page spread of entrées, each one looked more succulent than the next. His mind panicked and nearly shut down at the overload of potentials. He just sat there letting his gaze roll across one photo to the next. He began reading the descriptions of each meal. His stomach gurgled loudly, but he didn't seem to notice.

"Well, have you decided yet, Sam?" Frank asked expectantly.

The others had already put down their menus and were eagerly waiting to place their orders or, in the case of the children, to have their mother place their orders for them. Kenny and Luke were busily drawing on their placemats. Emma was watching Sam closely, with a very satisfied smile on her face.

"Uh, it's just that," Sam stammered, "there are so many things to choose from!"

It was still difficult for him to grasp the reality of his situation. He paused, seemingly flustered. He didn't say any more.

Emma was the first to notice that Sam's eyes were tearing up. Sam took his napkin and dabbed them quietly.

"I – uh, I –" was all he could stammer.

"Just pick your favorite," Joyce coaxed.

"I've never had a favorite," Sam replied honestly. "I've always just taken whatever was given to me, or whatever I could find. I've never had the luxury of a choice before."

Joyce and Frank were moved at this humble reply. They thought of the many days and nights he must have spent scrounging for food, and wondered just how often he had gone to sleep still hungry. This led to the wonderment of where he had slept and how he had kept warm. There were so many questions, so much they could not even imagine about this man. Their musings were interrupted by Emma, however.

"Why don't you just pick the steak!" Emma said. "Dad says there's nothing better than a good steak!"

"A STEAK?" Sam said, a bit overwhelmed. "I don't think I could eat a whole steak! Besides, it must be awfully expensive –"

"Sam," Frank interrupted quietly. Leaning forward he said in earnest, "Please, don't worry about the cost. I'm not a wealthy man, but I can certainly afford to buy a new friend a decent meal. Please, let us do this for you."

Sam could see the sincerity in Frank's eyes. He looked over to Joyce and saw her nod in silent agreement. She blinked to confirm it.

Sam was on the verge of responding, when the waiter returned and interrupted them to ask for their orders.

"Well, I guess I'll have the steak," Sam said, giving quick furtive looks to Frank and Joyce who nodded in agreement.

"Great!" Emma said with excitement. She realized that she had never been excited about someone ordering dinner before.

"Would you like steamed vegetables or a salad with that?" the waiter asked.

"Salad or vegetables?" Sam exclaimed with surprise.

"Yes, it comes with either one you choose," the waiter explained.

"It comes WITH it?" Sam said. Seeing the waiter nod, he added, "Vegetables, I guess. I'm told you should always eat your vegetables," he added with a wry smile.

He folded his menu and tried to hand it back to the waiter, ready to be done with this ordering business. The waiter graciously took the menu and then asked, "And, would you like fries, mashed potatoes or a baked potato with that?"

"More? Do potatoes, come with it too?" Sam was beginning to feel a bit overwhelmed.

The waiter smiled and nodded and began to wonder why the family didn't take "Gramps" out more often.

"Uh, baked potato, I guess," Sam replied. Turning to Frank, he added, "I've always liked baked potatoes. At least I think I have. I can't remember the last time I had one."

The waiter had to again interrupt to ask about chives, sour cream and a seemingly endless array of other questions. Sam was greatly relieved when he finally moved onto the others for their orders. He was so stressed out that he believed he was beginning to sweat.

Sam was too preoccupied to notice a waitress who had approached their table and was now standing next to him, coffee pitcher in hand. The waitress stood there patiently waiting, trying to gain Sam's attention, but failing to compete with the daydreams of food that were now taking hold of Sam's attention.

"Luke," Joyce whispered to her son.

"What?" Luke asked.

Without speaking, Joyce nodded at the waitress and then at Sam. Luke had been too engrossed in his own menu to have noticed the logjam that sat beside him. He looked back at his mother and repeated his query. She nodded again, more emphatically. Luke caught on and his face lit up with understanding.

"Hey, Sam," Luke said in a loud voice.

Sam didn't notice, so Luke elbowed him hard enough to gain Sam's attention. He didn't wait for Sam to ask what was wanted.

He simply said, "Hey, Sam, the waitress wants to give you coffee."

"Never touch the stuff," Sam said, eyeing the back of Emma's menu. He was too busy enjoying his visual heavenly fantasy to care to elaborate.

Frank, Joyce, and the kids were all somewhat surprised at Sam's reply, and wondered if Sam knew what he was turning down. They wondered if it was truly possible that the man that Frank had earlier accused of being a drunk trying to bum beer money from them, actually abstained from coffee. It was almost unthinkable.

"We never drink it either," Emma replied.

Sam didn't reply, he was busying himself looking at the dessert menu that was propped up on the table.

"I said, we never drink it either," Emma repeated, purposely increasing her volume.

"Huh?" Sam asked. "Well, good for you, you'll live longer." Looking around uncomfortably, he added, "I can't believe I'm sitting here. I can't remember the last time I sat in a fine restaurant like this, if ever."

He continued to look around admiringly.

"Yeah, uh, right," Luke said, trying to not slight Sam's impressed treatment of what he felt was an ordinary family restaurant.

If Sam's reaction to the menu had been extraordinary, it was nothing compared to his disbelief as a baked potato and a steaming steak were slid before him. Sincere tears of joy and gratitude began streaming down his weather-worn face.

"You people are just too much!" he exclaimed.

Emma beamed. Luke was embarrassed and felt uncomfortable sitting next to a grown man that was crying over a steak. Kenny smiled silently.

"Well, dig in everyone," Frank said, breaking the awkward silence. "We're glad to do it, Sam. We just hope you enjoy it."

Several minutes later, the family had finished their meals. Sam, meanwhile, had only eaten about a quarter of his potato and less than half of the steak. Throughout the meal, he would take a bite and then lay his fork and knife down on his plate while he chewed. His chewing had grown continually slower, with the gap between bites taking longer and longer.

Finally, he pushed the plate back and straightened. He shook his head regretfully.

"You haven't even finished!" Luke exclaimed.

"Luke, be polite," Joyce reprimanded.

"I'm sorry folks," Sam said forlornly. "I'm just not used to so much food. Leastwise, not so much food at one time!" He looked at his plate with yearning, but knew he couldn't take in more than he already had. "I'm sorry," he repeated.

"So much food?" Luke whispered to himself.

"Don't be sorry," Frank replied. "We just wanted to make sure you got some dinner. It looks like you did fine. Just fine."

"Yes, do you want some dessert?" Joyce asked.

"DESSERT?" Sam exclaimed aghast. "Oh, no! I couldn't possibly!"

"I could!" Luke interjected while Kenny nodded vigorously in agreement.

"I'm sure you could," Frank smiled at his boys. He was about to add, "but, we have to hit the road," then thought the better of it. He let everyone order something. Sam chose not to place an order. He just sat and enjoyed the feeling of food in his stomach while the others ate. Before long, the family, and Sam, were back on the road again.

Chapter 9
A Night's Stay

The sky was black. Only a few stars peered down on the car as it sped along the lonesome highway. Sam sat with his head near the window and his eyes glued to the outside. He watched dark shapes whiz by, guessing at their substance. Occasionally, he could see them pass another car heading in the other direction. He'd watch its headlights grow until their intensity seemed to burn his eyes, then suddenly they were gone, blanked out in the moment they passed, and he would turn to see the red taillights shrink off into the distance.

Joyce turned back to check on her family. Little Emma had snuggled up against Sam and had fallen asleep. Joyce had lost most of her concern about the man. He seemed sincerely nice. Emma looked so peaceful and content with her head against Sam's arm that Joyce couldn't help but smile. She felt a warmth well up within her and nudged Frank. He was stirred from his driving stupor and asked what was up. Joyce simply motioned with her eyes and a nod of her head.

Frank looked in the rearview mirror and saw his daughter at peace.

"Yeah, I know," he said. "Kind of cute, isn't it?"

"She's really taken to him," Joyce whispered. "Hasn't she?"

"Well, who wouldn't?" Frank replied. "He's a darned nice man."

"You weren't too taken by him when we first saw him," Joyce pointed out.

"Oh, yeah. Well, that was different," Frank mumbled.

"You know, I wonder how many people were just like us?" Joyce asked. "Passing him by and not giving him a care."

"And, how many more are there like him?" Frank added. "Decent people down on their luck, who just need someone to take a moment and care."

They sat in silence only a moment until Frank mused, "And, I wonder how many times Sam had gone over to that gas station, only to be turned away by that guy."

"He sure seemed to know all about him," Joyce agreed.

"Apparently, not. He only THOUGHT he knew all about him," Frank corrected.

"I wonder what more there is?" Joyce wondered. "I mean, what's his story?"

"I've been wondering that too," Frank admitted.

"He seems decent enough," Joyce said. "You'd think he'd have a job, a family, a home, something somewhere."

"Maybe he lost his job one day and never got another," Frank said.

"I don't think it's that simple," Joyce said, sneaking another look back at their passenger.

"You think his wife died and he lost it and just wandered off?" Frank asked.

"Oh, I hope not!" Joyce said with a start, and then added, "But, I would think it would take something like that. I can't imagine a man as nice as he is going through life single. Surely he must have been married once. He's not a bad-looking man."

"Eh? Maybe I should grow a scruffy beard," Frank said with a teasing glint in his eye as he tugged at his chin.

"I don't think so," Joyce said without hesitating.

"We're coming up on a town," Frank interrupted. "I think we're near enough to Salt Lake City. Let's call it a night."

"There's a Travelodge up ahead. Let's just stay there," Joyce suggested.

"Sounds good to me," Frank agreed.

Kenny and Luke were awakened by the stopping of the car. Their bleary-eyed heads slowly bobbed up, followed by questions of where they were and what was going on. When they saw their mom heading into the motel office, their questions were answered. It wasn't long before she returned and got back in the car.

"Do they have a pool?" Luke asked expectantly, as Emma stretched awake.

"They sure do," Frank replied.

Their shouts of "Yippee!" were quelled when they saw their dad point straight ahead and say, "It's right there!"

The light layer of snow covering the slide, steps, and lawn chairs surrounding the pool was not a welcome sight.

"Never mind, Kenny," Luke said glumly, looking at the empty cement hole before them. "It's an outdoor pool."

"What do you expect at a motel?" Emma asked with a sensible flare that annoyed Luke even more than the snow.

Frank drove over to the room Joyce had indicated, and the family piled out of the car, Sam included. Joyce walked over to Sam and handed him a key.

"I was able to get you the room right next to ours," she explained.

"Room?" Sam asked, bewildered. "I can just stay in the car." He made feeble gestures with his hand.

"Not when it's snowing!" Frank exclaimed.

Sam was about to explain how much warmer the car would be compared to what he was used to, when he was interrupted by Emma.

"Why can't he stay with us?" she protested.

"Because there are only two beds," Frank replied.

"Well, can I stay in Sam's room?" Luke asked eagerly.

"No, I don't think so," Frank said. "I think Sam would like his privacy."

"But! -" the kids all tried to protest.

"But, nothing!" Frank said firmly. "Now, go with your mother."

Joyce took the cue and with a firm, kind voice ushered her kids into action. They gathered bags and took them into their room. Frank turned to Sam and pointed to the other door.

"Well, Friend," he said, "this would be your room."

He walked Sam to the door and put the key into the lock. He gave it a turn, twisted the knob, pushed the door open, and then stepped back. He put his hand on Sam's shoulder and gently guided the bewildered man forward and into the room.

Sam crossed the threshold and stood within the room as if in a daze. So much had happened already that day, he didn't think he could be more overwhelmed, but he was. Frank flipped on the light and startled Sam as features of the blackened room burst into view.

He looked down at the brown, shag carpet and straight across the room to the mirror outside the bathroom. There was a TV on a dresser to the left, next to another large mirror. Opposite it, and filling most of the room, was a large bed, flanked on either side by nightstands bedecked with lamps. Sam stood speechless, his eyes growing moist as he looked at the broad stripes on the bedspread.

"It's all yours, Pal," Frank said at last, not knowing what else to say to ease Sam's mind and make him feel at home.

"I don't - I don't know what to say," Sam stammered.

"Say you'll be ready for breakfast by 8 and I'll be happy enough!" Frank said, forcing himself to sound calm and cheerful. This was all new territory for him as well. He felt awkward and uncomfortable, but also more than a little good about his efforts.

"I don't - I don't deserve this," Sam said, as he turned back toward Frank. He kept his head bent toward the floor and his hands came close together so that his fingers fidgeted nervously with each other.

"Sure you do, Sam," Frank said reassuringly. "You deserve this and much, much more. Have a good night's stay, Friend!"

Frank tried to think of something more to say as Sam continued to stand motionless, but brimming with emotions. For lack of other words, he simply said, "Good night," as he stepped out of the room and closed the door quietly.

Sam continued to stand alone in "his" room, trying to come to grips with the wonderful treatment he had received, when he was startled by a light tapping at the door. He stepped to it and opened it slowly.

"Yes?" he queried.

It was Frank.

"I – uh," he stammered, "I seem to have forgotten to give you your key."

He gingerly pressed the key into Sam's hand. Sam took it, still very bewildered as Frank again backed out of the room and said his farewell, closing the door softly behind him. Sam peered down at his hand and looked at the large, oval key holder and the brass key that was connected to it. He held the key up to his face, letting it dangle from its forest green plastic key ring.

"My key?" he whispered as a tear streaked down his cheek.

* * * * *

"Is everything all right?" Joyce asked as she and Frank began to prepare for bed.

Joyce had gotten the kids through their evening routine while Frank was next door. The boys had already brushed their teeth and were in their pajamas, jumping on one of the beds as Emma shook her head called them both "childish" as she climbed into her rollaway bed.

"Boys!" Frank said in a stern, hushed tone, "Knock it off! Just get in bed. We have another long day ahead of us, tomorrow." Turning back to Joyce, he replied softly, "Yes, everything's fine. I think this is all a bit much for him, though."

"What do you mean?" Joyce asked, concerned.

"I just don't think he's had so much attention in quite some time," Frank explained. "And, there are so many changes for him. A 'new family,' eating in a restaurant, new clothes, having to groom himself, a roof over his head. Imagine begging for food from day to day, year upon year, and then suddenly knowing that you're guaranteed a next meal. I think it's just all a bit much for him to comprehend. Not to mention getting a new name! How can you not know your own name?"

"That poor man," Joyce sighed wistfully, as she brushed through her hair. "That poor, sweet, old man."

"You've got to wonder just how long he's been on the street," Frank agreed picking up his toothbrush and loading it with paste.

"Well, hopefully things will turn out better for him in Oklahoma," Joyce surmised.

"Yeah. What is it about Oklahoma anyway?" Frank asked with a mouthful of minty suds.

"Maybe he has family there or something," Joyce mused, joining Frank in the toothbrushing routine.

"Maybe," Frank agreed. "If so, they're not exactly very supportive, are they? If they've let him slide all these years, who says they'll be any help once he shows up again?"

"You never know," Joyce said, trying to be positive.

"Yeah," Frank countered, "maybe he doesn't even have any family out there. Maybe he's just some old, delusional man with a spontaneous yearning to go ANYWHERE away from where he was."

"True, but why Oklahoma?" Joyce asked. "Isn't that some sort of odd coincidence?"

"Yeah, very odd," Frank agreed. "You're sure none of us said anything about going to Oklahoma before he mentioned it?"

"I'm certain," Joyce said. "You were the first one to talk to him. You didn't mention it, did you?"

"Of course not!" Frank exclaimed. "Why would I?"

"It must have just been a coincidence, then," Joyce said.

"That's some coincidence," Frank agreed as he put down his toothbrush and headed to bed.

"Well, we'll just see what tomorrow brings," Joyce said, as she headed for the bed.

"Aren't we going to have a family prayer?" Emma asked eagerly.

"Of course we are," her dad replied.

The family knelt by their beds and bowed their heads. Frank asked Emma to be the voice of the prayer. The prayer she gave was full of the traditional thanks and requests, with one key addition, "...And thank you for helping us find Sam! He's wonderful. Please help us get him back to his family...."

Emma was still beaming as she lay down in her bed and Frank shut off the light.

*****

Sam stood over the sink, staring at his reflection. He saw the deep creases in his forehead and bewildered look in his own eyes. He reached up and touched his cheekbones, pulling on them with his fingertips, trying to remove the deep circles under his eyes.

He absently stroked his scraggly beard with the back of his hand. He did this a few times before he realized he was doing it. He squinted a moment and nodded his head with determination. He grabbed the toiletry kit that Joyce had given him, and pulled out the scissors, razor and cream.

He looked at the scissors a moment, then back at his reflection. He nodded again and pulled a patch of whiskers tightly with one hand as he brought the scissors up and then clipped it off. As the sink began to fill with discarded whiskers, Sam couldn't help but smile. There was something freeing about the experience. He felt as if he was shedding his old life and preparing himself for a new one.

His trimming became increasingly energetic and enthusiastic.

Chapter 10
On the Road Again

"Everyone all set to go?" Frank asked as he and Luke came back into the room.

They had just finished securing the luggage back on top of the station wagon. Luke had turned back to get another view of it as he entered.

"We even got Mom's makeup case up on top this time, Kenny," he said to his brother, who gave a grateful smile and nod. "That ought to give you more room in your fort," he added, in reference to the space between the middle seat and the rear seat. Kenny nodded even more enthusiastically.

"I've checked under all of the beds and Emma checked the drawers," Joyce said, as Emma came out of the bathroom.

"Nothing's in there either, Mom," Emma dutifully reported. "I think we're clean."

"Great! Then we can hit the road," Frank slapped his hands together and rubbed the palms back and forth in anxious anticipation.

"Does Dad really like driving that much?" Luke asked his mother while Kenny looked on with an equally puzzled expression.

"No," she replied. "It's more the opposite. He dislikes driving that much."

"Huh?"

"The sooner we hit the road, the farther we go," Frank explained. "The farther we go, the sooner we're done! So, let's get going!"

"Haven't we forgotten someone?" Joyce asked.

"Yeah, where's Sam?" Emma put in.

"Sam?" Frank, an incurable tease, feigned a blank look on his face. "Sam? Sam who? Sam Hill?" he continued as he winked to his wife.

"Sam, our new traveling friend," Emma said flatly.

"I'm sure he's still right next door, Sweetheart," Frank said with a smile. "Why don't you go get him and let him know we're ready to be on our way again?"

While Emma disappeared out the door, the others took yet another look around the room.

"Man, Mom," Luke moaned, "how many times do we need to tell you the room's clean?"

Kenny shook his head, shrugged his shoulders and rolled his eyes in agreement.

"You just never know," Joyce replied in that know all, you-just-wait-and-see air that only moms can duplicate.

She pulled on the blanket on the boys' bed and whipped it up towards its scattered pillows.

"Joyce, you're not making the bed, are you?" Frank asked in a polite voice that had a husband's hint of exasperation with a tinge of come-on-we-need-to-get-on-the-road-already.

"Of course not," Joyce said with a hum. "That's part of the nice thing about sleeping in a motel." As she spoke, her eyes scanned the bed. She pulled on the blanket once more to pull it straighter. "It's just that –" as she said this, she reached down between a fold and grabbed something small, flat and square. Bringing it up to reveal her find, she said in triumph, "– you never know what you might find."

"Our cards!" Luke said with a mixture of surprise, dismay, and relief. Turning on Kenny, he added accusingly, "I thought you said they were in the car!"

Kenny just shrugged his shoulders and gave a sheepish smile. Frank reached down and tousled his son's hair.

"Well, I guess we all learned something this morning," he said with a laugh, and then slipped into the bathroom.

"Yeah, never trust Kenny," Luke said out of the corner of his mouth, while giving Kenny the evil eye.

Kenny just gave his mom a big hug, took the cards and mouthed a sincere "Thank you!" Joyce was giving Kenny a big smile when Emma burst into the room, frantic.

"He's gone!" she cried out through misty eyes. "He's gone!"

"Who's gone?" Frank asked, coming out from the bathroom.

"Sam!" Emma blurted out. "He's gone! I just know it!"

"He wouldn't be gone!" Luke said with that annoying lilt that brothers reserve for sisters, especially sisters who are in a panic. "We're his ride!" He rolled his eyes to emphasize the idea that surely she had no clue on how to tell if someone was still in a motel room, or not.

"Luke, that doesn't help," Joyce said to her son, attempting to quell his know-it-all moment. Turning to Emma she asked, "What makes you think he's not there?"

"I knocked and knocked and he didn't answer!" she exclaimed.

"Well, maybe he's a late sleeper," Frank offered.

"I thought of that," Emma continued, "but I knocked louder and louder and he still didn't answer."

"How loudly?" Joyce asked, beginning to feel concerned.

"As loud as I could!" Emma stated, on the verge of breaking down.

"Maybe he died," Luke said flatly.

"Oh!" Emma bawled inconsolably.

"Thanks, Luke, you're a great help," Frank said, as he walked to the door.

"Well, he is old!" Luke defended his assessment.

Kenny nodded in reluctant agreement, while silent tears began to streak his cheeks.

"Well, if he was asleep, all this blubbering ought to wake him up," Luke observed callously.

"Luke," Frank shot out, "you're REALLY not helping."

"Oh, Frank," Joyce said, as she knelt with one arm around Emma and reached out for and pulled Kenny toward her. "What will we do?"

"Do?" Frank puzzled, not believing the death theory. "I'm going to go over there and find Sam, that's what I'm going to do."

He headed out the door and over to Sam's door. He knocked, and paused. There was no reply. He knocked again, more loudly. There was still no reply. The third time, he also called out. Joyce and the others could hear him calling. They held their breath, waiting for a reply that never came.

Frank tried to peer in through the peephole. He just saw a blurred blackness. He tried the knob, but it was locked. He worked his way over to the window, but the blinds were fully shut and offered no vantage to the inside. He returned to their room. Everyone stared at him. This time, even Luke looked concerned.

"He didn't answer," Frank explained before any of them could ask. "I'll go get the manager and have him open up the room."

"Oh, Frank!" Joyce said with a quavering voice. "Do you think – ? "

"I don't know what to think, Joyce," Frank interrupted. "That's why I'm going to get the manager."

A few minutes later, the family stood in their doorway as Frank hustled a man, with a concerned look on his face, toward Sam's door. He wasn't the manager, just the night clerk. The manager usually didn't show up until ten. The clerk wondered how he was going to explain this. As far as he knew there had never been a death in the motel before. Did he need to call the police? What would the manager say? Would he blame HIM for it? Would he lose his job?

His mind was racing with questions as he fumbled with his keys at Sam's door. His hands were shaking. It didn't help that the family was gathering around, each one urging him to hurry and sounding on the verge of panic or tears themselves.

"Hold on!" he cried out exasperated, turning around sharply and holding a hand up for silence, but not looking anyone in the eye. His eyes were busily scanning the keys in his other hand. "Give me a moment to open the door already. Can you all please just stand back?"

The family moved back reluctantly, but leaned in as he declared "Aha!" and put a key into the door which worked when he turned the door's handle. He then cautiously pushed open the door. The room was dark except for a faint light bleeding in through the heavy curtains, and the light piercing in through the opened door. At first, they saw nothing as they stood there holding their breath. The clerk saw a lump on the bed and gave out a gasp, which caused Emma to whimper. The clerk stood, staring for a moment when his racing thoughts were interrupted by a voice behind him.

"Well, shouldn't we go in there?" Frank asked.

"Shouldn't we do what?" the clerk stammered.

"Go in," Frank repeated in a determined tone. "It looks like he isn't here. We should find out what's up."

"But," the clerk hedged, then as his eyes and mind adjusted to the situation, he realized that what he saw and believed to be a body lying on the bed was much, much smaller than he had at first thought. He also saw that it was only at the foot of the bed, which would have been an odd place for a body.

He stepped forward and Frank pushed past him and walked up to the bed. He bent over and slowly picked up Sam's duffle bag. It was full of clothing. He looked around as the others slowly and cautiously stepped into the room. They all looked around in bewilderment. Except for the duffle bag, the place looked entirely uninhabited.

Frank wandered over to the shower room and out again, "It looks like he didn't even bother to stay the night," he surmised.

"But, why?" Joyce asked, confused. "Why wouldn't he at least spend the night?"

"Yeah, it's got to be better than hanging out on the street again," Luke agreed.

They were all theorizing on Sam's peculiar behavior and potential demise when they were interrupted by a voice and silhouette at the doorway.

"What's all this?" a cheery voice asked.

"We're trying to figure out what happened to -" Joyce cut her words short as she turned around and recognized Sam.

"Sam!" Emma cried out running to him and wrapping her arms around him so suddenly and tightly that he almost lost his balance. "Sam! You didn't run off! You didn't get murdered!"

"Murdered!?" Sam said with a start. "Of course not! I'm right here, child." He patted her on the back and looked up at Joyce and Frank. "What is this about being murdered?"

"It's, uh, it's," Frank stammered.

"We thought someone came and MURDERED you!" Luke said with animated excitement.

"Murdered me?" Sam said with shocked amazement. "Why on earth would someone want to murder me?"

"But, you weren't here," Emma stated emphatically.

"Well, sure," Sam replied, "but that doesn't mean I was DEAD!"

"But, where were you then?" Luke blurted out.

Before Sam could answer, the clerk excused himself and made his way out of the room, muttering that he was glad that all had turned out so well and that he was greatly relieved that he didn't have a mess to explain to his manager.

"I just went for a walk," Sam smiled. "Just a walk. I'm fine. I assure you, I'm fine."

"We're so glad," Joyce said. "We were worried when you didn't answer our knock."

As she calmed down, Joyce was able to look at Sam and truly see him.

"Say!" she said with a smile and a wink, "I don't know what it is, but there seems to be something different about you!"

"Hey!" Luke exclaimed, "He's cut off his beard! Wow! Do you ever look different!"

"I think he looks even more handsome," Emma observed.

"I think you're right," Joyce agreed.

"Yes, he sure does," Frank agreed. Then, trying to get his family moving, he added, "Why don't we all get in the car and hit the road? Sam can tell us all about his walk while we're driving."

* * * * *

They had found a place to eat breakfast and then driven quite a ways before Frank brought up the subject again. He was a little hesitant, not wanting to rudely intrude, but his curiosity was getting the better of him.

"So, uh, Sam," he asked, trying to not let the others overhear.

Joyce was knitting and looked over at him, knowing what he was going to ask, but remaining silent as she looked back at her knitting. All three kids were in the back, playing cards in the rear seat. Sam was sitting by himself, gazing out the window with the typical blank stare passengers on an all-day drive manage to maintain. He didn't respond.

"Sam," Frank repeated.

This time, Sam turned his head away from the window and looked up toward Frank.

"Yes?" he asked somewhat distractedly. "What is it?"

"I, uh, I was just wondering," Frank fumbled, "where you went for your walk."

"Oh, nowhere in particular," Sam said honestly, casually turning to gaze out the window again. "Just wandering around a bit."

"It must have been a bit chilly for a walk," Frank said, trying to engage in conversation.

"Chilly?" Sam asked. "I didn't really notice. I guess I'm used to that."

He shrugged and uttered a deep infectious yawn. He brought the back of his hand up to his gaping mouth to cover it and looked as if he was going to inhale his hand. Frank looked up in the rearview mirror and couldn't help seeing the massive yawn. It generated an involuntary yawn in himself which he tried in vain to quell.

"I just thought you'd still be a- a-" Frank had to pause as a yawn won him over and he found himself slowly sucking in a great deal of air with his mouth wide open and his eyes forced into a watery squint. The yawn finally released him and he was able to continue. "Oh, my! Excuse me! I was saying I just thought you'd still be asleep."

"No," Sam replied, letting out another equally devastating yawn. "I wasn't asleep. To be honest, I didn't sleep much at all last night."

"No?" Frank asked. "Why not?"

"I don't know," Sam said, "and I'm sorry to say that. You people have been very kind to me. Most generous and kind. It was a fine room. Really it was. I just couldn't manage to sleep in that bed."

"The bed?" Frank queried. "What was wrong with it?"

He cast a furtive look at Joyce who subtly acknowledged him, but continued to study her knitting and pretended to not be listening.

"Oh, there was nothing wrong with it, I suppose," Sam conceded. "It's just been so darn long since I've slept in one! Pardon my language. I just guess this old body isn't used to such frills."

This time it was Joyce who shot a glance to Frank. It pained her to think of an old man who was so unaccustomed to sleeping in a normal bed that such an experience would actually drive sleep from him. She involuntarily shook her head out of pity and concern, but continued to say nothing. Her knitting continued, but she would later find it necessary to undo all of her work from this period as she just wasn't concentrating enough.

"After a nice long, hot shower – I must say it was VERY nice – I lay in that bed for what seemed like hours," Sam confessed. "I tried lying on my back, on my side, on my other side, on my face. I felt like some sort of sausage getting cooked on all sides." Sam laughed at his metaphor. "I finally just plumb gave up. I crawled out, washed my face again, and sat down in a corner. I sat all curled up with my back in the corner and finally fell asleep.

Even still, it wasn't a deep sleep. It was just too warm in that there room. I'm not used to sleeping indoors, you know. I'm used to the brisk, cool air served up by Mother Nature herself. I tried to open a window, but it was painted shut. So, I opened the door instead. After a bit I thought it might look suspicious to someone outside if they looked over and saw a room door open. So, I closed it.

"I sat back down in my corner. Before I could manage to fall asleep, though, it got too stuffy again, so I got back up and opened the door again. I looked out and could just barely make out that the sun was working its way up. The sky was a deep purple, instead of black, with just a hint of orange along the horizon. You had to really look for it, but I saw it. I knew dawn was coming. The sky's beautiful at dawn!"

Sam looked up with a dreamy look of contentment in his eyes at this moment. Frank knew that Sam really meant what he said about the sky. He seemed to have a deep appreciation for nature. That seemed appropriate, Frank thought, as Sam must have spent so much of his time out in it. He found himself wondering why that would cause Sam to "love" nature instead of curse it as an enemy.

He decided it must have been Sam's perspective, no, his attitude. He decided that Sam simply must have a good heart. He realized Sam was still speaking and tore his thoughts away from his musings to listen to the interesting character he had so recently met.

"I knew I wasn't going to get any more sleep before morning, so I just stepped out the door for a walk. I stopped and made up the bed first, though, so the motel folks wouldn't be too annoyed with me. And, I packed up my stuff so's it would be ready when I came back."

"Actually, the motel people don't need you to make your bed," Frank was surprised to find himself say.

"Why not?" Sam asked innocently.

"Well, they remake it with clean sheets for the next person," Frank explained.

"But, those sheets were clean!" Sam pointed out. "I didn't hardly sleep on them at all, and I was clean before I laid down on them. Cleaner than I've been in, in years!"

"Yes," Frank said. "That may be true, but they'll put on fresh sheets anyway."

"But, I was clean!" Sam sounded a tinge offended.

"It's not you, Sam," Frank consoled his friend. "It's the law or something. They are required to change the sheets in between each visitor who stays in the room. They can get fined if they don't."

"Sounds like a waste of time and money to me," Sam muttered.

"Welcome to the U S of A," Frank smiled back. "It's just part of what makes this country great!"

"Wasteful washing?" Sam asked, befuddled.

"No," Frank smiled, "the absolute guarantee of clean sheets!"

He laughed and caused Joyce to laugh as well. Sam shook his head at first and then shrugged and laughed along with them.

"Why don't you catch up on some of your sleep during the drive?" Frank asked.

"Thanks, I think I will." Sam said.

"Luke. Luke!" Frank hollered, looking in the rearview mirror at the back of his boy's head.

"Yeah, Dad?" Luke answered. "What's up?"

"Find a pillow for Sam," Frank said. "He'd like to take a nap."

Kenny pulled a pillow out from under his arm and enthusiastically handed it to Emma.

"He can have Kenny's," Emma said cheerfully. "He's not using it!"

"Great!" Frank said. "Just pass it up."

It took only a few moments before Sam was fast asleep with his head leaning toward his door, with Kenny's pillow wedged between his head and the window. He looked very peaceful. If the truth could be told, he was now sleeping more relaxed and carefree than he had in many a year.

Chapter 11
Another Night

"Thank you again for such a wonderful meal," Sam said, almost bowing to his new family as they stood in the doorways in between their motel room and his, "and I promise to sleep better tonight!"

"I'm sure you will," Joyce replied. "I told the man to make sure you had a window that could open."

"DID you, now!" Sam beamed. "Well, that's right thoughtful of you! What a sweet lady to take such excellent care of an old beggar like me!"

"We don't think of you as a beggar," Joyce corrected. "You're a friend. And, it's our pleasure to help you out!"

"Well, I do appreciate it," Sam said humbly. "I appreciate those kind words very much."

There was a pause, interrupted by the sounds of Luke and Kenny jumping on the beds. Emma was sitting on the edge of her rollaway, desperately guarding it from any unwanted jumpers.

"Kenny! Luke!" Frank called out in a rather hushed shout as he bounded into their room. "Cut it out, guys! You know we don't do that in hotels!"

"Yeah, but this is a 'MOTEL'," Luke pointed out as Kenny grinned and shook with silent laughter.

"We don't do it in MOTELS, either, Son," Frank retorted. "We don't ever do it at all. Now, be good and get ready for bed."

His voice filtered out through the open door, past Joyce and Emma, and into the parking lot. Joyce could tell this was the case and lowered her eyes with embarrassment. Sam tried to hide his smile. Emma just intoned the word "Boys!" in a way that implied that she, of course, was much too mature for such childish behavior.

"Well, at least they know how to have fun!" Sam smiled back to Joyce, encouragingly.

"They certainly do know THAT!" she agreed, returning the smile.

"Well, thank you again, and good night," Sam said, as he turned and put his key into the lock.

It turned and Sam was able to enter, but not before having to return a couple more "good nights" to Emma and the boys.

He flipped a switch and bathed a good portion of the room with light. There was no master switch. Each lamp needed to be switched on separately. Sam left only the one light on as he closed the door behind him and went to the window.

He examined the lock and gave the window a push. It slid sideways, allowing a steady flow of cold air to breathe into the room. He could see its fog curl through the screen and evaporate before it hit the floor. He sighed with contentment and smiled.

"It will be a good night," he said, as he found his new toothbrush and headed to the bathroom.

When all was ready and done, he went to the bed and knelt beside it. He gave a prayer of thanks for his many blessings and this good family that had plucked him out of despair. He lifted the blanket and sheet and climbed into the bed. He slid in between the sheets. The pleasant smile on his face continued until it gradually relaxed as sleep overtook him.

* * * * *

Cold air continued to creep into Sam's room. The lights were out. There was the occasional sound of cars passing by in the night. He was oblivious to it all as he slept snuggly in the bed. His body was wholly relaxed in the peace of sound sleep. His breathing was rhythmic and steady. His closed eyes began to move randomly in REM action as his mind drifted lazily into and out of dreams.

Throughout the night, there were various dreams. They were pleasant dreams. They were insignificant dreams. They were dreams of life and experiences, many of which were not based on his own experiences. Perhaps they were wishes in the form of dreams.

At one point, he experienced his most detailed and extreme dream. He found that he was sitting on a lonely curb in the middle of a vacated town. The streets were of hard-pressed, dried dirt. A cold wind swept over the streets whisking up waves of dust as it blew past him. There were no sidewalks, and yet he sat on a strip of a lone cement curb. The street was lined with empty buildings. Some of them had doors or windows left open. Their shutters flapped in the breeze, making a haphazard clunking noise as they lazily beat against the buildings.

The town seemed to be a paradox of remnants of the Old West mingled with modern structures. There were stretches of plank-laid sidewalks interrupted sporadically by sections of modern cement sidewalk. He saw, however, that the cement was missing, leaving only the hint of where the modern sidewalks should have lain. These walkways passed before a series of buildings.

One appeared to be an old-time saloon complete with large, fragile glass windows and fancy lettering that he could not decipher. Another was a modern convenience store with advertising that was apparently for lottery tickets, in its windows. Although he saw signs and ads here and there, he could not read any of the writing. Letters seemed askew, backwards, or even foreign in places.

The buildings along the road continued to alternate, with one being at least a century old, the next two looking modern, then a couple ancient structures and so on down the street. To the waking mind it would have made no sense, but to his dreaming mind it seemed natural and proper.

From where he sat, he could see into many of them. There was just a black void inside each. The building directly across from him appeared to be a restaurant. As he gazed intently inside its doorway – the front door was missing – he saw only darkness there, too. His gaze drifted down towards the bottom of the doorway.

He felt that light from the brilliant, oppressive sun should at least be able to light up the entryway, allowing him to see the floor. As he stared intently at the blackness covering the entry, he puzzled over why such an excessively warm day would allow such a bone chilling wind to sweep through the town.

He gave it little thought, however, because as he watched the doorway, a very small section of the entryway became visible as if someone had literally splashed a small puddle of light on the floor. He watched as the light on the floor flowed into the building, like a thick liquid seeking lower ground. It flowed slowly, but steadily and persistently. Like a lazy river, it meandered left and right, illuminating the carpet as it went.

A good twenty feet inside, it bumped into a wall and split. While the main portion continued to meander across the floor, the other portion climbed and began spreading over the wall. It was an amazing sight. The light on the floor continued to bump into objects. The liquid light illuminated the portions of the objects it touched. He saw the better part of an armchair drip into view, then the legs of a table and part of its tablecloth.

Along the wall, the river of light bumped into a wall lamp and brought it into view. Half a painting soaked up the light and became visible, but not discernable. He could see objects and things appearing, but none of them were making sense, or at least giving him enough information to know where he was or what he was really seeing. He still couldn't quite tell if he was looking into a restaurant, a hotel, or a bank. In ways it seemed to be all of these, and yet none of them.

He tried to stand and enter the building which was slowly swirling with light, so he could see better and possibly understand. His legs wouldn't move. He twisted at his waist and flailed his arms, but he could not get up. He didn't know if he was paralyzed or cemented to the curb. He suddenly grew a little fearful.

He called out, but his voice died on his lips. There was no echo. There was no reverberation. There was no sound. Even the shrill moaning of the wind had suddenly dissipated. It bothered him tremendously to find that he could make no sound at all. He tried to scream out, but it was as if his tongue was swollen and blocking off all sound in his throat. He reached for his throat as he opened and closed his mouth, but nothing could be done.

He was desperate to make a noise, to be heard, to attract someone's attention. He clapped his hands, but they too were muffled. Just as suddenly as it had died off, the chill wind began to howl and moan again. It whipped up dust until he could no longer see the building across from him. He couldn't see the street. He could barely see his feet or the curb on which he sat. He was in some sort of blinding dust storm, with a numbing wind whipping about him while a blazing sun beat on him from above. The conflicting sensations were agonizing.

He grew aware of people milling about. All he could see were swirls of dust. In his blinded state, he twisted left and right, frantic to reach someone – anyone – who could help him. He continued to cry out, but his voice remained muted. A feeling of panic began to take hold of him. He was in desperate earnest, at his wit's end, when he felt a soft tapping on his shoulder.

He turned and saw a young girl of about nine standing beside him. She was dressed in a knee-length white dress. She had shiny black shoes with stockings that had frills around her calves. Her long, brown hair was pulled back and held in place by a white head band. She had a pleasant smile on her face.

He wondered how she could stand there so peacefully with such a terrible dust storm devouring the town. He noticed that her dress and hair were not being blown about. Instead, she just stood there happily smiling at him. He looked around and saw that the storm was gone. The town was peaceful. The dust was gone, revealing a paved street.

Cement sidewalks lined both sides of the street. The curb on which he sat lined a strip of luscious green grass. Behind the girl was an inviting city park with trees, benches, and a river meandering through it. The girl continued to smile as she held out her hand to him. It was clear she wanted him to take her to the park. He smiled and nodded in agreement. He could think of nothing that would make him happier.

Suddenly, a bitterly cold wind whipped up dust and obscured his view of the girl. He looked around, frantic to find her. He reached out with his arms and hands, but could not feel her. She was nowhere near him. He sensed something across the way and looked. Somehow she was now on the other side of the street, standing in front of the building that was still in the process of being bathed with light. She beckoned to him again, holding out her hand.

He thought he heard her say, "All is as it should be," but didn't see her lips move.

Still sitting, he reached out his hand, desperate to catch hold of hers. Somehow, he was able to reach all the way across the street, while still sitting. It was an impractical reach that only makes sense while dreaming it; never afterward. As his fingers stretched outward toward hers, he could feel the icy wind beating against and between them. It howled menacingly, hurting his ears. He tried to call out, but could only hear the wind. Just as he was despairing that he could not reach any farther, the tips of their fingers touched.

Her fingertips were warm and endowed with a healing touch. The howling wind ceased immediately. The sun dominated an inviting, brilliantly blue sky and appeared as if it had always belonged there. He looked around. All was colorful and new. He was standing before the girl and before the building, although he had no memory of standing up or crossing the street. He turned his gaze down toward her to thank her, but she was gone. All was gone.

He lay in bed for awhile longer, slowly replaying the dream in his conscious mind, trying to make sense of it. He wanted to keep it near him, and not forget it as so many other dreams had been forgotten by him. If the truth were told, he could not remember the last time he had awakened with any recollection of ANY dream, let alone such a vivid recollection as this one. He could swear that his ears were still vibrating from hearing the wind blasting along the street.

"What a puzzlement," he remarked as he sat up in bed and rubbed his eyes.

Then, he wondered where the word "puzzlement" had come from. Something about it seemed familiar, as if it was from some event in years gone by. Somehow, that one word seemed to hearken back to a happy time in his life. He sensed a reminder of someone who was a dear friend. It was a memory of someone who was close to him. He had no memory of such a friend, neither could he understand why a single word would hearken back such feelings for an unknown, unremembered, perhaps even imaginary, friend.

"It is indeed a puzzlement," he said with a smile. "A very strange puzzlement!"

The sun was just beginning to creep through his window shade and he could hear the sounds of morning coming through his open window. He had slept away the entire night – in a bed.

"Perhaps, it is a GOOD puzzlement," he said, as he stood, repeating the word yet again, with a bit of a laugh.

Chapter 12
Contemplation in the Car

$\mathcal{D}$ad sat behind the wheel again. The kids were busying themselves in the back. Mom was knitting and chatting with Frank. The radio was softly playing Bing Crosby's rendition of "Pat-a-Pan." Sam sat in the middle seat, looking out the window. Frank looked back at him through the rearview mirror. Sam's face looked very peaceful, even serene.

He looked more relaxed than he had been previously. The trip seemed to be doing him good, or maybe he was becoming more acclimated to his surroundings and the family. Either way, the look on Sam's face gave Frank a nice warm feeling inside.

"Looks like Sam is starting to really enjoy the ride," Frank whispered to Joyce as he nodded back toward their guest passenger.

Joyce turned and looked back toward Sam. Sam noticed movement and turned to see her. She gave him a warm smile that he returned, as well as a nod of approval followed by a bigger grin. Joyce felt he looked as giddy as a schoolboy.

"I'll say!" she whispered with a smile to Frank. "I don't know what's come over him, but he certainly seems pleased."

As the final chords of "Pat-a-Pan" faded away, they were replaced by the familiar words, "On the first day of Christmas..."

"Oh, no!" Frank exclaimed, in a mock panic.

"What's wrong?" Joyce asked, concerned.

"I really don't like this one," Frank said. "It goes on and on forever."

"Oh, don't be a Scrooge!" Joyce smiled and pushed on his shoulder. "You've got nothing but time on your hands. Just enjoy it!"

"Hey, turn it up!" Luke hollered out excitedly from the back.

"Yeah! I like that one!" Emma echoed.

Joyce leaned over and turned the knob. Soon, the family was vibrating the car with their ever-hastening refrains, while Sam looked on and smiled. Even little Kenny pretended to play cymbals from the back seat, while Emma and Luke held up imaginary mikes to their mouths, and shook their heads from side to side as they boisterously bellowed out the words, "five GOLDEN rings!"

* * * * *

The radio softly played Christmas tunes. Joyce was driving while Frank slept with his head against his window and his mouth sagging open. Emma sat reading in the middle seat, across from Sam. Luke and Kenny were playing cards in the back. Sam sat quietly looking at the passing countryside. Every now and then he'd doze off and his head would bob back up. He'd blink a few times as he looked around.

Finally, he gave in and slid back in his seat to give his head a crook to lean on in between the wide seat and the door frame. He turned diagonally to give his legs more room and slid his feet to the center of the car, trying politely to keep away from Emma's half, although she would not have minded any such infringement. It wasn't long before his body relaxed and his mouth began to sag open like Frank's.

*****

Sam's snoozing gradually drifted into a dream. It would be difficult for him later to describe his thoughts and feelings about this. While he was not necessarily experiencing a lucid dream, in which he knew he was dreaming and knew he could influence events in his dreams, he was at least aware of the fact that a dream was occurring. This thought excited him. He was anxious to see what events awaited him.

He felt like a ticket holder entering a live, interactive production of some new play. He had no idea what the plot or storyline would be, but he was anxious to find out. What he soon saw, heard, and felt made very little sense to him. Inexperienced as he was with this new concept of dreaming – or at least the concept of remembering his dreams – he had no way of knowing if sense or reason were a part of dreaming, or if they were foreign concepts to the experience.

He again found himself on a dirt road. This one rolled off to the horizon before him. Turning, he saw that it rolled off to the far horizon behind him. To either side he saw nothing but barren weeds and scant brush. The concept of simply appearing at a point in the road was too nebulous for him. He somehow assumed he had traveled to his present spot. He further assumed that he had come from the direction behind him, and had been traveling forward in the direction he had faced when he first became aware of developments in the dream.

There was no point in his simply standing there. There was nothing for him to see or hear. He knew he needed to move and that he should choose forward or back; the thought of leaving the road never pressed upon his mind. He felt he could go forward and see what lay along the road, or he could turn back and see what was behind him.

Even in his sleeping mind, he realized that in these short few days he had known his new friends, his greatest and most pressing mystery was not the future, but the past. These new people had asked him casual questions that he could not answer. Questions no other human had bothered to ask of him, not even himself. He realized that until now, he had simply "existed." He was alive, but nothing more. No growth. No goals. No yearnings. Just "existence."

He had known the importance of at least continuing to exist. He knew that to do so he needed to find sustenance on an ongoing basis. And so, his existence consisted almost continually of seeking – of begging – for food and finding shelter.

Did he have a life before such a bleak existence? He did not know. He only knew it was the only life he had ever experienced, or could remember experiencing. If there was something before that life, what could it have been? Surely, it had to have been better than the life he now lived, the life he had chosen to live. Or, was it a life that had been chosen for him? He did not know and could not say.

To him, the future was irrelevant compared to the past. He had to find his past, and, in so doing, find himself. To him, then, there was no decision to make. He turned his back to the future – if that was the future – and faced his past – if, indeed, this road represented something as profoundly poignant as his past – and began to walk the chosen path.

He raised his foot and put it before him. The moment he pressed it to the dusty path, the entire scene changed. He was no longer on a road. There was no wide expanse to either side of him, littered with brush and sage. The sun was gone entirely. The sky and all about him was black. He felt wet all over. It was a wet that was dripping and crawling about him. He became aware of a howling pressure pushing against him. He gradually recognized these sensations and it dawned on him that he was in a rainstorm.

His initial fear immediately faded and he smiled. He smiled big and wide. He didn't mind the rain. He held his arms out and looked up allowing the rain to embrace him. As he stood there with his arms outstretched and the rain pouring onto his blissful face, he heard a menacing noise which shook him from his reverie. He pulled his arms back toward him quickly and flipped his head back into position.

He was hearing unintelligible shouts of anger, mingled and confused with other sounds. He sensed danger and looked this way and that at the appearance of each new sound. It was all around him. He heard sharp, sudden noises, mixed with the constant, threatening drone of angry voices. He looked left, right, before him, behind him. He was spinning around frantically, but seeing nothing. His heart was pounding; his mind racing. He felt short of breath and in spite of the rain, he was sweating.

Someone pulled at his shoulder. He turned to see who it was. Blackness was replaced by blinding light. Slowly, groggily, he opened his eyes. He pressed them shut again to block out the light. There was another tug at his shoulder, and a voice. He cautiously opened his eyes to peek out into the light. His sight adjusted and he began to make out images. He could make out the image of someone sitting behind a fabric wall, with objects whizzing by behind her. He blinked more and recognized the form.

"Sam? Sam?!" Emma asked again, with a very concerned look in her face as she tugged at his shoulder. "Are you all right, Sam?"

Sam sat for a moment, dazed. He brought his hand to his brow and held it there a moment as he blinked some more and allowed consciousness to regain itself. He was surprised to find his hand was sweaty. He lowered it as he straightened in his seat. Even without looking around, he could sense that everyone in the car was staring at him with wide eyes.

"Hey, are you all right, Friend?" Frank asked while looking back through the rearview mirror.

Sam noted benignly that Frank and Joyce must have switched drivers while he was sleeping. It must have been a very deep sleep, he thought.

"I'm fine, fine," Sam tried to reassure the others.

"Well, you certainly gave us a fright!" Joyce said. "Are you certain?"

"Yes," Sam smiled as pleasantly as he could. "I'm afraid I just had a bit of a bad dream."

"A BIT?" Luke scoffed. "Seemed more like an all out nightmare!"

"What do you mean?" Sam asked bewildered.

"You were moanin' and groanin' and tossin' around," Luke said, as Kenny nodded with an equally concerned look on his tiny face. "Then you started kicking your arms and legs around."

"Oh, dear!" Sam said wiping his brow. "I do hope I didn't alarm you too much!"

"Do you have bad dreams often," Joyce asked with concern.

"No, no I don't," Sam replied honestly. "In fact, I hardly ever dream at all."

"You don't dream?" Emma said, amazed.

"Naw, everyone dreams!" Luke said. "Even Kenny dreams!"

Kenny nodded his head up and down in agreement.

"I think Sam means that he doesn't remember his dreams," Frank pointed out.

"I guess that's right," Sam agreed. "But, as I can't remember my dreams, it's really hard to say if I have them, then, isn't it?"

Sam laughed a bit uncomfortably, trying to ease the tension in the car.

"So, what was this dream about?" Emma asked.

"Emma, don't pry!" Joyce interjected.

"But, I'm only – ," Emma stammered.

"It's all right," Sam assured them. "You can't go kicking about in someone's car and then not tell them why. It was a strange dream, or, at least I think it was a strange dream. I seem to be new at them. At any rate, I'm not sure what it was about. All I can remember are bits and pieces."

"What are the bits?" Luke coaxed.

"Well, I was standing on a road in the middle of nowhere. It was a dirt road. It was the only road. It went way out one way in front of me and one way behind me, so I was in the middle of it. I decided to turn around and go back and suddenly everything went black. It was raining. I heard noises and voices. They were angry voices. They seemed to be coming after me. That's when I woke up."

Everyone sat still for a moment, thinking. Luke was the first one to finally speak.

"Well, that's an easy dream to interpret," he said triumphantly.

"Really?" Sam asked, intrigued.

"Yeah," Luke said, puffing up and acting professional and analytical. "You're on this long road that goes forever and you decide to turn back. It's obvious. YOU'RE TIRED OF SITTING IN THIS DARN CAR!" and he laughed.

The others joined in, but only briefly.

"What were the voices saying?" Emma pressed, after the pause.

"I don't know," Sam admitted. "I couldn't make out any of them. They were just voices. They sounded angry."

"Did you recognize any of the voices?" Frank asked, as Joyce shot him a surprised look that he would pry.

"No, no, I didn't," Sam said. Pondering, he added, "It does seem that it felt like I knew them, though."

"You knew these guys? How?" Luke asked.

"I don't know," Sam said. "It was just a dream, though. It wasn't real."

"That's right," Joyce confirmed. "It was just a silly dream, Luke, like the time you thought you were being chased by a huge, yellow duck!"

"Hey, that was a long time ago!" Luke protested.

"A huge, yellow duck?" Sam smiled and turned.

"I was only ten!" Luke explained. "It seemed so real! But, that was a long time ago! I don't dream about that now!"

"Yeah," Emma smiled with a teasing lilt. "That was all of LAST YEAR!"

"All right, knock it off!" Frank interjected, as the two started to throw accusations back and forth about previous dreams.

"Well, it's good to know I'm not the only one who dreams!" Sam observed. Then, changing the subject, he turned to his window and asked, "Has anyone gone skating today?"

The three kids all rushed to the windows with vigorous squeals about racing each other. Joyce laughed and shook her head as she turned back to her knitting. Frank smiled and flipped on the radio. Soon, the car was rollicking down the highway with "Rockin' Around the Christmas Tree."

* * * * *

Joyce was driving, while Frank slept. Kenny was snoozing in his little fort. Luke was in the back, lazily flipping through his cards. It wouldn't take long before unconsciousness overtook him. Emma had drifted to sleep with her book across her lap.

Sam looked casually out his window. The car ran over a pothole, jostling him and the others. He looked over at Emma and saw the book slipping from her hands and toward the floor. He bent over and lightly took hold of it. He folded it closed and set it down on the seat beside her, giving her a kind smile. As he sat back up, his eyes met Joyce's. She happened to look at him through the rearview mirror.

"She's a very sweet girl," he told her softly.

"Yes, she is," Joyce replied. "And, you're a very sweet man."

"Uh, thank you," Sam blushed.

"I mean that," Joyce continued. "I really do. I'm very surprised to have found you - uh, that you were - uh -"

Her words trailed off and it was her turn to have her face flush as she realized she had inadvertently treaded into a tactfully dangerous topic. She didn't know how to continue, and decided to stop. Sam knew this and looked out the window. They rode in awkward silence for a few moments, before Sam interrupted it with a clear response.

"What you were trying so carefully not to say," he said, as he continued to peer out the window at nothing in particular, "is that you are surprised to know that I'm a bum, a shopping cart man."

"Well, NO, not that," Joyce bumbled back frantically apologetic. "I meant simply that I can't believe that you didn't have a home, a family, uh, a place to stay."

"And a job?" Sam added wistfully, giving a glance toward the front of the car, but not making eye contact with Joyce in the rearview mirror. "In other words, I'm a bum." In response to Joyce's protests, he continued, "Call it what you will, but that's what I called it back in my day. At least, that's what I think I called it."

His voice trailed off and he glanced out the window again. Joyce fidgeted uncomfortably, her mind swimming for a fitting response that just wouldn't come.

"Have you always –?" was all she managed.

"Have I always been a bum?" Sam stated flatly. "I don't know. I honestly don't know. I honestly hope not. Fact is, though, I can't remember ever being anything else."

"Surely, you worked at some point," Joyce coaxed. "You went to school. Your family cared for you. What led you to lose your job, your family, your home?"

"I really don't know," Sam said, scratching his head. "I have no memory of family, friends, home, or work. But, I must have had them." He paused. "You know," he added philosophically, "I don't think I've ever even bothered to give it any thought before now."

He seemed as shocked at this revelation as Joyce was.

"I guess I just lived day to day," he surmised, "looking for food and shelter, and being more concerned about the here and now than the past and gone. I mean, what's the point of thinking of Mom and Dad, if they're long dead and you will be, too, if you don't get at least a quarter or two from some willing stranger?"

"Dreadful!" Joyce mumbled and shook her head.

"But," Sam added, "ever since I met you fine people, I've had time to sit back. See my life, so to speak. Figure out who I am, where I'm going. And, I can't help but start to wonder where I've been, where I came from, and such."

"And?" Joyce pursued, as Sam's voice trailed off leaving a heavy silence between them.

"And, I just don't know!" Sam said, with more than a hint of frustration in his voice. "I just DON'T KNOW!"

He beat his fist into the palm of his hand and looked out the window again. He stared and could almost make out his own reflection in the glass, but the light was too bright to see it clearly. He could only see portions, but it was enough for him to recognize his face.

Actually, he barely recognized his clean-shaven face. He brought his hand up and caressed his bare chin, noticing the stark difference in the sensation to what he had become so accustomed.

"The eyes are the same," he observed quietly.

"Pardon?" Joyce asked.

"Huh? Oh, nothing. I was just talking to myself," Sam confessed, turning back to her. "I'm sitting here racking my brain, trying to remember my past. Trying to remember where I come from. Trying to just remember my own name! But, it just DOESN'T come!"

"It must be very frustrating." Joyce tried to sound comforting, as she felt tears welling up in her eyes.

"Am I daft, I wonder?" Sam asked.

"I – I don't know," Joyce said, "but you don't seem daft to me."

"No? Well, what sort of fellow can't remember his own name?"

"I would think that if you were daft," Joyce answered, "you wouldn't have the sense to ask that."

"I, well, I suppose you're right," Sam concluded. "I suppose you're right."

"Why don't you try to take a nap?" Joyce offered. "It might do you some good. I'll play some soft music."

"Thank you, but I'm not too sleepy at the moment," Sam said.

Chapter 13
Something Happened

Sam looked over at Emma, sleeping beside him. He turned and looked at Luke and Kenny sleeping in the back. They looked peaceful, almost angelic.

"You sure have a nice family, ma'am," Sam said.

"Thank you," Joyce replied with a smile and a glance in the rearview mirror.

"I'm privileged to have met you," Sam added. He looked back at Kenny and took on a pensive look. "If you don't mind my asking," he began, but then stopped. "I'm sorry. It's really none of my business."

"What? What isn't?" Joyce asked.

"I don't mean to pry," Sam said.

"Really, what is it, Sam?" Joyce asked.

"I'm sorry, I shouldn't have brought it up," was all he replied.

"You're wondering about Kenny, aren't you?" Joyce surmised.

Sam nodded.

"He's just –" Joyce began, then broke off.

"He's a wonderful young man," Sam finished. Joyce silently smiled her thanks to him.

"You're wondering why he doesn't talk, I bet," Luke said from the back.

Sam turned, a little surprised to hear Luke's contribution.

"I thought you were asleep!" he smiled.

"I was," Luke said. "But, I'm not now. Can I tell him, Mom?" Joyce agreed. "He talked just fine up until about two years ago."

"What was it that made him stop talking? Was there an accident or something?" Sam was understandably intrigued.

"Sort of," Luke continued. "My dad took us boys up in the High Sierras for a campout. It was fun. We went fishing and slept out in tents and hiked and stuff. We were there for three whole nights, then it was time to head back home. We were packing everything up. Kenny asked if there was anything he could do to help. Dad didn't need any help, but he would give Kenny little jobs. He was even smaller then – he was only five, you know – so there wasn't much he could do.

"Well, we were nearly done, and Kenny would finish one thing and then run back to Dad and ask for something else to do. I guess Dad was expecting it, because he had kept a canteen out. As soon as Kenny came up to Dad, he held up the canteen and asked him if he could fill it. Kenny smiled and nodded, and went running over to the river by our campsite.

"It wasn't far. We could see it. We camped right there because Dad liked listening to it at night."

Luke paused a moment before continuing.

"Well, Dad got all done packing and Kenny wasn't back yet. We couldn't see him and figured he must have gone downstream a little. He called out, but Kenny didn't come. He told me to run over to the river and get him. 'Gotta get on the trail!' he said.

"Well, I went over there and walked downstream a ways and I couldn't find him. I hollered good and loud, but never heard him. I went pretty far and was getting worried, so I ran back to camp.

"I told Dad I didn't see him. He said he must have gone upstream instead. I ran upstream calling out for him, but still couldn't find him. I ran back and told Dad. By this time, Dad was getting worried, too.

"He told me to stay at the camp with the gear. He told me not to leave camp no matter what, in case Kenny came back. He ran upstream hollering. I listened and could hear him holler. He kept yelling, but his voice got so far off that after awhile, I couldn't hear him anymore. Then it got real quiet.

"I don't think I've ever heard it get that quiet before," Luke said very seriously. "I could still hear the river and all, but it was real quiet. It was like I was the only person in the world. You know what I mean?"

Sam nodded.

"I didn't like it. It made me worried. Real worried. I got worried that I wouldn't see my dad or Kenny ever again. I wanted to leave; run up the river and find Dad. But, he had told me not to leave no matter what. I wanted to run, but what if Kenny came back and I wasn't there? I had to stay, for Kenny. It was awful hard. Right when I couldn't take it anymore, I heard something.

"I hollered out, 'Who's there? Who's there?' It was Dad. I must have sounded scared or something, because he came running up to me and asked if I was all right. I told him I was and asked where Kenny was.

"Dad looked sad and kind of scared. He shook his head and said he couldn't find him. He said he was getting worried about losing me, too, so he said we better stick together. He said he wasn't sure what to do. I've never known Dad not knowing what to do. I think that was the most scariest part.

"Well, he ended up searching through our packs, real fast like. I didn't know what he was looking for, but he was looking as fast as he could and mumbling to himself and tossing stuff out onto the ground. I asked what he was looking for. He said he wanted a paper and pen to write Kenny a note.

"My eyes went real big and I asked if we were going to just leave him there. He said he didn't know what to do. He said we needed to go get help searching for him, and he didn't want to just leave the camp, in case Kenny came back and we weren't there. He wanted to leave a note for him, telling him we'd be back just as soon as we could.

"I went to my pack and pulled out my notebook and pencil. Dad told me he wanted to write a note saying to stay there, that we'd gone off looking for him, that we'd be back soon, that we loved him, and that he should stay safe and not get scared, but Kenny was too little to read all that. So, Dad just wrote, 'Kenny Wait here!' hoping he could read it. He was only five, you know.

"Just in case he couldn't read it, Dad drew a little smile face. He said he hoped it would make Kenny feel safer. Dad stuck it up high, about as high as Dad's head, on a small tree, so Kenny would be able to see it even from far off.

"Then he looked at me and got very serious. 'Luke,' he said, 'We need to pray. We need to pray that we'll find Kenny and that he'll be all right.'

"I said, 'OK!' and we knelt down in the mountains there and Dad prayed for Kenny. He was pleading and praying real hard. But, you know what kind of surprised me?" Luke asked Sam who had sat with his eyes focused on Luke, taking in this heart rending account.

"No, what?" Sam asked, urging Luke to continue.

"When Dad prayed," Luke explained. "It sounded like he was TALKING to God. Not just praying, but actually talking to God. Like God was right there next to us and he was talking to Him and expecting an answer or something. I've never heard anyone just TALK to God before. You know, it made me think He was really real.

"I mean, I know God is real and all, but to hear the way Dad was talking to Him and asking Him to keep Kenny safe, and help us find him, it made me think that Dad thought He was really listening, that He cared, and that He would really do those things. I've never thought of prayer like that before. I always thought prayer was just prayer. Dad made me think that prayer was to someone real who was actually listening to him.

"Dad got done praying and I opened my eyes. I half expected to see Kenny come walking into camp. We called out, while still on our knees. We didn't hear nothing more than the river and the birds. We got up and kept calling as we looked around.

"Dad said we had to make our way downstream. The river followed the trail pretty good, or I guess the trail followed the river, so he said if we went downstream, we'd also get closer to getting help. Before we left camp, Dad stopped and asked for more paper.

"I asked what for and he said he was going to write another note and put it out on the trail. He was going to write it so that if any other hikers came along, they'd see it and know that we needed help looking for Kenny, and that if they found him, they should get word to the ranger station as quick as they could.

"Dad told me to stay on the trail and that he'd follow the river. We made our way along for probably two miles like that, both of us hollering for Kenny. We could hear each other fine, but we never saw anybody, no other hikers, and not Kenny.

"After about two miles, Dad got real concerned and came running up to the trail to me. He said we needed to get help and we had to hurry because it would be getting dark soon. It was still six or seven miles back to the Ranger station.

"Dad said he'd run on ahead and have me follow the trail, but he was too afraid of losing me, too. So he asked me if I could be real brave and strong and run the trail with him. I said I'd do anything if it got Kenny back safe.

"We ran that whole trail, or mostly. I just HAD to stop sometimes. My heart was pounding and my lungs felt like rusty metal. It hurt real bad, but I felt worse every time we stopped. I kept praying to God that he'd make me strong for Kenny. I kept trying to pray like Dad did. I don't know, but I think it really helped. I've never run that far in my life before. I was sure glad to see that ranger station.

"Dad ran ahead and burst through the door and shouted that his son was missing. Some guy came up and asked a bunch of questions. Everyone started hurrying around and talking into radios and stuff. A guy in a jeep wanted to take Dad up the trail to where we were. Dad wouldn't go without me.

"We rode up pretty far, but then the trail got too narrow, so we had to hike it again. We were tired, but we went as fast as we could. We got to camp and found all our gear and the note Dad had left, but there was no Kenny. We couldn't find him anywhere.

"I could hear a helicopter flying around overhead. There were guys on horses, and guys with megaphones. It got dark too soon. We didn't find him."

Luke stopped talking for a moment. He shivered at an all-too-vivid memory. He was a bit teary-eyed when he continued.

"Kenny was out there all night by himself. Dad and I built a BIG fire, hoping he'd see it and come back to camp, but he never did. We kept calling. I fell asleep, but I don't think Dad ever did. He kept calling. Kenny was out there alone all night long."

Sam looked at sweet, little Kenny, sleeping peacefully in the back. Sam wondered what that night must have been like for little Kenny, who was even smaller then.

"We looked all day the next day. ALL DAY. We still didn't find him. At nighttime, I asked Dad if God had heard us pray. Dad said that God hears every prayer. I asked why He hadn't brought Kenny back yet. Dad said he didn't know. God does things – or lets things happen – in ways that He feels they need to happen. I asked why God thought Kenny had to be lost.

"Dad said he didn't know. He said maybe it was to test us to see if we'd still believe in Him, even when we're scared. I said it sounded mean. Dad said that I felt that way because I didn't understand God's heart. He said He sometimes has to let bad things happen, so that we can appreciate the good better.

"I asked what good would ever come from Kenny being lost. He asked if I missed Kenny. I said I sure did. He asked if I loved Kenny. I said I did. He asked if I loved him even more now that he was missing. I said I never loved or missed him more than I did right then. He said, 'See, you've learned to appreciate Kenny even more than you had before.' I hadn't thought about it that way before.

"That night I couldn't sleep. We built an even bigger fire. There must have been 200 people searching the mountain for Kenny. All of them camped out on the mountain that night. It was the longest night of my life. I'd heard some searcher say that if you don't find them in the first three hours, the chances of ever finding them alive dropped with every hour that went by. It'd been three hours before we even got to that ranger station.

"The next morning, I prayed again REAL hard. I got up and didn't walk to the river. I went to the other side of the trail. There was a ravine there. I climbed down it. I saw something orange and went over to it. It was covered with leaves. It was Kenny's coat. I went to pick it up and it wouldn't come. Kenny was in it. I'd found him!

"I shouted out and everyone came running – at least those nearest did. I knelt down and touched Kenny. He was cold and a little wet – even though there was no water nearby. His clothes were torn up real bad. He was dirty and had scratches all over his face. He didn't wake up for me.

"They got him out and carried him down the mountain in a stretcher. They had to take him to a hospital. It was two whole days before he finally woke up. Mom cried for those two days.

"When he woke up, it was the happiest day of my life. He looked at us from his hospital bed and rubbed his eyes and felt the bandages on his face and hands. He looked at us, but didn't say a word. We asked him what happened, but he wouldn't talk to us. The doctors told us not to push it, so we didn't.

"He hasn't talked since. Not once. I'll tell you this, too," Luke added, leaning toward Sam and speaking in a softer voice, as if afraid the sleeping Kenny would overhear. "One of those searchers looked at the tears on Kenny's clothes and said they weren't from falling down. They looked more like they were from some sort of animal like a mountain lion or a bear or

something. He said some animal was probably stalking Kenny and may have
even attacked him. That's how he figured he got those tears in his clothes. He
said it was a wonder Kenny had survived. Said he wondered how Kenny
managed to get away....

"So, if Kenny doesn't want to talk, that's OK with me. I'm just glad I have
him back. He's my brother, and I love him," Luke concluded with an
unashamed tone of support.

"My word," Sam said aghast. "Did they ever find out what had chased him,
or stalked him, or whatever it was?"

"No," Joyce said in a trembling voice. "It might have been a mountain lion,
or a bear. It was very rocky and they couldn't tell from the tracks. There
WAS something, though."

Joyce continued to wipe tears away from her eyes.

"Well," Sam said, trying to console her. "I'm sure Kenny will talk again
someday, when he has something important enough to say. Let's just be
grateful he's all right. My goodness. God must have truly been looking out for
that little man."

"When it's 'important enough'? I hadn't thought of that! I wonder if he's
right?" Joyce asked herself, as she continued to drive. A small glimmer of
hope twinkled in the corner of her mother's heart, "Maybe. Just maybe," she
thought.

Chapter 14
Another Episode

$\mathscr{F}$rank was driving and fiddling with the radio tuner. He sighed as he gave up.

"Maybe you can find something good, Sweetheart," he said.

"I'll see what I can do," Joyce smiled and reached for the knob.

She fiddled with the radio dial until she heard familiar words from one of her favorite Christmas hymns, "O Come, O Come Immanuel" melodically emanate from the speakers.

"This sounds like a nice station," she smiled and kept the volume low. She could see that all of the kids were asleep and Sam's head had begun to sag and bob. "Why don't you just get some rest?" she suggested to him.

"Yes, thank you," Sam said. "I suppose I will."

He propped a pillow into the corner of the window and the seat, and leaned into it. Joyce looked back to check on Sam. Before they had passed more than two mile markers, she could see that Sam's breathing was calm and rhythmic. She smiled at the relaxed look that slipped over his face.

"Is he asleep already?" Frank whispered.

"Yes, he is," she confirmed. "He looks very peaceful, too."

* * * * *

There's no telling how his dream began; where he was; what he was doing, thinking, or seeing; or, if there even was a beginning. The one thing that is certain is that he again found himself standing in the dark. He was wet, a little cold, and very concerned. The wind howled and pelted him with unforgiving droplets of water that splashed in his face and eyes.

The voices came almost immediately. They were angry, threatening voices; deep, guttural voices. He whipped around left and right looking for the source of the voices. They were getting nearer, but he could see nothing. Only blackness. He reached out his hands instinctively, feeling in the blackness, and hoping to feel something that might help him.

Suddenly, one of his arms was grasped in a powerful grip. It was whisked behind him just as suddenly, as if in one fluid motion. Searing pain shot through him as joints and tendons stretched unnaturally. He began to see flashes of lights. The scene became disjointed, out of order, hectic.

At one moment his arms reached out before him. In another, he found himself with his arms somehow bound behind him. Voices continued to shout. He tried to make out the words. He knew he should be able to understand them. They were so clear, but they were so perplexing that he could make out nearly none of the words.

Again there was a flash of light. He thought he saw faces in the flashes. They were men. Men with hats. Men with wet hats and water streaking down their angry faces. They didn't seem to notice the rain. They just kept shouting at him. Grabbing him. Holding him. Hitting him.

He suddenly realized he felt the force of their blows. The flashes continued. Was it lightning? Was it headlights? Who were these men? Why were they so angry?

He pulled loose and tried to back away but was stopped by some large wall. It was an odd, metallic wall whose shape made no sense to him. He still couldn't see well and didn't have time to feel about and observe it. All he knew for certain was that it had cut off his escape.

A flash of light and he saw a hand holding a pipe high in the air. A fist hit him solidly in the belly. He was unable to bend, to groan. Powerful hands held him upright. Another flash. Another punch.

There was that pipe again. It was moving swiftly. It was moving toward his head. A flash of light and the pain was too much. All was darkness.

He kicked his feet out straight again, pounding the back of Frank's seat. Frank lurched forward asking a confused and irritated, "What?!"

Sam groaned and twisted as Frank turned to see him apparently still in the throes of another terrible dream.

"Sam! Sam!" he called out, as he reached over the seat and tried to shake him awake. Emma stirred and her father said, "Emma, wake up Sam! He seems to be having some awful dream."

Emma was dazed, but seeing the troubled expression on Sam's unconscious face, she obeyed and nearly jumped on the man and began to shake him.

"Sam! Sam!" she cried out. "Wake up, Sam!"

It took a moment, but soon he was blinking and groggily asking what was happening.

"You seem to have had another episode," Frank explained. "What were you dreaming?"

"I – I don't rightly know," Sam said slowly, thinking. "It was dark. Raining and dark. There were these voices. Men's voices. They were angry. They started hitting me. Then one of them had this pipe. He knocked me on the head real hard. I swear I could really feel it!" Sam looked at the family with an earnest gaze as he said this.

Kenny and Luke had heard the commotion and were kneeling on the back seat watching Sam and listening to his report. Kenny looked scared.

"That pipe!" Sam continued. "It hit me right here!" He reached with his hand and pointed to the back corner of his head and touched his hair as he did so. "Say!" he continued, now very perplexed, "when did that get there?"

"What?" Frank coaxed. "When did what get there?"

"This here bump," Sam said surprised. "Only, it's not a bump. It's more like a dent!"

"A dent?" Emma gasped.

"Let me feel!" Luke said, intrigued.

"Luke, don't!" Joyce blurted out, horrified at the thought of a groove in a man's head.

"It's all right," Sam assured her. "I don't mind. Fact is I'd appreciate someone checking to see if it's real or imagined!"

Luke leaned forward and stretched across Kenny's little fort, his feet on the back seat. He reached out to Sam's head, paused a moment, but then couldn't resist. He touched Sam's head right where Sam's fingers had been.

"Wow!" Luke said with wide eyes. "It's real all right! Cool!"

Luke ran his fingers across the dent.

"Hey, it goes for a bit," he said, impressed. "A couple of inches at least! It feels perfectly round like the inside of a straw or something. Feel this, Kenny."

Before Joyce could protest, Kenny leaned forward and was running his fingertips along the poor man's groove.

"Have you always had this?" Luke asked impressed.

"Don't know," Sam said. "I just now noticed it. Never had much use for admiring my head before."

Sam had a bit of twinkle in his eye when he said this, which caused Luke to laugh, as did Kenny, in his own, silent way. No one asked much more after this, but Frank looked over at Joyce and quietly asked, "He has a dent in his head?"

Joyce nodded as they continued to drive.

Just then, the song on the radio finished and "Winter Wonderland" started to play.

"Hey, Dad!" Luke said enthusiastically. "Turn that one up!"

"Sure, Son," Frank said as he reached for the knob.

"I'm not so sure that's a good idea, Frank," Joyce warned him.

"Why not?" Frank asked. "It's a good song."

"Don't you remember how it goes?" she asked.

"Sure, it's a classic," he shrugged.

"Not the way your son sings it!" Joyce pointed out.

"A beautiful sight!" Luke chimed out. "We're happy tonight! Walking in our WINTER UNDERWEAR!"

Emma burst out laughing, Kenny's little body just shook in a silent giggle, as Luke bounced his head back and forth and then tried to strut in place, holding his arms out as if showing off his long johns.

"I see what you mean," Frank rolled his eyes. "Oh, brother."

Luke was all warmed up and belting out the second verse as Frank turned the dial.

"Hey! No fair!" Luke protested. "I LIKE that one."

"Yeah, well, your mother likes this one," Frank replied as he stopped the dial on "Carol of the Bells," already in progress.

It was a recording with just bells, no singing. The ding-ding-da-ding was constant and infectious. Sam listened to the radio repeat the ding-ding-da-ding several times. He liked the soothing sounds he was hearing. Ding-ding-da-ding. He leaned his head back and closed his eyes. He even smiled a little.

The ding-ding-da-ding repeated several more times. Sam found his mind wandering as he relaxed. With the ding-ding-da-ding chiming away, he could see in his mind a set of train tracks. Enhanced by the vibrations of the car, he could picture himself traveling quickly down that set of tracks. Ding-ding-da-ding. Something about that vision seemed oddly familiar to him. Ding-ding-da-ding.

Chapter 15
The Last Leg

They stopped in Limon, Kansas. This was their goal, and they couldn't have come upon it soon enough. Even the best of kids get restless at the end of a long day's drive. These three were no exception. Pretenses of playing together to pass the time had disappeared and morphed into pokes, jabs, insults, and rude comparisons between the kids' natural facial features and various unappealing animals or insects until Joyce had declared the need to "Stop!" followed closely behind by Frank's irritated, "That's enough!"

Frank had ticked off the miles for the final one hundred miles with a descending countdown of, "Only 90 miles to go...," "Only 80 miles to go...," "Only 70 miles to go..." and so forth. For the last thirty miles, everyone else joined in. In a bizarre way that only makes sense to long-distance travelers, it became a bit of a game. The kids actually stopped pestering each other long enough to all declare the remaining distance in unison at the appropriate times.

The volume and enthusiasm behind each declaration increased as the distance diminished. The cheering that let loose when they passed the sign announcing Limon was so great that one would have thought they had arrived at Disneyland. Even Sam applauded.

As Frank pulled off the Interstate, Luke reminded him of the importance of the motel having a pool. "INSIDE this time!" he added. Remarkably, this requirement was met. They pulled into the lot of a large, two-story white motel that spread along three sides of the parking area. The rooms on the bottom floor opened out to the parking lot, but the second story was recessed and encased by a hallway that spread before it, giving that level a hallway and a pseudo-hotel feel.

In the middle section, behind large windows, the kids could clearly see a pool. The cheering that erupted from Emma and Luke dwarfed that at the city limits. Kenny did his best to contribute by clapping and whistling with all his might. Sam covered his ears and looked around, trying to maintain a pleasant look on his astonished face.

The car, and all of its luggage, had been unpacked in record time. The kids spent no time declaring which bed was theirs. Especially since Emma always got the rollaway. Instead, they knocked anxiously on the bathroom door, one after another, begging the person inside to "Please hurry!" as they changed into their swimsuits.

Frank had to remind them several times that there was "No running!" in the halls as the kids skipped through the hallway, with their white towels

billowing behind them. Kenny wore his like a cape and dashed along in a
zigzag between walls.

Their room was on the second floor, which meant that the hall led to a
balcony which overlooked the pool area, with stairs at either end of the
natatorium. When they reached the nearest stairs, Luke began to tear down
them, but was stopped by Emma, who had grabbed his arm and uttered the
bewildered word, "Look!"

Luke's feet almost went out from under him as the top half of his body
stopped, while the bottom half wanted to continue. He managed to keep
himself vertical by clinging to the handrail. His "Look at what?" was answered
by Emma's pointing. Following her outstretched arm, he looked down to the
pool.

There were only three kids in it. They weren't really swimming, just sort of
standing around. Two of them were tossing a beach ball back and forth while
the other tried to amuse himself by fanning his arms along the top of the
water. Two adults sat in lawn chairs on opposite sides of the pool. It was
apparent that two of the kids were siblings and the third was evidently by
himself, trying to manage to have a good time solo. It wasn't the kids that had
caught Emma's attention though. It wasn't even the rectangular pool itself. It
was its contents. The water, for reasons that escaped both Emma and Luke,
was a distinct shade of green.

"Cool!" Luke surmised with a grin. "It looks like the pool is full of lime
Kool-Aid!"

"What makes the water so green?" Emma asked.

"Probably not enough chlorine," Frank said, as he caught up to them on
the stairs.

He eyed the water suspiciously, wondering if he should let his kids swim in
it. He knew that prohibiting them would lead to no small amount of
squawking, especially when he noted the other kids idly standing in the water.

"Maybe that's why they call this place 'Limon'," Luke proposed as he
headed on down the stairs.

Frank rolled his eyes and his mouth inadvertently curled into a grin. He
shook his head, trying not to out-and-out smile. It would only encourage more
observational puns. When Emma and Kenny looked up at him, he motioned
with his arm and told them to "Go on!"

Luke was the first one into the water. He didn't carefully descend the
ladder like the other kids in the pool had. Instead, he had flung his towel
toward a chair, dashed to the pool and, ignoring Frank's admonition of "No
running!" streaked through the air completing a perfectly executed
cannonball.

He sprayed water across half the pool and at least six feet up into the air. Emma didn't use the ladder either. She bent down and kept one hand on the side of the pool as she hopped in, keeping her face dry. That only lasted for an instant as it was quickly wetted by Luke who had already exited the pool and struck the water again sending sheets of it at her, while she chided, "That was no cannonball!"

Little Kenny did his best imitation of Luke's form, holding his body tightly together while arching in the air. The minimal splash that it exuded would have made an Olympic diver proud, however. One little "Blip!" and Kenny had disappeared under the surface, only to reemerge a moment later with a big, silent smile.

"Now, THAT was a cannonball!" Luke said encouragingly. Turning to Emma, he confided, "How the heck does he do that?"

She shrugged and then sent a sheet of water at Luke. Joyce had come to the stairs just in time to get a laugh at the dousing of Luke. Soon, the three kids were having a blast in the water, a bit more literally than the unknown parents seemed to care for. The kids with the ball tossed it over to Luke, who gave it a punch back toward them shouting "Keep it off the ground!" Even the loner boy joined in at this.

They were still playing as Sam peaked around the top of the stairs.

"Sam!" Luke cried out. "SAM!"

Emma and Kenny both looked and waved and told him to join them. As he neared the pool, he held out his empty hands and pantomimed that he didn't have a suit. As the kids splashed each other, he went over and sat by Joyce and Frank. They watched the kids play with the ball, swim about, and have an impromptu cannonball competition.

It wasn't long before the kids declared Sam to be their judge. He laughed and laughed and told each one as they surfaced that their splash was even bigger than the one before. Joyce marveled at how much Sam seemed to be enjoying himself.

When it grew late enough, and the kids had ALMOST had their fill of the pool, Frank called them out. They eventually emerged and grabbed their towels. Still grinning, Sam went over and thanked Joyce and Frank, saying that he honestly could not remember the last time he had laughed like that.

* * * * *

Frank had again ensured that Sam's window could open to allow the cool night air to enter. Sam brushed his teeth and marveled at how smooth it made his teeth feel. He washed his face and looked into the mirror. Several times he found himself touching the newfound oddity on his cranium. The pool had taken his mind off of his earlier incidents. But, as he prepared for bed that night, the memory of his peculiar dreams returned and he slipped between the sheets a little more leery than the night before.

*****

Sometime, deep in the middle of the night, Sam stirred awake. Snatches of memories of flashes, rain, angry voices, and pummeling were fresh on his mind, but faded quickly, too quickly for him to consciously make sense of them. He rolled out of bed and wandered over to the sink. He splashed some water on his face and looked into the mirror in the faint light that shown through the curtained window. He gingerly touched the dent a few more times before returning to bed.

*****

"Emma?" Sam asked quietly.

In spite of his soft tone, everyone was somewhat startled to hear Sam speak. They had driven in relative silence for well over an hour. Kenny and Luke were in the back seat amusing cars with their card tricks. Frank was driving, humming along to "Bring A Torch, Jeannette, Isabella," while Joyce knitted.

"What is it, Sam?" Emma asked, looking up from her book.

"Would you mind reading to me?" he asked.

"Certainly!" she brightened up enthusiastically. She considered this an honor and a treat. "What do you want me to read?"

"Just from your book, if you don't mind. I thought it might help me relax and give me something new to think about."

"Did you have another of those awful dreams last night?" she asked concerned.

Sam said nothing, but nodded.

"I understand," she said. "I'd be happy to read to you!"

She flipped the pages back to the beginning of the chapter she was on. She explained that Nancy Drew was at a camp with her friends trying to figure out who was pretending to be haunting the lake and paddling around in a canoe late at night. Sam nodded and smiled, trying to be interested. Emma began reading.

Sam tried to pay attention, but it was, unfortunately, not a story that interested him. He looked out the window and saw the barren wintry fields roll by. He wondered what sorts of crops they bore in the summer. Now and then they would pass a pair of tall silos and he would guess, "Corn?" or "Wheat?" to himself, trying to surmise what they held.

Emma read at the same steady rate. Her enthusiasm never ebbed, even when she could see Sam's head slowly droop downward and then bob suddenly upward as he fought to keep alert. She was pleased to help him relax and was even trying to use her voice to coax him to sleep, the way her mother used to do with her.

Little did she know how aggressively Sam was trying to stay awake. He had come to dread sleep. The dreams were just too intense. He had fought to stay awake after last night's dream, and was continuing to fight. It was a fight he was not destined to win, however. The steady vibrations of the car, coupled with Emma's smooth voice, soon overcame him.

At first his head drooped to his chest, then his eyelids slid closed. He shifted in his seat and leaned his head back on the pillow he had wedged between his seat and the window. His jaw slowly fell open and a rhythmic breathing commenced. Emma observed all of this with a smile. She read a few more sentences, looking up at Sam more often than the book. Finally satisfied that he was truly asleep, she gave a big grin to her father, who winked at her in the mirror, and turned back to her book and began to read on in silence.

Sam's sleep was deep and well needed. For awhile, he had the blissful look of a newborn. After glancing back, Joyce remarked to Frank how peaceful Sam looked and how good it seemed to be for him to be on this trip. Just as she and Frank began to speculate on where Sam would end up, Sam began to twitch.

He pulled his legs toward him, then shot them away from him. His face jerked back and forth. His brow furrowed. Beads of sweat formed on his forehead and dripped down toward his ears. His one hand was clenched. He held the other in front of him as if trying to shield himself.

"N-no! No!" he said in a muffled, distant voice.

"Frank, I think it's happening again!" Joyce said with concern as she looked back at the guest.

"What do you want me to do? Pull over?" Frank asked, then continued, "Emma! Emma, wake up Sam! It looks like he's having another of those dreams of his!"

"Uh, yeah, Dad, sure!" Emma said, flummoxed and a little scared.

She closed her book quickly and leaned over to him and shook his arm.

"Sam! Sam! Wake up, Sam!"

There was no sign of Sam rousing. He continued to twitch and grown. Emma grabbed hold of his arm and shook it in earnest.

"Sam! SAM!" she cried out, frantically. "You have to wake up!"

"No! NO!" Sam muttered.

"What's going on?" Luke asked from the back.

"It's Sam. He won't wake up!" Emma said with her eyes tearing up. "You have to help me!"

Luke joined in and helped shake Sam awake. His eyes opened and then he blinked and shook his head quickly. He pulled his arms and legs close to himself. As his senses returned, he looked around cautiously.

"I, uh, guess I was dreaming again," he said sheepishly.

"I'll say!" Luke said. "We could barely get you to wake up! What the heck were you dreaming?"

"Watch your language, Luke," Frank reprimanded his son. "Sam, old friend, you really had us going there for a bit."

"Yes, we were very worried," Joyce added. "What on earth were you dreaming?"

"I, uh, it's just the same thing," Sam said. "It's dark. I can't see. It's raining. I don't know where I am. Then there are blinding flashes of light, angry voices. I try to get away, but I run into the big metal wall. Hands grab me and people are beating on me. It makes no sense. I don't understand. I don't understand ANY of it. It's all just bits and pieces. Fragments, really."

"Do you know any of these men?" Frank asked.

"No, I can't see their faces!" Sam answered.

"Yes, but, do you recognize their voices?" Frank pursued.

"No, no, I can't really hear what they're saying. It's all such jumbled noise," Sam shook his head. "No, no, wait," Sam stopped a moment. Then, with a look of someone suddenly remembering a forgotten secret, he added, "One of them did seem familiar. I can't place him. I can't really hear his voice now, but there was something familiar about him."

"Did you catch any words at all?" Frank asked. "Did you see his face?"

"No, no, but," Sam paused again, "it seemed like he was the one holding the pipe –"

"You got beaned by your friend?" Luke asked.

"Luke!" Joyce cautioned. "Please!"

"No, I didn't say that," Sam said. "I just – I just don't know. I wish these dreams would just go away, or at least make more sense. I'm terribly sorry to upset you fine people."

"Don't worry about us, Sam," Frank replied. "We just want to make sure you're well."

"I'm well," Sam said. "I'm well enough." In his mind he added, "I think."

"Sam," Joyce said, "we just want you to know we're concerned. We care about you."

"Yeah," Emma said, "you're family!"

"I'm – ?" Sam choked up and couldn't continue.

"That's right, Sam," Frank confirmed. "We consider you family. So, if there's anything we can do, you need to level with us."

"Thank you!" Sam said sincerely. "Thank you very much. I deeply appreciate that."

"You know, Sam," Frank added, "maybe these odd dreams have something to do with your lost memory."

"What do you mean?" Sam asked very intrigued.

"Maybe they are about something that happened just before you lost your memory," Frank explained. "I've read about stuff like this. Something awful happens that people can't deal with, so they just forget it."

"How can you just FORGET something?" Emma asked.

"It's not a conscious choice to forget," Frank explained. "Their subconscious just blocks it out until it's forgotten."

"You mean all this bit about rain and shouting is something that Sam really experienced, not just in a dream?" Luke asked with wide eyes.

Kenny looked frightened.

"Well, possibly," Frank said.

"Sheesh! No wonder his brain chose to forget it!" Luke replied. "It sounds creepy!"

"I don't know," Sam said slowly.

"Well, not that it's really my business, Sam," Frank said, "but that's just the point. You wouldn't know."

"What do you mean?" Sam asked.

"If something terrible, I mean REALLY terrible happens to a person," Frank explained, "something so terrible that they don't want to have to deal with it because they just don't know HOW to deal with it, then their mind will block it out."

"Forever?" Luke asked.

"Well, mostly forever," Frank added. "Or, until the person becomes comfortable enough that their mind feels they can finally deal with it. Then it comes back to them piece by piece. It isn't a fun experience, but they are able to deal with it and move on with their lives."

"So, Sam's gonna have more nightmares?" Emma exclaimed with concern.

"I don't know," Frank said. "I'm just telling you what I read. I can't speak for Sam."

The kids all looked at Sam with awe, bewilderment, a touch of horror, and not a little pity.

"I'm sorry, Sam!" Emma exclaimed as she leaned over and gave him a teary-eyed hug.

"We don't know if this is true," Sam comforted her. "It's just a theory."

"That's right, Emma," Frank confided. "I probably shouldn't have said anything at all."

They sat in silence for a bit. Looking out her window Emma saw something and tried to change the mood and the conversation.

"Hey," she said, "there's a train. It looks like a long one. Why don't we count the cars?"

"OK," Frank agreed. "Emma, you start counting. Everyone make a guess as to how many cars there are."

"I say 95," Emma declared.

"Kenny," Luke turned to his brother and asked, "how many do you think?"

Kenny flashed all of the fingers on both hands and opened and closed his hands ten times.

"Kenny says 100," Luke said. "I say 150!"

"150?" Frank said with surprise. "I doubt there's THAT many! I'll go with 125, though. Joyce?"

"Oh, 105," she guessed. "Sam?"

"87," he said flatly.

"87?" Frank asked. "That specific?"

"That's just how many I figure," Sam said. "Am I not supposed to get specific?"

"No, no, that's fine," Frank said. "87 it is."

"Why not 84 and ½?" Luke teased.

"Because I think there's 87," Sam said, turning around with a smile.

Emma was deeply engrossed in counting and made no comments. She began to count out loud. Luke asked which car she was on.

"45 – 46 – 47 – that yellowish one – 48 – 49," she said quickly, pointing.

Luke and Sam joined her in the counting. Kenny and Joyce watched as they passed the train. They were nearing the end when Emma said, "80! – 81 – 82 – ".

"Looks like Sam may have it right!" Frank said without being able to do more than cast quick glances at the train as they overtook it.

"86 – 87!" Emma announced, impressed. "Wow! How'd you do it, Sam? You got it right on the button!"

Sam made no reply. He sat with his eyes wide in a blank stare emanating from a pale face. Beads of sweat were gathering on his forehead.

What the family couldn't see was that he was having a waking dream. He had some sort of flashback to a dark train whistling by and the sound of the tracks. It disturbed him and he froze in mid-count, in the way that the family eventually saw him.

"Hey, Sam," Luke said, reaching up and touching his shoulder. "What's up, Sam?"

Sam still didn't reply and Joyce turned back and saw that expression on his face. She was immediately concerned and called to Frank.

"Frank! It's Sam!" she said. "Something's happening to Sam again! Emma, Luke, wake him up!"

"He is awake!" Luke pointed out.

"Well, he's in a trance or something!" she said. "Touch him! Bump him! Get his attention!"

Luke pushed back and forth on his shoulder while Emma took his hand. It was cold, clammy and limp.

"Sam! Sam!" both kids shouted anxiously. "Wake up, Sam!"

Sam stirred and reacted. He blinked several times and shook his head, then brought his hand to his forehead.

"I think I now know," he said, shaken, "what that wall is in my dream."

"What wall?" Frank asked anxiously.

"That wall that I keep backing into," Sam said. "The one that keeps me from getting away from the voices. It's a train."

"You get run over by a train?" Luke said with amazement.

"No, it's not moving," Sam said. "It's just sitting there, like in a yard or something."

"Someone's got a train in their yard?" Luke asked.

"No, silly, a train yard," Emma rolled her eyes.

"Hmm," Frank said. "Sounds like you've discovered another piece to your puzzle."

Just then, Kenny started acting very excited. He was fidgeting wildly and tapping Luke frantically as he pointed out the window. Luke, being distracted by the conversation, didn't catch on as quickly as he might have to Kenny's pantomiming. Kenny's outstretched, pointing arm suddenly whisked through the length of the car and he was now pointing behind them and acting just as excited and urgent as before.

"What is it, Kenny?" Luke asked, wide-eyed.

Kenny pointed emphatically behind them again, then down at the car. He had caught the others' attention by now, too. He then pointed straight ahead and held out his arms palms up, gesturing all around him and pointing at each person.

"We're all here?" Luke asked. "Of course we are."

Kenny shook his head and did something that made the situation more obvious. He held up his right hand with his thumb held close to his palm, but facing Luke. All of his fingers were tucked in, except for his index finger that stuck out, pointing.

"Where?" Luke said at first, looking in the direction Kenny was pointing.

Kenny shook his head, putting his hand down. Then he held it up in the same position, but slid it toward Luke, making sure to not point in the same direction again. He bounced it up and down slightly to emphasize it and even pointed at his right hand with his left. Luke scratched his head.

"You got me, little bro!" he said.

"I think he's saying we're in Oklahoma," Mom said with a smile.

Kenny got excited again and pointed to his mother, grinning. Then he held up all ten fingers and showed them to everyone.

"OH!" Luke said, also excited. "We're not in Oklahoma yet. It's still ten more miles. But, we're almost there!"

Everyone cheered, and Kenny beamed.

As the cheering subsided, Emma and Luke shouted out the same words together, surprisingly unrehearsed, "Hey! Let's eat at Braum's!"

Braum's was a hamburger chain that could only be found in and around the Oklahoma area. They were famous, at least to those in the area, for the world's best burgers and fries, but, more importantly, the most heavenly ice cream and shakes. It was almost a ritual for the family to stop off there for lunch as soon and as often as they could, whenever they visited Grandma.

"Why do you think we've put off stopping for lunch for so long?" Frank smiled back in his mirror.

The cheering that erupted now eclipsed that which had just happened. Sam covered his ears and looked around in amused astonishment.

"Sorry about that, Sam!" Emma said with a grin, "again."

"No, no!" Sam soothed, "a guy's gotta expect this sort of thing! Or, at least try to get used to it!"

"That's right!" Luke said proudly.

"It's nice to see you have things to be excited about," Sam said honestly. "But – and I almost hate to ask this – what's 'Braum's'?"

"What's Braum's?!" the kids asked in unison.

"Only the best burgers on earth!" Luke said, holding up an imaginary burger with both hands as he pantomimed taking a savagely large bite out of it.

"And, the world's best ice cream!" Emma added as Kenny pretended to scoop out ice cream from an imaginary bowl.

"Well," Sam smiled, "what are we waiting for? Let's go to Braum's!"

This was, of course, followed up by more cheering.

Chapter 16
The End of the Line

$\mathcal{T}$his lunch was a long-awaited festivity. The kids ordered their traditional allotment of fries, burgers and shakes. Emma chose vanilla, while both boys gorged themselves on chocolate. Frank favored strawberry, himself, while Joyce was also a chocolate lover. Towards the end of the meal, no one took particular notice when Sam excused himself to use the restroom. He just sauntered off while they each enjoyed the remainder of their meals.

"You gonna eat that last fry?" Luke asked Kenny, as he leaned over the table and gave his plate the once-over, which helped him spy the tiny fragment.

Kenny shook his head and Luke greedily and happily wolfed it down.

"I love this place!" he said with a satisfied grin.

"Me, too!" Emma smiled.

Kenny nodded in agreement.

"I'm glad you like it," Frank said.

"Yes, it's nice to see you finish your meals," Joyce smiled.

"I always –" Luke was interrupted by Emma who looked around and casually asked, "Hey, where's Sam?"

"I dunno," Luke said. Then seeing Kenny point, he added, "Oh yeah, he went to the bathroom."

"Restroom," Frank corrected.

"What's the difference?" Luke asked.

"Well, a bathroom has a – oh, never mind," Frank said, rolling his eyes.

"He seems to have been gone for quite awhile," Joyce observed. "I hope he's all right."

"He's probably just - well - I wouldn't worry too much," Frank said. "Let's finish eating. I'm sure he'll be back by the time we're done."

The family finished, and even cleaned up their tables, but Sam still wasn't back. They quickly ran out of things to do, and sat around the table waiting. They soon ran out of conversation too, and sat in an awkward silence, wondering what was keeping Sam.

"Luke," Frank asked, "why don't you go check on Sam and see how he's doing?"

"Uh, uh!" Luke replied, shaking his head vehemently. "Not me!"

"Come on, Luke," Frank continued. "Just let him know we're ready to go!"

"No way!" Luke pushed back, shaking his head vigorously. "Send Emma! I'm not going in there!"

"Luke!" Joyce countered, "You know Emma can't go in there! Just go let him know we're ready to go."

"OK, I'll go!" Luke said at last. "But, I won't like it!"

A moment later, Luke emerged from the restroom with a puzzled look on his face. He was coming back solo. As he approached their table, the family pantomimed the obvious question, "Where's Sam?" Luke's reply was to shrug his shoulders while he walked the final distance to the table.

"I don't know!" he said, when he arrived. "He's not in there!"

"Did you check all the stalls?" Frank asked.

"Yes! I checked all the stalls," Luke said with a frown. "I embarrassed myself too, when I found out that it wasn't him in that one." He rolled his eyes.

"What?!" Joyce said, starting to panic "Well, we have to find him! We have to find out where he went!"

They could see all around the restaurant. It wasn't very big. He had to either be in the restroom, or else he had to have left the restaurant entirely.

"Calm down, Sweetheart," Frank said with a practical tone.

"What?" Emma exclaimed. "What if someone took him!"

"I really don't think someone took him," Frank replied. "Maybe this is just his way of parting from us. Besides," Frank added, "he asked us to take him to Oklahoma. We're now in Oklahoma. Maybe having to say 'goodbye' was too much for him. Maybe he just wanted to try to slip away quietly."

The family tried to digest Frank's words. They continued to look around, even out the windows, but could see no sign of their beloved traveling companion.

"That does kind of sound like something Sam would do," Luke acknowledged.

"I'm afraid there's nothing more for us to do, but get in the car," Frank said.

"But, shouldn't we call the police or something?" Emma asked through tears.

"The police?" Frank exclaimed with surprise. "No, Sweetie. He wasn't required to stay with us. He's a grown man. If he decides to go, he's free to go."

"But! -" Emma said without finishing.

"Come on, Dear," Joyce said. "Your father's right. Let's go back to the car."

"But! -" Emma protested again.

"I'm not any happier about it than you are, Emma," Joyce said, "but there's nothing we can do."

"I need to get some gas," Frank said. "I'll move the car and let you walk over, or you can come along."

The station was only next door.

"I'll walk," Emma said. Everyone agreed.

Moments later, Dad was cleaning the windows while he was gassing up the car. As he worked his way around the car, his eye caught sight of some movement over behind the restaurant. He had his suspicions and put away the squeegee, then made his way over to the back lot.

As he approached the dumpster, he heard a noise that confirmed that someone was back there behind it. He came around and saw the back of a man, ducking around, apparently trying to hide behind the large trash bin.

"Hey, uh, Sam?" he asked hesitantly.

The figure stopped a moment, stiffened, then turned to face Frank. It was indeed Sam.

"Um, what's up?" Frank asked.

Sam didn't respond right away. He slowly turned to face Frank, but did not look up. It was clear that he was trying to calm himself. Frank could tell he had been crying and found himself growing emotional.

"Say, uh, Sam," he said in a halting voice. Trying to sound more confident, he continued, "Why don't you come back with us? We're in Oklahoma, sure, but isn't there somewhere in particular you'd like us to take you?"

"I – I can't," Sam stammered. "You people have already been too kind to me. Kinder than I've been treated in many a year – if ever."

"Well, uh," was all Frank managed.

"I don't want to be a burden," Sam said flatly. "You good people don't need anyone to be a burden on you. You've done your job with me, and now you can go. I'll make out fine."

"We've done our job?" Frank asked confused. "What job?"

"Your Samaritan job," Sam explained. "That's what you said, isn't it? You took me on because you wanted to be Good Samaritans, right?"

"Well, uh, yes," Frank agreed, "but, uh, it's not like that now. I mean, sure, that's what got us to pay attention to you to begin with." Frank paused, searching for words. "But, it's a heck of a lot more than that now."

"How so?" Sam asked.

"You became our friend," Frank said with clear, liberating honesty. He had found the right word after all.

"I, I – ?" was all Sam could manage.

"You became our friend," Frank repeated, emboldened with the truth. "And, friends don't leave friends hiding behind dumpsters. Come on, Sam, please come with us. We'll take you wherever you want to go. Really. Everyone's worried about you."

Frank held out his hand. Sam looked at it for a moment, then looked Frank in the eye. He appeared to be sincere. He stiffened and slackened his jaw a couple of times as he pondered the thought of friendship, true and honest friendship. He wiped his eyes and took a hold of Frank's hand.

"You won't tell them I was crying?" Sam asked.

"Not if you don't tell them I was," Frank replied.

"You?" Sam asked, startled.

"Well, I was just about to if you didn't come with me," Frank admitted with a smile. "Come on."

There was a squeal from inside the car when Emma turned and saw her father returning with Sam by his side.

"It's SAM!" she screamed. "It's SAM! He's coming back! Dad found Sam!"

"All RIGHT!" Luke hollered as Kenny clapped.

The car soon emptied of occupants and Sam found himself surrounded by well-wishers welcoming him back to their lives. They hugged him and then made their way back into the car. Sam let his tears flow freely at this, since there was absolutely no way he could have held them back now.

After the celebration, they all climbed back into the car. Emma guided Sam into what had become his traditional place and climbed in from the other side to sit beside him. Frank started up the car and they pulled out of the station.

"We're on our way!" Emma sang out the opening line of the family's traveling song.

"Pack up our packs!" the others joined in spontaneously as they all boisterously and jubilantly completed the traditional homage to family trips.

As the final echoes of the song died away, Frank glanced casually in the rearview mirror and asked Sam a question that he was a bit surprised that he had never bothered to ask before.

"So, Sam," he asked, "where exactly in Oklahoma did you want us to take you?"

Joyce and the kids were also surprised by this question as none of them had ever discussed it before. They were simply glad to have him along, especially after the fears of having lost him.

"Where?" Sam pondered, then repeated. "Where? I – uh – I –"

The uncomfortable pause made it clear that he hadn't given it much thought either. Emma looked at her friend and saw his eyes turned upward and his face screwed up in thought as if he was searching for the answer. Suddenly, his face cleared and brightened. The answer had come at last from depths or recesses of his mind that had been long repressed. It looked to

Emma that he was scrutinizing the answer in his mind before giving it, and when he was satisfied that it was the right answer, he decided to proceed.

"I guess that would be Bartlesville," he said with satisfied conviction, even though he hadn't the slightest idea of where that was.

"WHAT?!" Frank exclaimed.

"I'd like to go to Bartlesville," Sam repeated in a calm tone.

Frank slammed on the brakes and nearly careened off the road. Joyce grabbed the dashboard as Frank made his hasty maneuvering. Kenny was jiggled in his fort while Emma and Luke looked on. When the car came to a complete stop alongside the road, Frank turned, putting his right arm up along the top of the back of the front seat and turned his head to face Sam.

"Where exactly, did you say you wanted to go?" he asked in a calm but puzzled voice.

"I – uh," Sam said with hesitancy, wondering if he should repeat it. Not wanting to be dishonest or deceptive, he decided he would be forthright. "I just said I wanted to go to Bartlesville. Is there something wrong with that? Is it too far out of the way?"

"Did any of you kids say anything to Sam?" Frank asked, ignoring Sam's question for a moment.

They all shook their heads, "No."

"At least, I don't think I did," Emma said.

"Me neither," Luke added. "And, I KNOW Kenny didn't. Maybe it was you guys."

Frank looked to Joyce.

"I know it wasn't me," Frank said.

"I didn't either," Joyce confessed. "At least, I don't remember doing so."

"What is all this?" Sam said, growing more and more concerned. "Is there something wrong? Should I not have said that? Is it too far? Is there no such place?"

"Oh, there IS such a place," Frank responded. "And, NO, it's not too far. It's just a bit odd. You see, that's the very place we're going."

"Yeah, that's where Grandma lives," Emma added.

"Well, I'll be!" Sam stammered slowly. "Who'd have thought it?"

"Yeah, who'd have thought it," Frank agreed. "Did you hear one of us tell you this earlier? Really, now, did you?"

"No, no I don't believe so," Sam said with honest self-inquiry. "I can't say as I've ever really heard the name before at all, least ways from any of you."

"Then what in blazes made you say it now?" Frank asked, perplexed.

"Frank! Watch your language," Joyce reminded him.

"Sorry, I'm just surprised," he smiled back.

"I – I really don't know," Sam confessed. "You asked where I wanted to go. I thought about it long and hard. I knew that this was probably my only chance to get to where I need to go. I doubt I'll ever meet another wonderful family like yours. So, this was very important to me to get it right. I thought as hard as I've ever thought before. That word 'Bartlesville' suddenly came to me, so I said it. That's all. Honest."

"Well," Frank replied. "I guess it really is a small world after all. Bartlesville!" He repeated that to himself as he pulled back onto the road.

* * * * *

They settled down after this odd coincidence and continued to drive. Frank turned east at Ponca City and drove the final seventy miles with the family growing increasingly antsy. It slowly dawned on them that with each mile they traveled they had one less mile to spend with their new friend whom they had grown to love in the short time they had known each other.

Of course they would say that they would keep in touch, but they had no idea of how to get in touch with Sam in the future. Sure, they could give Sam their address, but who knew if he would ever actually write? Typically human good intentions made it doubtful. With a wistful sigh, Frank accepted the inevitable fact that the family and Sam would soon permanently part company.

"I'll miss the old guy," Frank said aloud to himself.

"Pardon?" Joyce asked.

"Huh? Oh, I was just saying I'll miss Sam," Frank said with a touch of melancholy.

"Oh, me, too," Joyce said, looking back at her knitting.

"You know," Frank said, staring out at the road ahead, "we don't even know his real name!"

"That's right!" Joyce said with a bit of a ponderous start. "I've gotten so used to calling him 'Sam' that I'd entirely forgotten about that."

"Funny, isn't it?" Frank asked.

"The name?" Joyce asked.

"No, that you can meet someone and grow so fond of him in such a little time."

"I know what you mean," Joyce replied. "I know what you mean."

She looked back at their family. Emma was reading aloud to Sam. Sam was listening, but also gazing excitedly out the window. Kenny and Luke were both in the back seat getting ready to do more magic tricks. Luke had just said something or other about seeing if the Okies were as good an audience as the Kansans. He put such an emphasis on the word "Okies" that it was clear he just wanted to say the word, especially when they both started giggling. Or rather, Luke giggled aloud while Kenny's body simply shook as if giggling.

"I think it will be hardest on Kenny," Joyce said, as she turned back to look at Frank.

"Kenny?" Frank asked, surprised. "I would have thought Emma."

"Oh, it will be hard on Emma, I'm sure," Joyce replied. "But, Emma is a solid character. She has her books, and beyond that, she's so independent. I think she'll be sad, but all right in the end. Kenny, however, is much more fragile and dependent. I think it will be hard on him. He's really grown attached to Sam."

Even as she said this, Kenny, with his face beaming in a grin, reached up past his fort and tapped Sam on the shoulder so he would turn and see the silly antics Luke was doing with his cards balanced on his head, with one tucked behind each ear like pencils and another stuck to his forehead. He was wagging his tongue and crossing his eyes.

Chapter 17
Parting

"Well, Sam," Frank announced after a bit over an hour's drive, "this is Bartlesville!"

There was cheering from the kids as Sam looked out his window with intense curiosity.

"Any of this look familiar?" Frank asked him.

"No, no, I can't say it does," Sam said slowly, as he eyed the houses they rolled passed.

"Well, uh, you just let us know where you want us to let you off, then, Sam," Frank said with an awkward bluntness.

He didn't mean to be so blunt. He wasn't trying to dump the man. In fact, he found himself feeling very reluctant, and hoping that somehow Sam would say something that would indicate that he'd have to stay on for just a little while longer. Joyce and the kids felt the bluntness of the comment, though. Emma looked hurt. Kenny grew very quiet, even for him.

"Sheese, Dad!" Luke retorted. "Why don't you just pull a door open so we can boot him out already!"

"That's not what I meant, Luke," Frank said in a tone that was somehow a blend of offense, embarrassment, and chastisement. "It's just that Sam said he wanted to go to Bartlesville, and we're here now, and as much as I'd like to keep him with us forever, he does seem to have somewhere he wants us to take him, or drop him off."

"Hey!" Emma said brightening up. "That would be great!"

"What would be great?" Frank asked.

"If we keep Sam forever!" she said, as if the answer was so obvious and simple.

"We can't keep Sam forever!" Frank corrected. "He's not a puppy we found alongside the road! He's a man! He's - "

Frank's next words were cut off as Sam spoke up quietly, but decidedly.

"Take me to the corner of Arbor and Locust," he said in an odd voice.

"Where?" Frank asked. Not getting a reply, and noticing that Sam was looking absently out the window he repeated his question, "Where, Sam? Where did you want me to take you?"

Sam continued to gaze outside. Emma looked at him, then at her dad, and back to Sam again. Sam still didn't respond. She nudged Sam cautiously.

"Eh?" he asked, turning. "What's the matter?"

"Dad asked you where you wanted to be dropped off," she encouraged him, hoping to jar his memory.

"Oh, I don't know, anywhere will be fine," he said absently.

"But, you just told me where," Frank protested in a kind, patient, but curious and insistent tone.

"I did?" he asked.

"Yes, you did," Joyce added. "You told us to take you to 'the corner of Arbor and Locust'."

"'Arbor and Locust'?" Sam repeated as if hearing the words for the first time. "Well, now that doesn't sound like two streets that would get along very well, now would they?"

"Pardon?" Frank asked.

"Well, I'd think the locusts would eat the trees in the arbor, don't you?" he said, turning to Luke and hoping for a laugh.

When none was forthcoming, he noticed that the entire family was staring at him with concern.

"I'm sorry," he said at last. "I don't recall saying that."

"You don't recall giving me an address?" Frank began, but was cut off by Joyce putting her fingertips on his shoulder and shaking her head slowly, cautioning him to not make a big deal of it.

"We'd be happy to take you there," she said to Sam. "Do you know what's there?"

"I'm sorry, I'm afraid I don't," Sam admitted.

"Hey, we're going by the mortuary!" Luke said with excitement.

"What's so interesting about a mortuary?" Sam asked.

"It's funny!" Luke said.

"Funny? What's funny about a mortuary?" Sam asked.

"The owner paints the grass green in the winter time," Emma explained. "I guess he doesn't like it when it turns brown."

"It's not 'funny'," Joyce corrected. "He's just trying to keep his place looking nice, even in the winter."

"There it is. See?" Luke pointed.

"Well, I'll be." Sam said, looking out the window as they drove past a single-story building with a lawn painted a forest green, while all others were a pale, grizzly yellowish brown. "It does look nice, though."

"I think it's silly," Luke said, as Kenny waved at the grass as they passed by.

"You think EVERYTHING'S silly." Emma rolled her eyes.

They continued past the Phillips 66 headquarters, the Frank Lloyd Wright Building, and the new city center.

"Check it out, Sam," Luke said, as he pointed to the large, red-brick city center. "See how they made it look like a circus tent?"

"A brick circus tent," Sam observed. "I think I've seen everything now. Pretty clever."

"I think it's silly," Luke said.

"What'd I tell you?" Emma shrugged to Sam.

They continued through town, driving past neighborhoods and then through a stretch of fields and forests before coming to more neighborhoods.

"Well, there's Locust Street." Luke said, pointing.

Locust was one of those streets that fed into the main street they were cruising, but did not cross it. Frank made a right turn and began heading down Locust. He slowed down enough for the family to read the cross streets as they approached them. They drove a dozen or more blocks when they began to wonder if this was some sort of wild goose chase.

They slowly drove past houses decked out for the holidays. There were lights on nearly every home, reindeer on the lawns, Santas on rooftops and even a sleigh or two, in spite of the fact that Bartlesville was in absolutely no danger of receiving any snow. It was cool, but not cold. No one noticed the decorations, however; they were all intently watching for street signs.

It was Kenny who started pointing frantically that caught Luke's attention.

"I see it, Kenny," Luke agreed. "It's right there, Dad. Stop!"

"I see it, too," Frank said, as the entire family, including Sam, looked out their windows wondering which of the four surrounding corners was the one that Sam wanted. "We'll stop here. Good work, Kenny! You've got eagle eyes."

Kenny smiled as Luke patted him. Frank pulled to the side and parked.

"Which house do you want?" Joyce asked as she looked around.

She was looking at a nicely-kept one with green siding and glorious strands of Christmas lights along the eaves, as Sam looked to his right.

"That one there," he said, not taking his eyes off an old house with a hedge on one side and a flaking picket fence across the front.

"There?" Frank asked. "That looks like a vacant house. I don't think anyone's lived there for years."

"Are you sure this is where you want to be dropped off?" Joyce asked, as Emma looked to her with her eyes growing moist. "I mean what place is this?"

"I don't know," Sam confessed. "I can't remember, but I'm certain this is the place."

Everyone eyed the house hesitantly from within the car. Sam, however, got out immediately and began looking at the house with wonder. Frank climbed out. Emma dashed out suddenly, seeming desperately afraid that Sam would disappear without a proper goodbye. Kenny and Luke began beating on the back window frantically trying to get someone's attention so that they would open the wagon's back gate and let them out. Seeing that this was not to be, they leaped over the middle and climbed out Emma's door.

Joyce was the only one still sitting. Her head was down and her fingers were flying over her work. No one seemed to notice the look of concerted effort on her face.

Sam wandered up to a weary picket fence. Most of the white paint had long since fallen off, leaving only scraps of it now. It sagged in places and was missing a board or two here and there. Its little gate was closed, but askew. One of the hinges was broken.

The house had also been white at one time, but was more gray than white now, with peeling paint throughout. It was a modest home with a second story that was half the width of the first. It had five cement steps leading up to its front door which had at one time been painted a dark green. The screen was missing.

The windows on either side of the door were dark and full of grime. The one to the left was much smaller. Evidently, it was for the kitchen or dining room. The one to the right was a broad picture window that was obviously for the living room. Along the foundation, they could see the top half of windows peaking up above window wells along the bare cement.

The yard was brown with thin, sickly grass and weeds nearly two feet long that had withered in the colder weather and fallen down in an entangled mess. There was trash and debris here and there that had accumulated over years of neglect.

Sam turned to look at the family, who, all except for Joyce, had lined up at the entry to the yard and stood there breathlessly staring at him, anxious to find out what would happen next.

"You're welcome to come with us," Frank offered.

"Yeah! You'll LOVE Grandma's!" Emma coaxed with bright excitement.

"I'm sure I would," Sam smiled, then turned to Frank and explained, "I think I'll just wait here awhile longer and see if anyone shows up."

"Really, we don't mind," Frank said, trying to be more polite than realistic.

He knew that Sam's journey with them was coming to an end, and it was time for Sam to find out what had pulled him to this location from across the country. He was a bit wistful in realizing that he would not find out how that journey would end, but was satisfied to have at least played some small role in it.

"But, why do you have to stay, anyway?" Emma moaned.

"I want to find out about my past, my life, where I came from and why I left it," Sam replied patiently and soothingly.

"But, what if you find out it was no good?" Luke questioned. "What if you left because you wanted to, or because you had to? And, it wasn't nothing you wanted to be a part of anyhow?"

"'Anything', 'anyway'," Frank couldn't help correcting his son, who was so engrossed in the conversation that he didn't hear his father.

"Well, Luke, then at least," Sam replied, pausing for emphasis, "at least I'll have my answer. Somehow my past has been taken from me. For good or for ill, it's my past and I'd like to find out what it was. I know I can never have that part of my life back, but I'd like to take what I can with me into the future. And, I believe that all needs to begin here."

He turned and looked at the dilapidated house again. The family followed his gaze. Little Kenny shuddered.

"Well, we can't just leave you here alone," Frank suggested as Joyce finally exited the car and joined them, carrying a small bundle in her hands. "It'll be dark soon."

"I'll be just fine," Sam smiled. "I'm used to finding my way around in the dark, as well as finding a place to spend the night."

"Yeah, uh, I guess that's true," Frank acknowledged.

"Really, I'll be just fine," Sam insisted. "You people have been so kind to me. So very kind. I don't know if I'll ever be able to thank you enough."

"Well, we have one more thing for you that you simply must accept," Joyce said, stepping forward and handing her bundle to Sam.

"What's this?" Sam asked.

"A little Christmas present," Joyce replied.

"A Christmas present?" he said, choking back tears. "I can't remember the last time anyone gave me a –"

"Open it!" Joyce said, holding back her own tears.

"Now?" Sam asked. "Shouldn't I wait?"

"We won't be here then," Joyce pointed out, "and I want to see how you like it!"

Sam obeyed.

"Where'd you find Christmas paper?" Frank whispered to his wife.

"You have to plan ahead," Joyce replied coolly.

"Plan ahead? How on earth did you know we'd be taking on a passenger?" Frank asked incredulously.

Joyce just rolled her eyes at him with that "you simply don't understand what I'm saying" look. She turned away from him and watched Sam eagerly unwrap his gift. It didn't take long until something soft, fluffy, and made of a familiar color of yarn tumbled out of the paper into Sam's outstretched hand.

"It's beautiful!" Sam declared with a shaky voice, as he looked at the pile in his hand.

Joyce reached over and held up the pieces one at a time so that they became distinguishable.

"It's a hat and scarf," she declared. "I don't want you to ever be cold again!"

She handed them back to Sam, who took them graciously and bowed his head in thanks as Joyce hugged him and kissed him on the cheek. She stepped back and wiped her eyes as Sam looked at his treasures. He pulled on the hat and wrapped the scarf ceremoniously around his neck.

"You look very handsome!" Emma declared.

"Thank you!" Sam replied, nodding to her with an eloquence that, though it had been hidden for years, now somehow seemed natural to him. He looked as if he would say more, but no words escaped his mouth. He tried to look at the family he had grown to love, but could only manage to look down toward the sidewalk at the moment.

"We'll miss you, Sam," Frank said, holding out his hand to shake Sam's in farewell. "You take care, old friend. We want to hear good things about you!"

"Yes, yes, I will," Sam promised.

He took Frank's hand and pulled it to him and embraced the man who had pulled him out of the gutter and brought him to a new life with a more promising future. Frank returned the embrace and was stunned to realize just how much his heart hurt at the thought of leaving this former stranger. Emma and the boys joined in and soon they all stood there in a group embrace.

"I – I just don't know how I'll ever thank you good people!" Sam declared, as they finally backed away from each other. "You are more than Samaritans! You are angels, pure and simple. You are angels. My guardian angels. I can never thank you enough."

"It has truly been an honor and a pleasure to have had this chance to get to know you, Sam," Frank replied. "Thank you for all you have done for our family."

"I haven't done anything!" Sam objected.

"Oh, yes you have," Frank replied. "More than you can know. It has been a wonderful thing for our family to have been able to spend these few days with you. Here, take this."

"What is it?" Sam asked as Frank handed him a small slip of paper.

"It's my mother's address and phone number, as well as ours back in California," Frank explained. "If you ever need us, you can contact us at one of these. And, if you get the chance, you can drop us a line and let us know how you're doing."

"I'll do that!" Sam promised. "Thanks so much, again!"

Several more words of loving gratitude were exchanged between the man and the family on that cold sidewalk in the unfamiliar neighborhood before the family was finally persuaded to leave their dear friend where he stood, and get into their car. It was upon returning to the car that Emma realized Sam's clothes were still inside it. She grabbed his bag and hustled it over to him.

He thanked her again and gave her another hug before she climbed back into the vehicle. As they drove off, Emma rolled down her window so she and Luke could bless Sam's ears with a refrain of "God Rest Ye Merry, Gentlemen" while Kenny waved goodbye through the back window.

Sam stood there waving a tearful goodbye until the car was finally out of sight.

"I'll be fine!" he repeated again to them, even though he knew they could not hear him. "I'll be just fine, now."

He stood there watching even after they were gone, then he turned back to the house. He opened the gate and walked up to the front door. He pressed the old doorbell and waited. He didn't think he had heard a bell, but paused a moment just in case. He pressed it again, and this time was certain that he hadn't heard anything, so he knocked loudly on the door and waited again.

He tugged on his sleeve and held it with his fingers. Using his palm, he wiped at the grimy window making a clear spot for him to peer in. He could see into the hallway, but no farther.

He suddenly had the flash of a scene inside that house, in which he saw a little child running with a young woman chasing after him. Although he could not see her face, he could sense that she was smiling and laughing as the child passed from his view. He sensed the presence of a man who was also laughing and felt somehow that it was himself. He blinked and the sensations were gone. He was staring into the empty house.

He knocked again and waited some more, but the only sounds he heard were the light whistling of the wind and random background noise from neighboring homes. He gave them a shrug and stepped down from the porch.

Chapter 18
Homecoming

$\mathcal{F}$rank drove the family across town, past the railway station and headed toward Grandma's home. They had sung a few carols along the way, but gradually grew quiet as the distance between themselves and Sam widened. The quiet didn't last however, and was replaced by the kids' antsy, restless anticipation of seeing their grandmother.

As the din slowly but surely increased, Frank turned to Joyce and grinned, "I knew it couldn't last."

"That would have been too much to ask," Joyce agreed.

They finally turned into Grandma's neighborhood and all three kids piled into Emma's middle seat and fought for the windows, particularly Emma's window on the right, since that's the side of the street on which their grandmother lived.

"There's her house!" Luke shouted out, looking ahead three houses.

"And, look!" Emma added as they passed the yard before their grandmother's, "there's Uncle Steve hanging his lights!"

Emma rolled down her window as the kids yelled and waved to an elderly man standing precariously on a ladder with a string of lights that was half on his eaves and half trailing down his back. Frank even obliged the kids by giving a quick toot on the horn. The man turned in surprise. Recognizing their faces, he smiled warmly and waved back with lights dangling from his free hand.

"I sure like Uncle Steve," Emma said.

"Yeah, me, too," Luke agreed. "Say, Dad, how long have we known Uncle Steve?"

"I've known him a long time," Frank replied as he pulled the car into the driveway. "He's always been around so far as I can remember. He's always been a wonderful family friend and a blessing to my mother. He seems to care for her every need. Makes me feel good to know he's here for her when I'm so far away."

They piled out of the car, with the three youngest trying to race each other to the door. Grandma beat them all and had it open with herself standing on the front step, her arms extended, before they could clear the distance from the car to the door. There were many hugs and greetings.

"Uncle" Steve wasn't really their uncle. He was only a very good and longtime friend. He managed to climb down from his ladder and come over and greet the family as well. Emma had reserved a hug for him.

As Grandma invited the family indoors, Uncle Steve asked Frank how long they'd be able to stay.

"At least a week," Frank managed to reply as he was pulled into the house by Luke.

"Grandma's already got dinner ready!" he said with excitement. "I can SMELL it!"

Before long, they all sat down around the table. Kenny's face was gleaming in eager anticipation as he took his traditional seat next to Grandma, who sat at the head of the table opposite Frank.

"Oh, boy!" Luke cried out. "I just LOVE Grandma's cooking!"

After a blessing on the food, which included thanks for a safe arrival, they all dug into mashed potatoes, corn, and shredded roast beef. Grandma not only knew they were coming, but she also knew their favorite meal.

"Grandma!" Emma declared, as she piled a scoop of yellow corn on top of her potatoes, "We've been Good Samaritans!"

"You've been what, Sweetheart?" Grandma asked, puzzled, while Frank and Joyce exchanged slightly anxious looks at each other. They had wondered how to explain what they had done without it sounding foolhardy at best and dangerous at worst.

"We've been Good Samaritans," Emma repeated. Seeing the confused look in her grandmother's face, she continued, "you know, like the parable in the Bible. The one where the guy gets robbed and left on the ground and everyone passes by him except for one Samaritan who takes care of him. We found a guy like that that everyone was ignoring, but not us! We picked him up and took care of him!"

"Goodness!" Grandma exclaimed. "What do you mean you picked him up? Did you give him a ride somewhere?"

"I'll say we did!" Luke laughed. "All the way to Oklahoma!"

"What?" Grandma exclaimed, looking first at the kids and then at their parents.

Seeing the concerned look in her eyes, both parents started speaking at once, trying to explain. Meanwhile, Emma and Luke embarked on their own excited telling of their odyssey. Even little Kenny got into the act, gesticulating and miming his own version of the tale. Grandma looked around her with increased concern and massive confusion. Finally, she waved her napkin in the air signaling defeat.

"Wait just a moment!" she exclaimed, as the family's various renditions slowly ground to a halt. "Just a moment! I can't understand all of you at once! Frank, tell me what this is all about."

Frank felt a bit uneasy as his mother stared unblinkingly into his eyes with that searching look he had become so accustomed to as a teenager, whenever he'd come home later than scheduled, or done something suspicious. He swallowed and then began.

"You see, Mother," he began, "it's all perfectly harmless." Ignoring her upraised eyebrow, he continued, "We passed an RV..."

"That stands for Recreational Vehicle, Grandma," Luke interrupted. "It's those big camping cars they have."

"I'm familiar with RVs, Luke," Grandma replied without taking her eyes off of Frank. "Please continue, Son."

"It had a sticker for the Good Sam Club and Emma asked what that was all about," Frank continued. "I explained that it stood for 'Good Samaritan' and that it came from that parable about the man who helped the wounded man – "

"I'm also familiar with that parable," Grandma pointed out.

"Yes, well," Frank pursued, "when we stopped for lunch, we came across a homeless man who asked for money." Grandma's look became very piercing at this, as she wondered how foolhardy her son had been. "We didn't give him any," and she looked a bit more relaxed, "because we assumed he just wanted to buy beer." She nodded her head in agreement.

"But, he wasn't!" Emma blurted out with a grin. "He really wanted to buy lunch!"

"And, how do you know that?" Grandma asked.

"Yes, well, we saw him come into our same restaurant while we were eating," Frank explained.

"And, he had a sweet, little, homeless lady with him," Emma added.

"And, he bought them both a children's meal and split it between them," Frank said, rekindling his feelings of guilt.

"A children's meal?" Grandma asked a bit shocked. "For them both?"

"Yes, it wasn't very much," Joyce added.

"I felt terrible when I saw this," Frank confessed. "Here I thought he was just going to buy beer. When he really was hungry."

Grandma sat back, knowing that she would have reacted the same way.

"Anyway, afterwards when I went to get gas, he came walking by," Frank said. "I saw this as a second chance to do right by him. We talked briefly and somehow I ended up offering him a ride. I didn't think he'd accept, but he did. Then he said he'd always wanted to go to Oklahoma. It was too strange, but somehow we all agreed."

"It's what the Good Samaritan would have done!" Emma declared.

"Yes, but taking a stranger into your CAR! With your CHILDREN!" Grandma was flabbergasted.

"He's no longer a stranger," Joyce explained. "He's a very sweet man."

The family then took turns explaining all of their dealings with Sam and how wonderful he was, and how they wished he had agreed to come with them to her home so she could meet him – at which Grandma's eyes looked shocked and she shuddered involuntarily – but, that he seemed to have found a home or at least a place to spend the night, and how they all hoped he would do well, and so forth.

"I don't know," Grandma said at length. "It all still sounds very dangerous. I'm just glad you're all here safe and sound. Where did you say you dropped him off?"

"Just some old abandoned-looking house on the other side of town," Frank said.

"That's odd," Grandma replied. "I would have liked to have met him, I guess. I wonder what will become of him."

*****

Back at the abandoned house, Sam wandered around the yard. He walked slowly through the overgrown weeds and across large, brown patches in what could have once been a flourishing lawn. He looked at the peeling, white paint that was streaked with gray and dirt from years of storms and neglect. Here and there he could see that some of the windows were cracked, but none had actual holes.

He continued his slow walk through the yard, touching objects as he did so. He did this because he began experiencing random flashes of visions or images. It seemed the longer he spent there, the more he would see. He was intrigued now, more so than scared by them. He couldn't know for sure, but he began to grow more certain that they weren't disjointed images, but pieces of memories. He wished they would linger long enough to help him place them, to put them into some sort of perspective, to make sense of them.

Touching the pole which used to house a laundry line, he saw a flash of white cloth billowing in the breeze. As the sheet billowed, he caught a glimpse of a woman standing at the line hanging clothes. He couldn't see her face clearly, but could tell that she was pleasant and most likely smiling. She stood with her own dress blowing in the breeze. He saw the dazzling light of midday sun shining on her blue, white-dotted dress. He walked toward her, but the vision vanished before he reached her.

Touching the corner of a shed, he caught the glimpse of an old push mower that vanished nearly as instantly as he saw it. Looking up at what he assumed was the kitchen window, he caught a glimpse of something that made the hair on his neck tingle and twinge.

He could have sworn he saw the face of a small boy peering out over the window sill. The face stared at him. It seemed to know him. A smile spread across the boy's face and his arm raised and he began to wave. Sam waved back. He blinked and rubbed his eyes as he did so. When he looked again, the face was gone. But, an intense sense of longing lingered in his soul.

It was only then, staring into the black emptiness of the window, that he realized that the boy had been bathed in light from within the house, and that the house – as he had then seen it – was also bathed in light and looked new and inviting. Now, it was cold, dark, peeling, and uninviting.

He shook his head slowly. Something odd was going on and he was determined to find out what. He walked up to the back door and found it locked. The window was bolted shut, and would not give when he tried to raise it from the outside. As he pushed and strained, it dawned on him that if he were seen trying to break in at this late hour, it would be difficult at best to explain his presence. He decided he needed to be more discrete, careful and seclusive.

He stepped down from the porch and walked along the back of the house to where there was an old woodbox. Its lock was old and rusted. He was able to remove it quickly with the tip of a decaying pickax he had seen leaning against the back shed. He pulled it off and yanked on the door. The door creaked upward and open. In the blackness, he could just barely make out the shapes of logs.

It took only a few moments for him to remove the logs and twigs. He wrapped his hand in an old cloth he found in the yard and waved it all around inside the box and then rubbed it along the ceiling, floor, walls and corners, to get rid of any spiders or critters that might be lurking within the shed. Satisfied, he grabbed his bundle of spare clothes and crawled in. The ground was unusually hard, but he was used to hard ground. Using his clothes as a pillow, he pulled his knit hat tight, wrapped his scarf securely around him, curled up and went to sleep for the night.

*****

Luke woke up to the sound of sizzling.

"Ya hear that, Kenny?" he asked, tossing his pillow at his brother's head. "That's sausages! Grandma's making sausages!"

Kenny smiled even as he rubbed the sleep out of his eyes. Within seconds, both boys were dashing out their bedroom door, bouncing off the walls in the upper hallway and then bounding down the stairs heading for the dining room.

"We're ready!" Luke announced as he and Kenny slid into their seats at the table and looked into the kitchen.

"I could hear you!" Grandma laughed. "How about putting some dishes on that table, or are you planning on eating with your fingers?"

"We'll eat 'em any way we can, Grandma!" Luke declared.

"Well, I'd prefer you use plates and utensils," she replied.

It wasn't long before the entire family was enjoying a morning meal of pancakes and sausage as they chattered randomly about how nice it was to be at Grandma's house again. The boys talked of the many things they wanted to do while they were there. Emma spoke of seeing the Christmas lights at Kiddie Park, which caused Luke to roll his eyes and point his finger down his throat.

This was immediately followed by a reprimand from Joyce and the declaration from Frank that that sounded like a grand idea. Luke rolled his eyes with a groan this time, which made Kenny laugh in his silent way. Kenny wondered if he should let his brother know that he enjoyed the lights there, too, though.

Chapter 19
New Surroundings

The door to the woodbox pushed open. Sam crawled out slowly and then stood and stretched. He looked about him. Somehow the yard looked even more deserted in the early morning sunshine. The air was cold, but it was nothing like he was accustomed to out west.

He looked around the yard. Retracing his steps from the previous night, he looked at the clothesline, the corner of the house, and the back window. He was disappointed to find that he was unable to recreate the illusions he had seen the night before. He knew he was tied up in the middle of some strange mystery and was hoping to bring it through to a successful end.

He didn't bother trying the doors on the house. He knew they would still be locked up tightly. A gurgling from his midsection reminded him that he was hungry. He patted his tummy, coaxing it to wait, and walked out of the yard. Stopping at the gate, he wondered which way to go. Instinctively, he turned to his left and made his way down the street.

Within a few blocks, he saw that he was entering the business section. A Denny's caught his eye and he made a beeline for it. He looked inside and the gurgling returned with even more vigor than before. He saw a waitress deposit a healthy stack of pancakes in front of a man and he found himself licking his lips. Coming to his senses, he backed away from the window, wishing he could enter.

He jammed his hands inside his pockets and began to walk away. When he did so, he discovered a small wad of paper in his right pocket. It was a folded piece of writing paper from a motel. He unfolded the paper and found it contained two green pieces of paper. He pulled them apart and examined two twenty-dollar bills. He stared at the bills a moment, holding each up to the sunlight.

He looked at the paper in his hand. It was a note, written in Joyce's handwriting. It read simply, "Thanks for bringing your warmth and love to our family."

A smile spread across his face and a warm feeling of gratitude filled his breast. He pocketed the money and headed for the door. As he reached for the handle, he saw his unshaven reflection in the window. He shrugged, brushed himself off and went inside.

He was somewhat relieved that a waitress was willing to seat him. She handed him a jumbo-sized menu. He was almost overwhelmed at the pictures on it. His stomach gurgled once more.

The waitress, bearing a badge that read "Sandy," returned to take his order. Inherently frugal, he said he would simply like a cup of hot chocolate.

"Is that all?" the waitress, Sandy, asked.

Surprising himself, he heard his voice add, "I'd also like one of these 'Grand Slams' with that."

Sandy took a note and turned to place the order, while he began to panic a moment, wondering how he would pay. But, remembering his newfound fortune, he settled down with anticipation.

When Sandy brought it out and set down the massive plate before him, his eyes bulged. He was still not used to so much food in a single sitting. He dug in and did his best, but ultimately, he could only eat half. When the waitress returned, he asked for something to carry the remainder in.

"You want to take pancakes with you?" Sandy asked in a puzzled tone.

"Yes, thank you," he replied.

She shrugged and made off to the kitchen, returning with a box, a bag, and the check. He gathered his goodies, paid the check and headed out to the sidewalk, wondering where to go next, and with the unfamiliar sensation of knowing that he actually had his lunch along with him. It was going to be a good day.

He wandered awhile, admiring the morning as he did so. He decided that there were few things in life better than viewing the world with a full stomach, especially when you knew you had another meal coming.

He turned a corner and continued on awhile. Before long, he discovered that he was near the rail yard. As he stepped over a track, he suddenly had another dark flashback of a train whizzing by on a rainy night. Unlike his most recent flashes, this one was distressing. He stopped and staggered a moment before he was able to clear his head and continue.

He looked up and saw the main office a ways ahead. He wasn't far from an abandoned railcar and quickly stashed his food in it before heading up to the office. It was a small, old brown building with siding that looked like long wooden shingles. There were windows on either side of the door. Boldly displayed over the doorway was a large sign with two-foot high letters that spelled, "Bartlesville, OK."

He paused a moment, not quite sure if he should knock or just go right on in. He was unaccustomed to entering buildings unbidden, and was on the verge of doing something he hadn't done in a very long time. In fact, he wondered when and if he had ever done it before. He was about to ask for a job. Summoning his courage, he closed his eyes, raised his hand and formed a fist to knock boldly on the door.

He was concentrating so keenly that he barely noticed that the door he was about to knock on was opening and his target had shifted into a balding head.

He opened his eyes just in time to stop himself from thumping on the forehead of a very surprised man in his fifties.

"What in tarnation?!" the startled man interjected. "What is all this?"

Sam stopped still as a picture, with his fist still raised towards the man's face. He saw the man backing up and glanced over at his own raised hand. He slowly realized he was in the midst of a very awkward moment. He withdrew his hand quickly with a sheepish, apologetic look.

"Well," the man repeated, "what is all this? Have you come to murder me?"

"Murder you?" Sam said with shock. "Certainly not! I was just coming to see you."

"See me?" the man asked. "Do I know you?"

"Oh, no, sir," Sam said. "At least I don't think so –" Sam's voice trailed off as he wracked his brain trying to see if the man's face was stored away inside there somewhere. He concluded it wasn't. "At any rate, I've come looking to see if you have any jobs I can do for you," he added.

"Any jobs?" the man replied. "You mean you're looking for work?"

"Yes, sir." Sam straightened, trying to look more confident and appealing to his prospective employer. "I will do whatever you need and am very dependable."

"Are you, now?" the man replied. He eyed Sam suspiciously at first, tugging at his chin, as he let his gaze take him in from top to bottom. At last, his gaze met Sam's and his face mellowed. He took a deep breath before admitting quietly to himself, "I could use an extra hand around here."

He finally answered in a friendly tone, "Come inside here with me. Let's talk."

Sam followed the man inside. The room was dark, lit mostly by the sunlight that bled in through the two dingy windows, and partially from an assortment of low-wattage bulbs, two of which hung from wires in the ceiling. Three others were nested in old lamps in the corners of the room. One was on a spindly desk lamp.

The desk lamp seemed to be drowning in a precarious sea of books, papers, and ledgers that were scattered about in rolling waves of piles on his wide-topped desk. Sam saw countless file cabinets with dented drawers lining one wall. Each wall was decorated with old, black-and-white photos of trains, engineers, and even men on horseback, whose smiling faces had been displayed there for what was probably decades.

Sam noted that, old as he was, the man he was meeting seemed too young to have been the one to post the photos. He concluded that he must have inherited the office, photos and all, when he took on the job. And, that he must have done very little - if any - redecorating over the years. He was obviously a man who was comfortable with keeping things as is.

The man motioned for Sam to sit, holding his outstretched hand, palm upward, toward the wall with the door. Sam turned and saw the window, and a clutter of items. Looking more carefully, he found a pile on top of what he surmised was a chair. He pulled off a stack of papers and old coats and aprons and set them to the side, on the floor. Then, he slid the wooden chair up toward the desk and sat down.

The man smiled and grabbed a paper cup that was stacked above a dusty water cooler. The cup was white in the shape of a snow cone cup. He filled it and sat down as the cooler gurgled. He then leaned back in his chair and smiled at Sam as his feet instinctively crept their way up to the edge of his desk to steady himself.

"Normally, I'd say, 'No'," the manager said, "but my runner just ran off to spend the holidays in Florida. I can't pay much, but I could use you, or else I'm going to get backed up. How soon can you start?"

"Right now," Sam said, holding out his hands, palm outward, to emphasize the point.

"Great! Put this on," the manager said, tossing him a denim blue jacket with dark blue pin stripes and a pair of gloves. "What's your name, anyway?"

"My name?" Sam asked, taken aback. He was a bit surprised that he hadn't even thought that he'd be asked for that. At first, he was tempted to say, "Sam," but something instinctive kicked in and he decided against that. He hesitated a moment and then replied, "Um, it's Louis. My name is Louis."

"OK, Louis," the manager replied, shrugging off the hesitation, "the first thing I need is to get this yard cleaned up."

With these few words, Sam's life had changed dramatically. He went from being a homeless shopping-cart man, to a man of means and employment. He went from begging for his subsistence, to earning his keep. He went from being wholly dependent on the benevolence of others, to putting himself in a position in which he could actually determine what he ate and when. He became able to take charge of his life in ways he could not yet imagine. He had decided that the name change would be good for him, as it would reflect this third stage of his life.

"By the way," the manager added, as Louis opened the door to the yard, "my name's Charlie."

"Charlie?" Louis asked. He walked over to the manager and held out his hand. "Good to know you, Charlie."

They shook hands and Louis gave Charlie a broad smile, which Charlie couldn't help but return.

"I think you'll be all right," Charlie added with a bit of a laugh. "Yeah, I think this'll be just fine."

"Me, too," Louis replied, just before he turned to the door. "I thank you for giving me the opportunity."

Louis nodded his head and then walked out to the yard with a new sense of purpose. It was no longer an old rail yard, but instead he viewed it as his means for a new life. It was abundant with opportunities. The weeds, scattered stacks of rotting wood and trash that were strewn here and there, driven by wind and rain, were not just garbage, but job security. If he were hired to clean up the yard, then the mess from years of halfhearted care was what had generated that need. He did not mind menial labor.

To the contrary, he was excited at the prospect of doing any labor at all. He felt more like a gardener of some great gardens stepping out of the palace doors to tend to his trimmings, as he looked around for a shed and a broom.

Before long, he was sweeping debris. Charlie checked on him later and could have sworn he heard Louis humming some obscure tune. He shrugged, smiled, and walked back into his office.

Around noon, Charlie came out again and hollered to Louis that it was time for lunch. Louis was carrying a bundle of rotting wood over to a bin. He nodded in agreement and said he'd be right there. After depositing the wood, he headed over to the railcar where he'd stashed his bundle of food and brought it with him back to the office.

"You're working like a tornado!" Charlie said, as Louis came in.

"Eh?" was all Louis could manage as he took up a chair next to Charlie's desk and put his bundle on his lap.

"I'm not used to seeing anyone work as hard or as quick as you," Charlie said with a smile. "Maybe ole Lefty oughta just stay in Florida!"

"Thank you, sir," Louis said.

"Don't call me 'sir'!" Charlie loudly objected. "I ain't no royalty. Call me 'Charlie' for Pete's sake!"

"Uh, sure, uh, Charlie," Louis said.

"That's more like it!" Charlie said. Leaning forward and grabbing a couple stacks of paper and sliding it aside briskly, he added, "Stick your eats here!"

"What?"

"Just stick your lunch here, Louis," Charlie said. "You can't very well balance it all on your lap."

"Oh, uh, thank you, Charlie," Louis said.

"Don't mention it." Charlie said. "So, where you from anyway?"

"From?" Louis said, uncertain of how to answer. "Here and there. You know. I've spent the last several years out West."

"Whereabouts?"

"Nevada," Louis said. "In the Reno area."

"Reno, huh?" Charlie observed. "Do any gambling then?"

"Every day's a gamble," Louis said.

"Ain't it the truth?" Charlie agreed. "Ain't it the truth? What'd you do for a living, then?"

"Whatever I could," Louis admitted, vaguely.

Chapter 20
Crèche

"Come on, kids. Time to go!" Joyce hollered out the back door.

Emma, Luke and Kenny stopped playing and turned towards their mom.

"Go where?" Luke asked.

"To the crèche exhibit," Joyce replied.

"A 'crash' exhibit??" Luke asked in surprise as Kenny shrugged. "What, is there a bunch of wrecked cars piled up somewhere?"

"Not 'crash', 'crèche'," Emma emphasized with an eye roll.

"Every year the same joke," Joyce mumbled as she watched the kids head towards the house.

As they walked toward the door, Kenny tugged on Luke's sleeve. Luke stopped and turned to his little brother. Kenny looked up at him and shrugged with a puzzled look.

"You remember, Kenny," Luke said. "The crèche display thing." Kenny still looked puzzled, so Luke continued, "We do it every year. It's those Nativity scene things that they set up at the church. You know, where everyone has a different set to display and we walk around looking at them and tell Mom how cool they all are."

He added that last part with more than a hint of sarcastic exaggeration, emphasizing the word "cool" in a way that made it clear that they were just trying to make their mom feel good about their being there. Kenny's eyes lit up comprehendingly and he nodded and smiled. Mouthing the word "cool" slowly, he made and "OK" sign and slid it slowly across the air to add emphasis to just how cool "cool" was. The two smiled and Luke laughed as they ran through the house and piled into the station wagon.

Before long, they were pulling into the parking lot of the LDS church building that played host to the annual crèche exhibit. It was an ecumenical effort that involved temporarily contributed displays from members of several of the local churches and community members. Several of the displays were quite unique and valuable.

Members of that church volunteered to serve as hosts during the day and guards during the night to ensure that no one touched, broke, or stole any of the exhibits and ensure that nothing happened to anyone's display.

"Remember," Frank said, as they got out of the car, "no touching anything!" Looking at Luke, he added, "And, no wise cracks. This is a nice tradition. Please don't poke fun at it."

"Who, me?" Luke asked, trying to look and sound as innocent as one of the miniature lambs he knew he would soon see lying beside a manger.

"Yes, you," Joyce replied, surprising Luke a bit that his mother would step in with that reply.

"I'm hurt," Luke said with mock indignity.

"Well, come on young man," his grandmother replied, putting her arm in his, "maybe some nice displays will heal you."

Luke smiled and crossed the parking lot with his family. Before going in, they walked to the front lawn to see the annual live Nativity scene there. They saw a couple dressed as Joseph and Mary, while a couple of men in robes looked on, holding shepherds' crooks. This year, there was a teenage boy kneeling beside them. He was also dressed as a shepherd and looked very uncomfortable. Seeing this new family arrive, he slyly reached up and pulled his hood farther down over his eyes, just in case it was someone that might recognize him.

There were even some sheep and a cow sitting by. One of the sheep seemed to be sleeping. Luke looked carefully until he was able to see where the chains on the animals were tethered to stakes in the ground, hidden by loosely piled hay.

Kenny pointed and waved his arm questioningly, nudging Luke as he did so. He gave his brother a puzzled look.

"Yeah, you're right," Luke agreed. "Hey, Dad, where's the wise guys?"

"'Men'," Frank corrected. "Wise MEN."

"Maybe their camels got loose and they're running after them," Emma laughed.

"Yeah, right, maybe," Frank said, not wanting to pursue that one any further, lest they be overheard by the volunteers. "Let's get inside. It's getting chilly out here."

"Yeah, I'm frozen STIFF," Luke said, as he took on a frozen pose.

"Come along, young man," Joyce said, wrapping her arm around Luke's shoulders.

Luke smiled and did as he was told. The family made their way to the cultural hall portion of the church, known anywhere else as a "gym." Frank had long ago explained to Luke that LDS churches all have a cultural hall to help its members stay physically fit, as well as spiritually sound. Luke didn't really care what the reason was. He just thought it was pretty cool. He always wanted to "shoot hoops" during Sunday School.

Even before they walked through the entrance to the gym, they could hear soft Christmas music filtering out into the hallway. Joyce was greeted by a sweet lady who smiled as she handed her a program detailing each of the crèches they would be viewing. It turned out that several were from foreign countries, and the program listed which country they were from, what they were called in their original language, how old the crèche was, who owned it, and other details of interest.

Frank and Grandma picked up programs, too. Emma tried, but Frank just handed his to her and rushed her into the gym.

Once inside, the kids actually got excited. There were Nativity scenes laid out on tables along all the edges of the room and set up on tables spaced throughout the gym floor. They were of all shapes and sizes. One must have been seven feet tall. Luke made a beeline to it with eyes and mouth agape. Frank followed quickly behind him, to ensure he didn't touch it, pulling Luke's outstretched hand back just in time, before his fingers began playing with the delicate tinsel along the fringe of the manger.

Kenny and Emma both headed toward the center of the room where an enormous artificial Christmas tree stood, covered from top to bottom with Nativity ornaments. Some were groupings of individual characters hung carefully so that they all looked toward the center figure of the Christ child in a manger. Others were self-contained carvings of miniature mangers, complete with wooden backdrops that had a star carved into their very tops.

The room was filled with families quietly moving around from display to display and pointing out anything they found of interest to each other.

"Come look at this!" Joyce said, ushering her kids to her.

She had made her way to a table that was bedecked with large wooden figures that were all elongated with indiscernible expressions. They were carved of a very dark wood and polished until they shined. There was a tall wooden statuette of a palm tree in the back of the figures. Instead of sheep and cows, it looked more like there were lions and gazelles placed around the scene.

"What the heck is this?" Luke asked.

"It says it's from Africa," Joyce said, leafing through her program. "Looks like there are several from around the world here, this year."

"Cool!" Luke smiled. "Hey, check it out! There's a monkey climbing the tree!"

He pointed and stepped aside for Kenny to see. Kenny would have laughed out loud, if he could. He smiled so brightly that it warmed Frank's heart and made him think that that one look made the whole outing worthwhile.

To their surprise, the family spent nearly two hours looking at the crèches. Based on previous years, the parents had anticipated giving the kids 15 minutes, tops. But, everyone seemed to be taken in by the oddity, splendor, and uniqueness of the varied displays this year.

"Perhaps the kids are finally growing old enough to appreciate them," Joyce thought.

"That was amazing!" Luke declared as he climbed back into the car. "I never thought I'd say that, but it really was."

"Better than last time?" Joyce asked.

"Oh, yeah," Luke said. "WAY better."

"It certainly was a bigger display," Frank added as he pulled the car out of the parking lot and turned onto the road. "They must have three times the number of displays as last time."

"The word's getting out and more people have contributed," Grandma explained. "It's nice to see everyone take part."

"Yes," Joyce agreed. "It's nice to see people celebrate Christmas together, rather than worry about which Church is doing what. Makes you feel good."

"I liked the music," Emma said.

"Yes, that was very pleasant," Joyce agreed.

"Speaking of pleasant," Luke said, "how's about we head over to Braum's for an ice cream?!"

"What has that got to do with – ?" Joyce began to ask, but was interrupted by Emma's seconding the suggestion and Kenny jumping up and down in his seat.

Frank was smiling and already turning in the direction of the ice cream shop before Joyce had a chance to say "yea" or "nay."

"This family sure likes ice cream," Grandma observed with a smile.

"Oh, yeah, baby!" Luke said with an artificially deep voice.

"Tell you what," Grandma said. "How about you drop me off at the house, so I can get dinner going, while the rest of you get your ice cream?"

"Ice cream before dinner?" Joyce protested.

"Yes, yes, yes!" the kids chanted.

"Yes," said Grandma. "Normally, I'd say 'no,' but I've got a stew I want to make and it will take a couple of hours to simmer. You'll all get much too hungry waiting for it. The ice cream will tide you over. Besides, the kids were all so well behaved, they deserve a treat."

At this, the kids went silent and suddenly shifted to beaming, exaggeratedly angelic faces. Luke even held his hands up to his face, palms down, resting his chin on his outstretched fingers in as innocent a pose as he could manage.

Frank looked in the mirror and burst out laughing. Joyce was forced to give in, as she could no longer keep from smiling herself.

"OK," she agreed. "Just this once. And, only because you were so good," she added.

The kids interrupted their angelic silence with cheers of joy that somehow fell into their singing, "God Rest Ye Merry, Gentlemen." Frank wondered at the connection, but shook his head as he smiled, and then joined in. Joyce soon followed suit.

*****

Satiated with ice cream, the family left the ice cream parlor and were making their way across the parking lot to their car, when Emma suddenly screamed out. At first, Frank thought she was hurt, but soon realized that she was just incredibly excited.

"It's him! It's him!" she repeated, pointing.

"What? Hey, yeah! Are you sure?" Luke wasn't as certain. "Maybe, it is?"

"Of course it is!" Emma said, running toward an old figure in the distance. "Sam! Sam! It's me, Emma!"

The old man was nearly half a block away and starting to cross a street when he heard her shouts. He turned and squinted, trying to determine where the noise was coming from. Stepping back onto the sidewalk, he saw someone running towards him. When he recognized her as Emma, he stopped and smiled.

"Well, I'll be!" he said, as he held out his arms and Emma rushed into them. They both embraced like long, lost kin.

The rest of the family soon caught up and greeted him with enthusiasm.

"I just KNEW we'd see you again," Emma beamed. "I just KNEW it!"

"Well, it's certainly good to see all of you again," he replied.

"How are you making out?" Frank asked, shaking his hand warmly. "Are you all right?" Leaning close in, so as to not embarrass him, he added, "Do you need any money?"

"Oh, no, no!" was the reply. "I'm doing quite fine. I'm well enough off. I got me a job!" he declared with noble pride.

"A JOB?" everyone repeated with surprise.

"So soon?" Frank asked, impressed.

"Yes," he confirmed. "A new job, a new place to stay, a new town, and a new name."

"A new name?" Emma asked, taken aback.

Realizing he might be injuring the feelings of the girl who had so recently christened him, he explained, "Yes, a new name. No offense intended to you beautiful people who endowed me with such a splendid name before, but it just slipped out. The man asked for my name, and I said, 'Louis' as if I'd been using it my whole life."

"'Louis'?" Joyce asked. "Do you think that's you're real name, then?"

"I don't know," Louis admitted. "It just came out, and it just seemed right. To be honest, I have a sneaking suspicion that it just might be. It just might be my real name."

"Does that mean your memory's coming back?" Frank asked.

"I don't know. I really don't know." Louis admitted. "But, it's possible, isn't it? Wouldn't that be nice? Imagine getting my memory back. This place could do that for me, I believe. It just seems like the right place for me to be."

"So, what's your job?" Luke asked as Kenny nodded with curiosity.

"My job?" Louis straightened and puffed out his chest and pointed his thumb to his chest as he stated, "You're looking at the new assistant at the Bartlesville Railyards."

"The rail yards?" Luke repeated. "Cool!"

"Well, congratulations!" Frank said, shaking his hand again.

"Will you join us for dinner to celebrate?" Joyce offered.

"Dinner?" Louis asked, very tempted.

"Yeah," Emma said. "You can meet our grandma!"

"Your grandmother?" Louis repeated. "That IS very tempting."

"Yeah, you don't have anything else going on, why not come?" Luke interrupted.

"Luke," Joyce reprimanded, "don't assume such things."

"I'm afraid I actually do have some things I need to see to," Louis replied. "I've come to this town to find myself. I already seem to be making some progress. There are some more things I'm anxious to look into. You people have done so much for me and I really would love to spend more time with you, but I'm afraid I won't be able to join you tonight. I hope you won't hold that against me."

"We'll be disappointed," Joyce said, "but we certainly won't hold it against you."

"What sort of progress are you making?" Frank asked. "Have you learned anything more besides your name?"

"I'm seeing things," Louis replied in a serious tone. "Just glimpses. Flashes. It's hard to explain. They don't all makes sense, but I think it might be memories coming back to me."

"Are they scary?" Emma asked with concern.

"Actually, some of them are," Louis admitted. "But anything is like gold to me. I'm grateful to get whatever glimpses I can, if they will help me solve this terrible mystery of mine."

"Well, I think that's certainly worth pursuing," Joyce encouraged. "We don't want to take you away from finding out who you are. We can always have you over another time."

"Yeah, but, how will we find him?" Luke asked as Kenny shrugged.

"I'm staying at that place you dropped me off," Louis said.

"Anybody show up?" Frank asked.

"No, not a soul," Louis said. "I suspect it's been vacant for several years. And, if I clean up the yard a little, I suspect that the neighbors really won't mind."

"Probably not," Frank agreed. "I just hope you know what you're doing."

"Do any of us?" Louis asked. "Besides, you can always find me at the rail yard. I'll be there. Working!" he added with pride.

The family wished him well and sent him on his way. He declined a ride, as he said that the walk in the fresh air in these surroundings might help spur his memory.

As the family drove back to Grandma's, Emma said, "It was sure great to see Sam again! Do you think he'll ever really get his memory back?"

"I sure hope so," Joyce said. "I sure do hope so."

Chapter 21
An Evening at Grandma's

As they pulled into the driveway, they saw Uncle Steve carrying a ladder from the side of Grandma's freestanding garage area over to his own garage. He stopped on the strip of lawn which separated their two driveways, and waved warmly as the family car rolled to a stop. The kids all got out in a hurry to greet him with hugs and smiles. He laughed and nearly dropped the ladder as they surrounded him enthusiastically.

"Careful, kids," Frank warned with a grin. "You don't want to smother him!"

Grandma heard the commotion and opened her back door.

"Are you done already?" she hollered over to Steve.

"Just about!" he replied. "I was just going to put the ladder back and give them a try."

He set the ladder against the wall inside his garage and walked back to Grandma's. He walked inside her open garage door and reached for a light switch, then paused.

"Wait a minute," he said. "Kenny, would you like to do the honors?"

Kenny's face lit up and he bobbed his head up and down eagerly.

"Well, have at it, then," Uncle Steve said. He lifted Kenny up to the switch that was above a workbench.

The family backed up a bit to brace themselves for what they hoped would be a wondrous surprise. Kenny reached out and flicked the switch. The world around them all suddenly shifted. Their faces literally glowed with the season as strings of Christmas lights that were hung around the eaves of both the garage and the house instantly lit up in a variety of cheery colors.

Everyone slowly wandered the yard and driveway, backing away from the house to be able to take in the full view. Their heads were all tilted back, their eyes opened widely, and their smiles were only interrupted by letting out occasional "oohs" and "aahs" as they took in the whole scene.

"I like the reds!" Emma declared.

"Yeah, but I like the blues best," Luke put in.

"I think they're all lovely," Joyce said.

"Thank you so much, Steve," Grandma said to Steve, who had made his way over to her as the family looked admiringly at the lights.

She had a peaceful, happy glint in her eyes as she, too, sincerely admired the lights. Steve stepped closer to her side and began to put his arm around her. She kept looking upward for a second as she stepped aside quickly, then turned to him and patted his extended arm and gave him a friendly smile.

"It really was very nice of you," she confirmed. "Now, children," she said, stepping farther away from Steve, "supper's ready! The stew is already on the table. Let's get in before it gets cold."

The kids took another lingering look at the lights while Joyce ushered them inside. Grandma gave Steve more thanks before she followed the kids indoors. Frank approached Steve with an outstretched hand.

"Thanks again, Steve," he said, as the two shook hands. "I really do appreciate how you've looked after my mother all these years. It's good to know that while I'm so far away, I can count on a good friend like you to watch over her and make sure she's safe."

"She's a remarkable woman," Steve said, looking toward the door where Grandma had disappeared into the house. "It's an honor to be of service."

"Well, thank you nonetheless," Frank said, giving Steve a pat on the shoulder before they parted.

Frank made his way inside and to the hall restroom, where he washed his hands. The rest of his family was already sitting at the table waiting for him when he sat down. The kids were fidgeting and eager. They loved Grandma's stew and seemed to feel it was the perfect cap to a perfect day. As soon as the prayer was ended, they were quickly passing their bowls to Frank in turn, who filled them and sent them back to have their contents devoured.

"Grandma," Emma said, after a few minutes and several spoonfuls, "guess who we saw!"

"I wouldn't know," Grandma admitted, puzzled. "Who did you see?"

"Sam!" Emma said with excitement. "We saw Sam!"

"Yeah!" Luke added. "He was heading home from work."

"From work?" Grandma asked, even more puzzled. "How does he have a job?"

"He got hired on at the rail yard," Luke replied, as he took another roll.

"The rail yard?" Grandma exclaimed, "How odd!"

"What's odd about it?" Emma asked.

"Nothing, nothing," Grandma lied. "It's just odd that he would be able to get a job so soon. This Sam of yours must be quite a remarkable man to come to a strange place and get a job the very next day. You say he hasn't worked for years before?"

"Well, that's what he told us," Frank said. "He said he's been homeless for as long as he can remember."

"And yet he comes to Bartlesville one night and has a job the very next day?" Grandma asked.

"Maybe Bartlesville is his lucky town!" Luke put in.

"Lucky indeed," Grandma acknowledged. "At any rate, I think it's wonderful when a man can improve his life through honest, hard work. If that's what Bartlesville can do for – uh – Sam, then I'm happy he's been able to come here. You should all be commended for having brought him."

"Say, Grandma," Luke began, savoring a roll, "what did Grandpa do for work here?"

Grandma, Frank and Joyce suddenly stopped eating and grew very still. Grandma turned her gaze away from the table. Joyce gave quick looks between her and Frank. Frank, who was leaning forward with his spoon halfway to his mouth, glared intently, but not angrily at his son. The tension was so thick that all of the kids noticed it at once. Luke looked around wondering what he had done wrong.

"We don't speak of your grandfather," Frank said coolly.

"Why not?" Luke asked.

"We just don't," Frank responded in a tone that made it clear even to Luke that the matter was not to be further pursued.

"It's not nice to ask too many questions," Joyce chimed in, seeing the puzzled and somewhat hurt expression Luke's eyes conveyed, and trying to add a friendly attitude to the bitter chill in the room.

Luke was about to ask, "But – ?" when he was suddenly kicked by his sister, who nodded for him to be quiet. The look she shot Luke let him know that the two of them could discuss it later.

"Now, who wants more rolls?" Frank asked, trying to move onto a new topic and drop the old entirely.

*****

"What do you think that was all about?" Luke asked Emma, while the two sat together in front of the TV.

Although it was much later, and there had been an entire dinner, complete with dessert, followed by clearing and cleaning the dishes and such, there was no need for Luke to explain the context of his question. The forceful finality of their father's statement to cut their inquiry short still reverberated in their minds. There was no way they could let this matter drop. Nor did they feel they could find a way to bring it up again with their parents. Not tonight, at least.

"I don't know," Emma replied. "It sure makes you wonder, though, doesn't it?"

"Yeah," Luke agreed. "And, I'm going to find out."

"What?" Emma exclaimed, looking at him with surprise, "You're not going to go ask Dad right now, are you?"

"No, I don't think I'll be asking Dad at all," Luke said with a sly tone that piqued Emma's interest all the more.

"Well, then," she asked, "what are you going to do?"

"Grandma's got an attic, remember?" Luke hinted.

"Yeah, so?" Emma questioned. "Wait a minute! You're not going to go snooping around up there, are you?"

"You're not going to stop me, are you?" Luke said with a warning glare.

"No," she confessed, "I'm going to go WITH you."

Luke looked surprised. His sister never wanted to go in on his capers. She was much too forthright, at least in normal times. Something about this didn't seem to be all that normal, however.

"When do we go?" she asked.

"Tomorrow morning," Luke said, looking around carefully and then leaning toward his sister, to make sure they weren't being overheard. "Just as soon as the coast's clear and no one will miss us. I figure a little after breakfast when they'll think we're outside playing or something. They shouldn't miss us then."

"Good idea!" Emma said with hushed excitement. "How did you think that up?"

"Hey!" Luke said, tapping his chest with the tips of his fingers and then holding out both hands widely like "the Fonz" on one of their favorite TV shows, "This is ME you're talking to!"

They both laughed.

* * * * *

"OK, Kenny, you know what to do, right?" Luke asked his brother as he sat in the tire swing that Uncle Steve had hung from the old walnut tree in the backyard, years ago.

Kenny nodded affirmatively and tried to put a serious look on his face, but he couldn't help smiling. It was just too much in his nature to do anything to the contrary.

"Good!" Luke said, giving Kenny a pat on the shoulder. "Just stay here and play. We'll be back as soon as we can, and we'll tell you everything we find out. Here, I'll give you a good push before we go."

He gave Kenny three or four good pushes, then a big "underdog", for which he ran under the swing and pushed Kenny high above him. It made the tire fling and jerk on the rope, and then twist as it rocked back and forth wildly. Kenny's face was lit up with glee as he clung tightly to the rope and let the world swirl around him.

* * * * *

"Did anyone see you?" Luke asked Emma as they climbed through the attic door and quietly closed it behind them.

"Of course not," she said with a touch of indignation. "Do you think I'm dumb or something?"

She scanned the dusty attic. There were old cardboard boxes stacked here and there. There were lamps and trophies, and a coat rack with old coats and dresses all covered with plastic. The place was poorly lit by sunlight, streaking through a couple of small rooftop windows, and a bare bulb hanging in the middle of the room. Its pull-chain still swung softly from when Luke had yanked it.

Luke was looking around quickly, trying to spy any box or bundle that might look suspiciously as if it could contain clues. Emma did the same, as they quickly split up and took opposite ends of the attic. Luke was persistent but soon had to give up on his end. He headed over to Emma, who was methodically making her way to the far corner.

"See anything yet?" he asked hopefully.

"No, nothing," she said, still scanning the piles for new boxes to rummage. "You'd think there'd be at least something that might give us a clue here."

She was nearing the end of the row, and Luke was closing in from the other side of the room, when she gave an old, faded sheet a tug. A puff of dust filled the air and they both began coughing. Luke was still rubbing his eyes, ready to give his sister "What for?", when she shrieked excitedly.

"Hey!" Luke warned. "Keep it down! Do you want Dad to hear us?"

"Yeah - I mean, - no," as she contradicted herself, still excited, and pointing. "What do you think is in THAT?"

Luke saw that she was pointing to an old trunk tucked away in the farthest corner. It was one of those traditionally mysterious trunks they'd seen in movies. It was all brown, with straps rolling across the top and down the front and back, like stripes. It even had a latch for a padlock, but no lock attached.

"Hey, hey, hey!" Luke said, hustling over to it. "I think you might have hit pay dirt!"

The two of them tried to pull the trunk out to the middle of the room, but it was wedged too tightly between other boxes.

"We probably don't want to move it where they could tell we looked in it, anyway," Luke surmised. "Let's just move some of this stuff and check it out from here."

"I can't believe it's not even locked," Emma said.

"Yeah, maybe it's not the one we want after all," Luke suggested.

Luke tugged at the latch. It took more effort than he thought it should, to move it. It seemed to have rusted in place, testifying that it hadn't been moved in many, many years. Luke tired of pushing and pulling on the latch and finally stood up and gave it a good kick. It flitted sideways.

"That'll do it!" he said triumphantly.

Emma reached down and slid the latch up, then reached down to pull open the lid. Luke had to help her, as its hinges creaked and groaned stubbornly. With the lid opened, they looked at the box and saw that its contents were covered by a small cloth. Emma gingerly pulled the cloth off and revealed what they were hoping to find.

The box was filled with old WWII paraphernalia. There was some sort of banner, a scrapbook, a photo album, and even a uniform, complete with a hat. The kids looked at the box in amazement, then at each other. They couldn't have been more shocked if they'd found the Holy Grail.

"What is all this?" Luke asked with hushed reverence.

"I don't know," Emma said. "Maybe we shouldn't be doing this."

"What? Stop now?" Luke nearly exploded. "You're off your rocker!"

"Well, just be careful," she cautioned. "It all looks very old and – and precious."

"You think this is worth something?" Luke said, screwing up his nose. "Maybe to some museum..."

"No, I mean it looks like it's special to someone," she explained.

"Hey, check it out!" Luke said, digging deeper. "Some old medals and stuff. Wonder if this is real gold?"

"What's this article?" Emma asked, picking up a fading newspaper clipping. Not only was it fading, but there were stains on it that made it very difficult to read.

"Let's see," Luke said, as he took it from her gingerly and read the headline aloud: "'Pilot Escapes!' Sounds good so far."

Luke continued to read as much of the article as he could make out. It was an account of a pilot who had been shot down over Germany, held in a POW camp for 18 months and then managed a very daring escape. He had been smuggled back to England and then, after recuperating, he would soon be returning to his hometown of Bartlesville, Oklahoma.

"'Bartlesville, Oklahoma'!" Emma exclaimed. "There's some war hero that came out of Bartlesville?"

"That's what it says," Luke confirmed. "Bartlesville."

"What was the guy's name again?" Emma asked.

Luke scanned through the article again from top to bottom.

"I can't really tell. I can make out 'Colonel' something, but I can't make out the name," he said. "See what you can tell. It's right here."

"I can't make it out, either," Emma conceded after looking as carefully as she could.

"Bummer," Luke shrugged.

"I wonder why Grandma has all this stuff?" Emma asked.

"You don't suppose she knew the guy?" Luke suggested. "'Course, maybe it's just that he was from Bartlesville. Everybody must have known everybody back then."

"Well, sure, but why would she have the guy's UNIFORM, though?" she asked.

"I don't know," Luke shrugged. "Who says it's HIS uniform?"

"Don't they put names on uniforms?" Emma asked.

"Hey, yeah!" Luke brightened. "Let's see!"

They looked for a name tag on the top, on the label, anywhere. For some reason, they could find no name anywhere.

"That's really weird," Luke moaned. "I'd think there'd be a name SOMEWHERE."

"Hey, here's another little box," Emma said, reaching into the bottom of the chest. She pulled it up and it had a miniature padlock on it. "Looks like the kind of box they used to keep letters in."

Luke was just reaching for the box when they heard their mother's voice. She was hollering out to the backyard that it was time for lunch. They sprang into action, quickly replacing everything they'd gotten out and stowing the trunk in the corner again. They shoved other things into place, hiding the trunk, and ran for the attic door, forgetting to be quiet. As they pulled the door open, they suddenly realized their carelessness and hoped that they hadn't been discovered.

*****

Lunch was a quiet affair. Emma and Luke were bursting at the seams to talk about what they'd found. Kenny was dying, waiting for their report. Meanwhile, Luke and Emma were also feeling both guilty for having snooped, and suspicious that they'd been discovered because of the noise they'd made. Their parents, however, were blissfully ignorant of their actions and oblivious to the flurry of thoughts that were racing through their children's heads. The kids just looked down at their meals in silence, casting occasional glances at each other and one or two furtive looks towards their grandmother.

"You kids sure are quiet," Mom announced. "What's up?"

"Nothing!" Luke interjected suspiciously. "Nothing's up! Why would something have to be up – ? "

He would have gone on in trying to point out that just because a person's quiet, it doesn't mean that something's up, but Emma wisely gave him a swift kick, lest he blow their cover and make it blatantly clear that something was indeed "up."

"We're just anxious to get back outside and play," Emma smiled coyly. "Kenny came up with a new game we want to play."

"Kenny did?" Dad asked with interest.

"Yeah," Luke lied, "we call it stickball. It's kind of like baseball, only you play it with a soccer ball and you use a stick to hit it with."

"Sounds fun," Dad observed. "Maybe I'll have to come out and play with you, too. Well done, Kenny."

Kenny smiled sheepishly as his dad tousled his hair and then ambled away.

"That was quick," Emma whispered, as soon as their dad was out of earshot.

"We used to play it with JP back home," Luke admitted quietly.

* * * * *

"The kids are sure quiet," Joyce commented to her mother-in-law as the two did dishes. They could see the kids sitting on the backyard swing set.

"Yes," Grandma agreed. "And, I don't see them playing any of that 'stickball' either."

"I'm afraid they're just bored," Joyce sighed. "It happens every trip. A couple days of excitement, then they get bored until they find something else to take up their attention."

"Well, they always seem to enjoy a trip to the old farm," Grandma suggested.

* * * * *

"So, why do you think Grandma HAS all that stuff up there anyway?" Emma asked Luke, as she idly pushed her swing back and forth with her toes.

"I dunno," Luke said. "But, I'd sure like to find out."

He looked up toward the house as he briefly considered asking his grandmother about the items directly. Right then, Grandma looked out from over her dishwashing and gave him a smile and a wave. He waved back instinctively, but blushed and quickly turned away.

"What do you think, Kenny?" he asked his brother.

Kenny just shrugged and shook his head slowly. They'd already filled him in on their discovery. He was as perplexed as they were.

"Maybe it belongs to a friend or an uncle or something," Emma suggested. Kenny's face lit up and he nodded, egging her on. "Maybe it was just some article about some guy. It was an interesting story. She might have just kept it because it was interesting..."

"...and happened to be someone from her home town," Luke finished. "Yeah, but how would she have gotten the uniform, then? Remember?"

"Oh, yeah. She must have known the guy."

Kenny tugged at Luke's sleeve and then pointed toward the kitchen window and then shrugged in his questioning way.

"Why don't we just ask Grandma?" Luke asked, interpreting Kenny's question. "Because it just wouldn't be right, Kenny. You don't understand. If it's hidden away, she doesn't want us to know about it. And, how would we explain how we found it? We're not even supposed to be up there, remember?"

Kenny nodded as he slumped back down into a defeated pose. He couldn't help looking back up toward the window to the face of the one person who would know the answers to the questions that were pestering his siblings.

Chapter 22
Back at the Rail Yard

$\mathcal{L}$ouis was hard at work, and enjoying every moment of it. He'd already cleared out the old shed that Charlie had asked him to see if he could get around to someday. Now, he was moving scraps and junk around, organizing and cleaning the things he saw that needed to be put in place.

He came across a large sheet of rotting plywood and bent down to get a hold of it. The corner tore off, but the sheet itself wouldn't move. He gave it a kick with his boot and was able to get it to budge. He grabbed the torn corner and managed to pull the sheet free from the earth. Dirt still clung to it as he flipped the board aside.

Underneath, where the board had lain, he saw an old metal pipe, covered with rust. At the sight of the pipe, he suddenly found himself deep within one of his flashback episodes, as he had begun to call them.

It was a terribly rainy night. All was blackness. He felt the rain pounding against his felt hat and dripping down the sides of his face. He wiped his eyes and could make out shouting and commotion. There were several flashes of blinding light that, in their wake, revealed angry faces.

He could make out a rain-soaked hand raising a metal pipe high into the air. He felt threatened, vulnerable, but somehow defiant. A piercing flash of lightning showed the pipe coming downward very quickly - toward him.

Just as suddenly, he found himself standing in the rail yard, looking at the ground. Inadvertently, he gently rubbed the back of his head, noticing the odd groove in it. He shuddered. He shook his head slowly, wondering.

He became aware of sounds around him. There was a voice. He realized it was real, or rather, current. He turned around to see his boss approaching.

"I said, is it a snake you've found?" Charlie repeated. "You know they sometimes like to hide under old wood."

"Huh? Oh, no, it's just some old pipe," Louis said, giving the pipe a kick.

"Yeah, those can sometimes look like a snake," Charlie said.

"Yeah, uh, they sure can," Louis agreed as he bent over and picked it up.

He could clearly see that it was not the same pipe from his flashback and tossed it over into the junk pile he had been making.

"You're sure a big help," his boss said. "Where are you from?"

"Here, I think," Louis said.

"You think?" Charlie scratched his head.

"It's been a long time," Louis said without exaggeration. "I've been out West for so long it seems like a lifetime ago."

"I know what you mean," Charlie nodded. "Do you have any family?"

"No, I don't think so," Louis replied, "other than the family that brought me back here."

"'That brought you back here?' What do you mean?" Charlie asked.

"I was down on my luck and they were heading out here and offered me a ride, so I went with them."

"Someone you didn't even know gave you a ride clear across the country?" Charlie looked as if this was the most remarkable statement he had ever heard.

"Yeah, they were my Good Samaritans!" He laughed nervously, hoping to change the subject.

"I'll say!" Charlie agreed.

With this, the noon horn blasted loudly and clearly.

"Well, let's get some lunch!" Charlie said.

*****

The kids were quietly playing cards in the living room. Frank was reading, while Joyce and Grandma, both of whom were knitting, sat and chatted.

"The kids are certainly well behaved," Grandma smiled.

"That's what troubles me," Joyce replied. "It's a sure sign they're up to something!" she said teasingly.

Luke heard this, but tried to ignore her. He gave his mother a nervous smile and then looked at Emma.

"Hey, it's time for family prayer and bed," Frank said, looking at his watch.

Before they knew it, the kids found themselves in the bathroom, brushing their teeth.

"I'm going to look at that box again tomorrow," Luke whispered through foamy lips to Emma.

"It's not our box," Emma cautioned. "We probably shouldn't pry."

"It's a little late for that, don't you think?" Luke pointed out, and then spat into the sink. "Besides, I just want to see it again."

*****

Louis wandered back to the house on Locust and Arbor. He looked around cautiously before going into the backyard. Once there, he headed directly toward the wood box. But, as he reached the back corner of the house, he paused.

Looking down, he spied a large rock in the weeds, nearly at the corner. He stooped and moved the rock. There, on the ground, under the impression of the rock, he found an old rusted key. He picked it up and stared at it long and hard. If ever there was vindication of a clue, this was it.

Suddenly, he encountered another of his flashbacks. It was a sunny day. He could see a hand inserting the key into the back door. Looking up, he could see a woman inside the house. She was in the kitchen, near the window. Although her back was to him, he could tell she was smiling, possibly even humming. There was a very pleasant air about her.

She neared the window. She looked like she was carrying something, possibly a pie, to put on the windowsill. His heart was pounding in his ears. He was going to catch a glimpse of her face. He could plainly see her apron. Just as she bent towards the window, she was gone.

He stood there, staring into the dirty, black window. A cold breeze whipped across the lawn and blew his hair into his eyes. He brushed it away without blinking. The window remained black. He had a tear in his eye and an unfamiliar aching in his chest. He sensed he had just missed out on a very loving welcome.

After several long moments, he held the key out in front of him. He looked at it and then at the door. He approached the door and tried the key in the keyhole. He was actually surprised to find that it didn't even fit into the hole.

He pulled it from the lock and rubbed it vigorously against his trousers. He looked at it and then rubbed it more between his finger and thumb, then used his nails to help fleck away the rust.

He tried it in the keyhole again. It fit and turned. He gave the handle a twist and the door freed itself. He pushed the door open hesitantly and started to enter.

Once inside, he had a remarkable experience. For an instant, it was as if he was actually in the flashback, rather than viewing it. The room was filled with light. It was a warm summer day outside. He heard a radio playing 1940's music. A pot was boiling on the stove. A slender lady was tending the pot. She heard him enter and turned to him, smiling broadly and welcoming him home, reaching out to him.

He reached out and began to step toward her, when he was distracted by the sound of a little boy on a tricycle. The boy came peddling in, ringing the trike's bell as he peddled. As the boy neared him, he bent down to catch him. Louis was smiling benevolently and felt a joy he couldn't remember having felt before.

As he reached for the boy, the scene vanished and was replaced by the aged room, filled with the darkness of the late evening. He heard a car honk as it drove by, startling him back from his daydream. He looked about and noticed the undisturbed filth of the abandoned house. Still stooping, he flexed his outstretched hands, wishing the boy was still there.

He stood up again. His eyes were filled with tears. He walked over to the sink and turned on the faucet. It sputtered, but would not pour out water. He moved the faded curtain aside and looked out the dirt-streaked window at the overgrown backyard.

"What is happening to me?" he lamented quietly. "Why do I keep seeing these things? Am I going insane? Why have I even come here?"

After gathering his wits together, he walked through the hall and headed upstairs. The banister was coated with dust. The walls had stains from where pictures once hung.

He stepped onto the landing and walked down the hallway, bracing himself for another flashback. He passed a room and pushed the door open and peered in without entering. The room was empty, but it was clearly a bedroom. Judging from its size, it was not the main bedroom, but more likely one for a child. He blinked, expecting a flashback.

Nothing.

He had grown so accustomed to the flashbacks, that he almost felt as though he could trigger them at will, or at least with any new, significant discovery. He was very surprised when viewing this room, perhaps the very room of the child he had seen previously, triggered nothing at all. He wondered why.

"Maybe it's not something that happens when you're expecting it?" he asked himself as he continued down the hallway.

He followed the hall to its end. It stopped at a graying, white door that looked like it had been closed for many years. He reached out and wrapped his fingers around its dusty knob. He gave it a turn and could feel it unlatch.

He hesitated a moment and then pushed the door open. He let go of the knob and let the door creak fully open, without entering. He was a bit gun shy and found that he flinched inadvertently, expecting a powerful flashback.

Nothing happened.

He stood in the doorway a moment and peered into the room. So far as he could see in the dim, evening light that filtered through the dingy window, the room was empty. He lifted his foot carefully and stepped across the threshold with the gingerness and cautious yet determined, trepidation of a soldier stepping onto a minefield. His heart pounded in his ears and he became acutely aware of his own breathing.

He half expected that, as he crossed the threshold, the room would burst alive with bright sunlight as well as images and noises of the home's former inhabitants. He found himself involuntarily squinting in anticipation of the light, as he leaned forward and placed his other foot firmly within the room.

He stood still in place – letting his eyes scan the walls – as he braced himself for the onslaught of another flashback.

Still, nothing happened.

"How peculiar," he mumbled softly, as if trying not to disturb some sleeping giant.

After another pause, he reached for the door and closed it, leaving himself alone in the room.

* * * * *

Emma lay on her bed. The lights were out. Her eyes were slowly closing.

"I wonder why all that stuff's up in that chest?" she whispered as she slowly drifted off to sleep.

* * * * *

The hovering dust created a marvelous sunbeam for the day's earliest rays. They fell almost directly onto Louis' tranquil face. He felt their warmth on his cheek and intuitively turned his head to face directly into it.

The light against his eyelids triggered his senses and he slowly gained consciousness. Blinking a few times, he stretched his curled body and then sat up. He was a bit stiff, but was also unfortunately used to such stiffness.

He stood up and inspected the room in the daylight. He could see scratch marks in the hardwood floor where a bed had once stood. The wall where its headboard had brushed against it was scuffed. He touched the scuffmarks, casually.

He moved to the closet and opened it. He was greeted by whirls of dust. In the corner, he could see a faint outline of where a dresser had once stood. He walked over to it, but continued to feel no sense of familiarity or onslaught of a flashback.

He left the room and wandered into the bathroom. A medicine cabinet still hung above the white porcelain sink. The faucets were old fashioned, even by his standards. There were two separate faucets, one for hot water and the other for cold. He tried them both. He heard a momentary creaking noise, but nothing came out.

He wandered through the rest of the upstairs, going into the two remaining bedrooms, and peered into the linen closet. He felt a sort of surreal curiosity about the place. He wondered why he had been driven to it, what the images he had seen meant, and perhaps, most of all, why he wasn't experiencing any more flashback at that very moment.

It seemed to him that if he had, in fact, spent time in this house years before. He felt that his presence in the house now – wandering from room to room, and purposely touching the doors, walls and appliances – should be triggering these spontaneous flashbacks that he had grown so accustomed. He wondered if he was even beginning to depend upon them.

He soon found himself downstairs again, inspecting the main floor. He opened every cupboard and closet before heading to the basement. He was leaning on the old, dusty furnace, wondering if it still worked, when the word "work" suddenly made him aware that he had to hurry to his own work.

He smiled in spite of himself, pleased that he actually had to be somewhere, doing something. It was a novel and rewarding expectation.

As he left through the back door, he marveled again at how strange it was that there had been no more flashbacks. He wondered if it was because he was trying to force them, or something. He shrugged his shoulders, unable to know, as he crossed the yard and approached the sidewalk through the gate.

As he turned toward the rail yard, he noticed the neighborhood for the first time. It was clear that lower-middleclass families lived there. He saw a man hanging Christmas lights on the eaves of his house. The man paused from his work when he sensed Louis and waved to him. Louis waved back, returning the man's warm smile, and kept walking.

He passed a newly painted home that had a "sold" sign in the front yard and noticed that the open garage was full of boxes waiting to be unpacked. As he passed the house, he saw through the front window a man and woman and some children moving items around. He realized that they must have just moved in.

"Very interesting," he said to himself, as he continued down the road.

He made what was fast becoming a regular stop at the Denny's. This time he ordered AND finished the Grand Slam.

"Well, Louis, you finally did it!" Sandy, the waitress, gave him a pat on the shoulder as she passed by doing her rounds.

"Yes, Sandy, someone had to do it!" Louis smiled, as he wiped his mouth with a napkin. He opened his wallet and saw that he was running very low on cash. He left Sandy a nice tip anyway. "It'll be payday soon," he smiled to himself, as he walked out to the street again.

"Hmm, I wonder when the last time was that I had a payday to look forward to?" he mused.

He gave it some serious thought as he walked along, honestly trying to remember. He was more than a block away before he finally shrugged and said, "Just can't do it! Can't remember ANYTHING it seems."

He didn't want to admit it, but the only thing he seemed to be able to remember clearly was a past filled with lonely, cold nights on the street and long hot days wandering about trying to scrounge up money and food.

"There's GOT to be more to it," he said in frustration.

Just then, the sky went black and cold. A thick rain washed against him. He felt an odd urgency about his wallet, or was it a bag full of money? It was something of extreme value that he couldn't place his finger on. He heard angry shouting and saw flashes of faces again. They were threatening. He knew he needed to run, or hide, or somehow get away. He knew he had nowhere to run, though.

He thought he should be panicked, but the feelings inside him were different. He was more – how was it? How could he describe it? He was more "indignant" than "frightened." He even felt both anger and disappointment towards the voices. It made no sense to him.

He looked up toward the sounds. He saw only the sidewalk and shops brightly lit by the morning sun. The vision – and the threats – were gone. He was left to himself again. He noticed he was breathing heavily and leaning against a lamppost.

"Most peculiar," he said, as he shook off the vision and continued on his way to the rail yard.

Louis arrived there slightly ahead of Charlie, who greeted him and complimented him on being so punctual.

"I'm not used to workers getting in on time," Charlie added.

"Well, we're even," Louis said with a smile. "I'm not used to working."

"Good one," Charlie snorted and gave Louis a hefty congratulatory slap on the back. "Now, let's see what we've got to do today."

Chapter 23
In the Backyard

$\mathcal{L}$uke and Emma sat listlessly on the backyard swings. While Kenny puttered with a truck in Grandma's sandbox, the two of them just let their feet dangle as they dragged their toes along the ground with the light swaying of their swings. They were both looking downward, deep in thought.

"What do you think?" Luke asked casually.

"About what?" Emma asked.

"You know," Luke replied. And she did.

"I dunno," she said.

After a pause, Luke finally said, "I think we should go up and look at it again."

"But, it isn't right," Emma said.

"We've already done it," Luke countered.

"But, what if we get caught?" Emma asked, with genuine concern.

"Then they'll have to tell us what all that stuff is," Luke said, brightening a little. "It would bring it all out into the open."

"Yeah, but –" Emma started, but was interrupted by a friendly voice.

"Hi, kids!" Uncle Steve said from over the back hedge. His arms were full with bags of trash. He was making his way to the series of silver-colored trash cans he kept behind his garage.

"Hey, need some help?" Luke said, hopping off the swing and running over to him. He was through the hedge almost before Emma was out of her swing. Luke adored Uncle Steve and was always eager to see him.

"Sure," Uncle Steve said, "pull the lid off of that one there. I think it's still empty."

Luke did and Uncle Steve began to unload his trash. Emma came sauntering up as he was putting the lid back on.

"Hi, Emma," he smiled. "How are things?"

"Uncle Steve," she began, "do you think people keep secrets?"

"Well now, that's an interesting how-do-you-do!" Uncle Steve replied, keeping his warm smile going. "I suppose everyone has a secret or two hidden away in their closet."

"Or, in their attic," Emma corrected.

"Emma!" Luke scolded, not sure it was the time to share their find.

Uncle Steve looked from Emma to Luke and back. He could plainly see that something was afoot between them. Leaning toward her, and keeping his voice in an artificial hush, he asked, "Have you got a secret?"

"Not me," Emma stated flatly. "My Grandma. I think she's got a secret."

Uncle Steve straightened upright with surprise.

"Well, why do you think she has a secret?" he asked.

"Emma, it's none of our business." Luke tried vainly to coax his sister into silence.

"Maybe," Emma agreed, "but like you said, this could bring it out in the open. Uncle Steve might know and then we won't have to go snooping around anymore."

"Know what?" he asked with growing curiosity.

"Grandma has a trunk up in her attic," Luke confided.

"A trunk isn't a secret," Uncle Steve said. "It's just a good place to store things."

"Yeah, well, sometimes some of those things might be secrets," Emma said. "We found some things."

"Old things," Luke added.

"So?" Uncle Steve coaxed. "They're old. That doesn't make them secrets."

"No, these things are different," Emma said.

"Different? How?" Uncle Steve asked.

"These things are from the war!" Luke said, emphasizing his words by holding out his hands, evidently feeling that this brazen fact would make everything clear to Uncle Steve.

"Which war?" Uncle Steve asked, "Vietnam? Korea?"

"No, much older," Emma said.

"They look like they're from WWII," Luke said.

"I see," Uncle Steve said, nodding slowly and tugging at his chin with his thumb and finger.

"You see?" both kids asked at once.

"Yes," Uncle Steve confirmed, "that's probably stuff from your grandmother's husband."

"Her HUSBAND?" they both repeated in shock. "Grandma was MARRIED??"

"Of course, she was," Uncle Steve said with a laugh. "Where do you think your father came from?"

The two began to pummel him with questions, but he just smiled and waved his hands and told them that they really should ask their grandmother about this, not him. At this, they looked over at the house in time to see their grandmother open the kitchen window and put a pie in the sill to cool. They looked at her with a slightly different, curious intent.

"Anyone want some cocoa?" she called out to them.

"Uh, yeah!" the kids said. "Be right there!"

The two gave Uncle Steve an awkward glance or two. Then they waved goodbye and ran to the house. Kenny was way ahead of them. Uncle Steve watched them go. He smiled as they left. He continued to watch as they disappeared into the house, then he shrugged, shook his head, and returned indoors.

*****

Louis was straightening up debris down near the tracks. He lifted yet another old board and a glitter of sunlight caught his eye. He bent down to see what it was. There was a tiny bit of old metal glinting in the grime. He reached for it and moved the dirt with his fingers until he was able to uncover it. It was a ring.

He picked it up and stood looking at it. It was caked with dirt and grime. He wiped it on his jeans and then scraped at it with his fingers. He poked his finger into the hole to push the dirt out. As he cleaned it up, he discovered that it was an old high school ring.

"Well, what do you know?" he said.

He took it over to Charlie. Charlie gave it the once over and said they should get the rest of the grime off, so they could find out whose initials were on it. They took it to a bathroom sink and ran it under water, then rubbed at it with paper towels. It was soon looking surprisingly good.

"Let me see that," Charlie asked.

Louis handed him the ring. Charlie looked it over carefully.

"Yep, it's a high school ring all right." He said, pointing at some initials to the left of the green faux jewel that it held. "See, right here 'BHS'. Local school even. That would be Bartlesville High School, unless I'm a fool. Now, let's see." He rubbed at it some more. "Here we go, '36'. That's the class of 1936. That narrows it down some. Now, if only we can get this last key piece cleaned up."

He rubbed the right-hand side of the ring carefully, but diligently.

"Here we go. It says 'WIS'. Probably belonged to someone named 'William'. I bet he went by 'Bill' though," he announced with satisfaction. "Somebody named 'Bill' that graduated Bartlesville High School in 1936! Ain't that something? We could probably find the owner, I'll reckon."

"Really?" Louis said. "Imagine knowing so much from a little piece of metal. If only brains could be polished up the same way."

"Huh?" Charlie asked.

"Nothing," Louis replied. "Let me see that again, if you don't mind."

"Certainly," Charlie said. "It's yours if you want to keep it. You found it. 'Course, it would be very decent of you to try to find the real owner."

"Find the owner?" Louis repeated. "How would I go about doing that?"

"Simple," Charlie laughed, "just go down to the high school, tell the office what you've found and they should be able to help you track down the owner. There can't be that many people with the initials 'WIS' who graduated from there back in '36," he added with a wink.

"You know," Louis said, "I think you're right."

"'Course I'm right!" Charlie laughed some more. "You've got a fair mystery on your hands, but one that's not too tough to solve. Let me know when you find Old Bill, eh?"

"I sure will," Louis said. "Thanks," he added as he wandered out the door back to work.

Charlie watched him go and gave him another smile before returning to his paperwork. Louis stared at the ring as he walked. He couldn't take his eyes off of it. He turned it over and over with his fingers, holding it up to the sun and such. He held out his finger to try it on for size and was surprised to see it fit.

He looked at it on his finger and suddenly the sun withdrew its light, leaving the sky in blackness. Rain pelted his face and moistened his clothes. He looked down at his soggy pants and saw that they had changed from jeans to brown slacks. He could see that he had on a coat over his shirt.

He held up his hand and still saw the ring on it. He started to look at it, but felt someone pulling on his left shoulder, jerking him around. As he began to turn, he could hear an angry voice. It seemed familiar, but he could not place it. He turned around completely, but there was no one there.

The sun was back in place. The rain was gone. His clothes were back to normal. He was still wearing the ring. He could see Charlie back up at the office. Charlie looked out through the window and waved pleasantly at him. Louis took off the ring, pocketed it, and got back to work.

* * * * *

The kids were very quiet during lunch. They wanted to ask about the box, but were too shy. Joyce looked over to Frank who was busily taking turns between bites of his sandwich and spoonfuls of soup. She continued to stare at him, as if he would somehow telepathically notice her gaze. She couldn't counter his tuning out of the world as he enjoyed his food, however.

She reached her leg under the table and tapped his foot. It took a couple of taps before he was pulled from his daze and looked over at her, still chewing. Her expression made it clear that he was to remain silent. He mouthed "What?" trying not to reveal too much of the sandwich he had tucked away behind his teeth.

She nodded her head toward Emma on the one side of the table and then Luke on the other. He looked at both blankly, then back to his incomprehensible wife, and repeated his mouthing exercise with the addition of hunching his shoulders, holding up his hands and scrunching his nose in total confusion. Joyce just rolled her eyes and sighed in frustration. Giving up, she decided to take a more direct approach.

"You're sure quiet," she remarked to the kids.

"Yeah, well," was all Luke said.

"You guys must be bored," Joyce added with a smile as Frank, who watched the exchange, and finally gave a comprehending, "Oh!"

"Uh," he offered, "maybe today would be a good day to visit the farm."

"You mean the Andersen's?" Luke asked with excitement.

"None other!" Frank replied, giving his wife a triumphal look, implying that he had solved the problem already. His gaze was met with a look that was a cross between relief and a physical manifestation of the tired phrase, "Oh, brother!"

"Do you think they'll be home, though?" Emma asked. "I mean can we just drop in out of the blue, unannounced on them?"

"I'm sure it will be fine," Frank smiled. "Besides, I'm sure Wade would be happy to see his old high school buddy again."

*****

Louis sat next to Charlie, chewing on a sandwich. He held the ring in his left hand, and turned it over and over again.

"Say, Charlie," he asked, "you have a hammer I can borrow?"

"A hammer?" Charlie asked in surprise. "You're not looking to smash the thing, are you?"

"No," Louis replied calmly, still looking at the ring. "I just need it for a project at home."

"You want to take it home?" Charlie asked. "You don't have a hammer at home?"

"No," Louis replied, "I just got in town, remember?"

"Oh, yeah, right," Charlie said. "Sure, help yourself."

"Thanks," Louis said, as he continued eyeing his new possession.

"Bet you're curious, eh?" Charlie asked.

"Well, yeah, I wonder what sort of story this ring holds."

"Story?"

"Yeah," Louis confirmed. "Well, I found it in a rail yard. How'd it get here? How'd it get dropped? Why wasn't it picked up? Whose was it?"

Charlie took a big bite of his sandwich and then said, "Why don't you go to the school and find out?"

"I will."

"I mean now."

"What? Now? But, the work..." Louis said, startled at the proposition.

"I can manage for a couple of hours without you," Charlie admitted. "Besides, it's the Christmas break. The school's only open a few hours a day. You'll have to get time off no matter what to catch them open. You may as well go now. Anyway, you've got me curious now, too."

"You, too?" Louis asked. "Then I better go." He smiled, finished his sandwich quickly and stood up to leave. He paused hesitantly and then asked, "Uh, Charlie, where's the school?"

"You really are new in town!" Charlie laughed. "Head that way four blocks, turn left, and you'll see it at the bottom of the hill. Can't miss it."

Chapter 24
Discoveries

The family station wagon was cruising towards Dewey. Joyce sat next to Frank, who was driving. All three kids were seated in the second seat, with Kenny in the middle. Luke and Emma were glued to their windows, watching familiar territory roll by. Kenny was leaning forward with his forearms on the front seat and his chin resting on his hands, as he peered out the windshield with a dreamy look on his angelic face.

"It'll be nice to see Susie again," Joyce said.

"I'm just glad I decided to call," Frank said. "They had planned on doing a little Christmas shopping, and we would have missed them. It would have been a shame to come all the way out to Oklahoma and not get to see them."

Soon, the car turned off the main road to follow a side road. It then turned into a drive that led to a large white farmhouse, with an even larger barn next to it. The front door opened and a bloodhound bounded out, followed by a boy and girl about the same ages as Emma and Luke. Their parents came out next, waving and smiling.

Frank pulled the car to a stop and everyone piled out and exchanged greetings. It wasn't long before the women were on the porch watching the kids play with the dog in the yard, as the men wandered over to the pasture to see the cows and chat.

* * * * *

Louis stood in front of the school. He must have read the large words carved into the cement facing three or four times. He looked at the logo on the ring and the name over the school again. They matched just fine. There was no doubting that this was Bartlesville High School. That wasn't what was holding him back.

He braced himself for another flashback as he entered the building, but none came. The school remained old and unfamiliar. With the help of a janitor, he negotiated his way to the main office, and was pleased and relieved to find someone there.

"Can I help you?" the office lady asked from behind a split door. As was customary, she had only opened the top half. The bottom half had a sort of shelf on it.

"Uh, yes," Louis paused and gave her a smile, to boost his nerves. He wondered why he was so anxious. "I found this here ring. I thought I ought to try to find the owner."

"Really?" she said very intrigued. "May I see it?"

"Certainly," and he handed it to her. "It has the initials 'WIS'. It must have belonged to someone named 'William' or 'Bill'."

"And, it's from the class of '36, I see," she added.

"Yes," he acknowledged.

"It's quite dirty," she said.

"Yes, I just found it, covered by a board at the rail yard and partially buried."

"Do you mind if I try to clean it a little?"

"No, by all means."

"Come on in here," she said, opening the bottom half of the door and letting him in. "I have some nail polish remover here. It might help."

"Oh," was all Louis said in reply.

She got out some facial tissue and unscrewed the nail polish and got to work. Before long the ring was shining. She rinsed it in a sink, then held it up to inspect it.

"Oh?" she asked as she held it up to her eye. She had a puzzled look that made Louis grow concerned. "I thought you said the initials were 'WIS'?"

"Yes, they are," Louis confirmed. "At least, that's what they appeared to be."

"I'm afraid that's not right," she replied handing him back the ring. "Take a look. What do you think now? It looks like 'LNS' to me."

"By golly, I think you're right!" Louis said. "I'll be."

"That would have sent us down the wrong path entirely!" she observed. "Now, let's find out who this 'LNS' is."

She disappeared into a back room. Louis heard shuffling noises. Finally, she immerged with a large, old book in her hands. She carried it delicately. The cover was blackened. A large portion of the book was missing, as if the book had been torn in half long ago. She set it down on a table and gingerly dusted if off.

"We had a fire in '54." She explained. "The whole school burned down and had to be torn down and then entirely rebuilt. It's a wonder this yearbook survived at all."

"I see," Louis said.

"The top half of the pages are totally lost," she said with dismay. "I wonder what the chances are that we'll be able to find who we're looking for."

Louis cracked open the book. Even though he took great care, fragments flaked off into his fingers.

"I'm terribly sorry," he apologized.

"It's all right," she said. "It can't be helped. Just be careful. The person you're looking for would have been a senior. Those are usually right up front."

Louis painstakingly turned the pages until he got to the senior photos. He made his way to the "S" section of names, and noticed that he could feel his heart beating. A couple more pages, and he was there.

"I can't imagine there'd be more than one person with those initials," she commented.

"No, neither do I," he agreed, as he scanned across the pages. His finger stopped on "Louis Nicholas Smythe."

"That must be him!" he exclaimed, looking at it and then stepping back so she could step up and look closely at the picture. "Do you know him?" he asked her.

"He does look slightly familiar," she acknowledged. "But, nothing comes to mind." She looked up at him shaking her head sorrowfully. "I'm sorry, but it's just not someone I know! Wait a moment!" she exclaimed with excitement.

She looked down at the picture then back at Louis. She repeated this action, and then exclaimed, "Why it's you!"

"What?" he asked, crinkling his face in disbelief. "No, no, it's not me."

"Why, yes!" she said with confidence. "Surely it is! Look at your eyes. See, the ones in the photo, they're your eyes. They have to be. What's your name?"

"Um, my name's Louis," he said hesitantly.

"Louis what?"

"I don't know."

"What do you mean you don't know," she asked, putting a hand on her hip.

"I was in some sort of accident several years ago or something and can't remember my early life."

"What? Oh, my!" she gasped. "That's dreadful!"

"Yes," he said. "I've been out West until recently. A nice family brought me back here. I'm trying to – trying to find myself."

"Well," she said, "it looks like you're off to the right start. At least you know your name, now."

"Do you mind if I look through the book some more?"

"Certainly!"

He spent a great deal of time leafing through the book. He eyed each person carefully, reading names, and staring intently at faces, trying to – hoping to – remember someone or something. He also braced himself for more unexpected flashbacks, just in case.

Turning toward the back, he found the team section and found a picture of himself as the track team captain. He stared at it, trying to remember a race, a teammate, a win, a defeat.

Nothing. Absolutely nothing came back to him.

"You were quite handsome!" the secretary teased, looking over his shoulder as she stepped forward to peek.

He blushed, and she moved away to give him some privacy. He leafed through some more pages, and lingered on a picture of a girl, but the name was burned off. He ran his finger over the half-burned picture. He could almost see her smile, but not quite. There was something very familiar about the picture. It filled him with longing, but no sense of recollection. He actually wished for a flashback, but couldn't manage it.

Finally, he turned the page and continued on. He came across a picture of a face he recognized all too well. It was the face of the man who had been haunting his flashbacks. The face in the book was somewhat younger and smiling, but it was definitely him.

He could picture the man's cruel face. He could hear his antagonist's voice shouting angry words at him. He could feel the rain pelting him in the face, blurring his vision. A thunderclap startled him and for a moment drowned out all other noise. He flinched, and then looked back at the man. He was gone. The book lay in front of him, idly sitting on the table.

He could feel that he was sweating, and worked to control his breathing, hoping the secretary hadn't noticed. He looked up and over to her. She was sitting, calmly going through paperwork. She noticed his glance and looked up at him, giving him a smile.

"Are you finding anything of value?" she asked.

"I think so," he said, as he turned back to the page.

He looked for the man's name, but, it too, was burned off. He scoured the book for more pictures of the man, anything that would reveal his identity, but could find nothing.

*****

Luke held out a handful of hay and wiggled his fingers. He watched individual strands break free and flitter noiselessly to the barn floor below. His good friend, Jake, was lying on his back in the hay beside him. Emma was lazily swinging her legs over the edge of the loft, while her friend, Sarah, sat beside her, doing the same. Kenny was busily pushing together massive clumps of hay and then jumping into them.

"Hey, we're Good Samaritans!" Emma said, out of the blue.

"What do you mean?" Sarah asked.

Emma proceeded to tell Sarah all about the RV they had seen, the story of the Good Samaritan, and then Sam. Luke and Jake listened as well. Luke was ready to correct any inaccuracies. Jake was just interested.

"What if he'd been a madman or a killer?" Sarah asked with wide eyes.

"Oh, he's no killer," Emma reassured her. "But, he can't remember his own name!"

"What's that?" Jake said with piqued interest. "He can't remember his own name? How's that?"

"We figure he was in an accident or something," Luke said. "It's kinda sad, really."

"It's kinda CREEPY, if you ask me!" Jake said.

"Only 'cause you don't know Sam," Luke replied, trying to not take offense. He knew if he were in Jake's place, he would have said the same thing.

"If he can't remember his name, how do you know his name's Sam, then?" Jake asked.

"We named him that," Emma explained. "'Sam' is short for the Good Samaritan!"

"That's cute!" Sarah laughed.

"I don't think he was hoping to be 'cute'!" Luke said with a smile.

"Where's he now?" Sarah asked.

"I don't know," Emma confessed. "We dropped him off at some old house. We've seen him once since then. He seemed happy. At least I'm pretty sure he is."

"How can you know that?" Jake asked.

"Because he doesn't have a load of hay shoved down the back of his shirt!" Luke shouted as he attacked Jake with hay. Soon, all of the kids were tossing hay at each other and wrestling like gangbusters.

*****

Louis wandered back to the rail yard, wearing the ring. The moment Charlie saw him, he came dashing out of the office and hustled over to him. He'd been pacing, as he was so anxious to hear what Louis had learned.

"Well, did you find out anything?" Charlie demanded anxiously.

"Yep," was all Louis said.

"Whose was it?"

"Mine," Louis replied as he held up his hand and let Charlie see it on his finger.

"Yours?"

"Yeah."

"Well, then, I guess you don't know any more of the ring's story now, do you?"

"No."

"But, I bet you're even more interested in it."

"Yes, that's for certain," Louis admitted. After a pause, he added, "By the way, my name's Smythe, Louis Smythe."

"Eh?" was all Charlie could say.

"It was in the yearbook," Louis explained. "It said that my name's Louis Smythe. Apparently, I was on the track team, too."

"Track, huh?" Charlie smiled. "Guess you've been a good runner all your life then, eh?"

"Huh," Louis grunted. "I guess so."

＊＊＊＊＊

"Well, did everyone enjoy the farm?" Grandma asked, as she took a helping of mashed potatoes and then passed the bowl to Luke.

"Sure did!" Luke replied, as he eagerly accepted the potatoes and made a massive mound on his plate before passing it along. He then grabbed a bowl of corn and piled some on top of the potatoes before smothering the stack with gravy.

Kenny just nodded and smiled in agreement as he took the potatoes from Luke and emulated his brother's ritual. Truth be told, ultimately Joyce was the only one at the table who didn't follow suit.

"What was so fun?" Grandma pursued.

"Everything!" Emma announced. "And, we got to tell Sarah and Jake about being Good Samaritans!"

"I bet that was a surprise!" Joyce smiled.

"I wonder what's become of him?" Frank queried.

"You don't think he's still at that place where we dropped him off, do you?" Luke asked.

"That abandoned house?" Joyce asked. "I'd certainly hope not!"

"I hope he's found a new home by now!" Emma replied as the others nodded agreement.

＊＊＊＊＊

The sun was still high in the sky, but slowly heading its way to the west as Louis walked home, deep in thought. He purposely chose to go a different route than normal. Even with the day's revelations, he still wanted to carry out his plan. And, the last thing he wanted was to be recognized or noticed by anyone on his normal route.

He walked several blocks out of his way, scanning every neighborhood as he did so. From his years on the street, he was used to blending in or being ignored. He willingly allowed himself to go unnoticed once more.

With each new block, he would scan the yards, seeking his target. Finally, he saw what he was after. He quickly made his way to a large house on the corner of a sleepy street. In the corner of the lot was a large "Sold" sign that had toppled over and lay on a stack of weeds, evidently abandoned.

He casually walked up to it, inspecting it as he did so. He stood next to it and gave it an unobtrusive nudge with his boot. There was some sort of wire caught on it, and some trash over the top.

He bent down, and picked up a side of the sign, sliding the trash away from him. He unlooped the wire that clung to his prize and freed it. He stood up and carried the sign away with him around the corner.

Without looking around, he quickened his pace and crossed the street and another corner. Once he was out of view, he laid it down on the ground, pulled out a pocket handkerchief, and wiped the sign clean, or at least mostly clean.

This done, he stood up and headed down a tree-lined lane, holding the sign casually in one hand, allowing it to be seen by one and all. He had long ago learned that sometimes the best way to go unnoticed is to be blatantly obvious.

He even began humming to himself. It was an old tune from the '40s. The tune simply came to him. He couldn't have named it if his life depended on it. All he knew was that he liked it. It made him feel happy.

He knew that as long as he wasn't seen taking the sign, or within sight of the home, he could walk the rest of the way, carrying the sign in plain sight, without people thinking anything of it. Anyone seeing it would have no idea where it came from, which would make it a generic sign, evidently being carried by its owner.

He arrived at his "home" and looked around to ensure he was not being watched. At this point, he pulled out Charlie's hammer and promptly hammered the "sold" sign into a prominent part of the front lawn. He didn't bother to admire his work. He simply entered the home quickly through the front door, using his key.

He had only been in for a few moments when he looked out and saw a couple walking in front of the house, pushing a stroller. He saw them pause, with the wife pointing to the sign.

"My goodness!" the wife, Brynn, said. "It looks like they've finally sold that old, white house."

"I didn't realize it was for sale," her husband, Tom, replied. "I thought it was just abandoned."

"Well, it'll be nice to have someone move in there," Brynn replied.

"Yeah," Tom agreed, "maybe they'll fix up that yard."

"Tom!" Brynn said. "Is that all you can say?" and she gave him a love tap on the arm.

Standing just out of sight, Louis watched them walk off. He smiled from within "his" home. He made sure they were safely out of sight, and that no others were nearby, before he secretively exited for one more errand.

Chapter 25
A Story Worth Telling

The dinner dishes were done and the family was sitting around the house, passing time. The kids were in the family room watching TV. The adults were chatting in the living room. Joyce was knitting.

Emma nodded to Luke, and they left Kenny with the TV and wandered into the living room with the adults. They sat down quietly and listened to the talk.

"Are you two getting sleepy?" Joyce asked, without looking up from her knitting, making it very clear that she was aware of their presence.

"No," they replied in unison.

"We just want to listen to the talking," Luke said.

"I seriously doubt that," Joyce said.

"More likely you're trying to get some clues as to what's in those presents," Frank said, pointing to the ever-growing horde that was accumulating under the tree by the front window.

Luke looked fleetingly at the gifts, then back at his grandmother. Frank couldn't help but notice.

"OK, what's up?" he insisted.

The kids hemmed and hawed so much that all three adults grew very suspicious and curious. The kids exchanged looks, then slowly went quiet and looked at the floor.

"OK, I mean it now, what's up?" Frank repeated.

"We – we found a box," Emma confessed after a long pause.

"A box?" Frank asked. "What sort of box? Where? Does it have presents in it?"

"No, not presents," Luke said. "We wouldn't snoop after presents!"

He looked up and tried to give a noble look, worthy of congratulations for having character enough to not sneak peeks at his presents.

"But, you've apparently snooped after something, though, haven't you?" Frank said, looking at them both. Any self-encouraging stature quickly melted away for both children. "Where did you find this box?"

"In the attic," Luke said.

Frank was very concerned by this news and began to scold them for being in the attic, a place where they had absolutely no right to be, and so forth. His lecture was interrupted by a quiet, discerning sigh from Grandmother.

"Oh! Oh my!" she said with dawning realization. "I'd entirely forgotten about that!"

"Forgotten about what?" Joyce asked.

Grandma's eyes were cast toward the hall that led to where the access to the attic was. She didn't seem to hear Joyce. The kids and their parents looked at her. Frank was beside himself with puzzlement. He wasn't angry, just very, very confused.

"What box?" he repeated.

"An old box with a latch?" Grandmother asked of the children, looking for and receiving a nod from them. "Dark brown and old fashioned?" The kids nodded affirmatively. "Inside there were old ribbons and clippings and a uniform?" Again, she received a positive nod.

"A uniform?" Frank asked. "What sort of uniform?"

"A soldier's uniform," Grandma replied. "From World War II."

"World War II?" Frank's eyes grew big as he stood and began to pace and circle.

"A hero's uniform," Grandma added.

"A HERO?" he asked.

"Yes, a hero," she replied.

"But, what – ?" Frank began, but did not finish.

"I'd entirely forgotten about that trunk," she said. "I haven't seen it since we moved here."

"But, what trunk is it?" Frank asked. "Whose trunk is it?"

"It belonged to your father," Grandma replied calmly.

"My FATHER?" Frank fell into the nearest chair. His face had gone pale with shock. His lips formed the words again, but no sound emerged. His mind ran over the thought, and then his face grew uncharacteristically angry. "Why would you keep something from that man?" he demanded.

"Because these were from a time he did something special, something noble, something worth remembering," she replied.

"That man NEVER did ANYTHING worth remembering," Frank said dismissively.

"You're wrong," she said. "He was a hero."

"A hero?" Emma asked wide-eyed.

"Yes, a bona fide, red-white-and-blue hero," Grandma said in a soothing tone.

"What did he do?" Luke asked intently intrigued. Joyce had long ago stopped her knitting. Now, she set her needles on the small table next to her chair to listen without distraction.

"I don't believe any of this," Frank said.

"You should," his mother replied. "You should hear it, at least once. There's a story you must know. A story worth knowing, worth telling, that I have never told you. It's about your father. And, I'm afraid that NOW seems to be the time to tell you."

"I don't need to know ANYTHING about HIM!" Frank countered.

"You should at least know this much," Grandma said. "Whether or not you choose to listen, this is what your father once did. He was a pilot during World War II. He was stationed in England."

"Were you married to him then?" Emma asked.

"No, Sweetheart," she replied. "Not yet, but we were engaged. We had wanted to get married earlier, but the War came on and put our lives on hold. In fact, we didn't get married until after the War, which meant we were pretty old to get married, but that's a much later story.

"I was telling of your grandfather in the War. He had flown several combat missions over Germany. He had only two more before he would have fulfilled his quota of 25 missions and been able to return for duty in the US – and we could get married. But, on a terrible day, his plane was shot down. I'll never forget when his mother ran to my home, crying her eyes out, to tell me that two officers had hand-delivered that horrible telegram. It said that his plane had been shot down over enemy lines and that all aboard were missing. When she pressed him for more information, the officer had shaken his head and told her that he was sorry to say, confidentially, that there was little hope that he had survived the crash. I nearly died that day.

"It was nearly two years before I learned what had happened. His plane was indeed shot down over Germany, about 50 miles west of Munich. All but three of his eight-man crew died in the crash. He and two others managed to parachute out, but he was terribly injured. He was captured and was in such bad shape that some German doctors put a metal plate in his head to replace the missing pieces of his skull. They interned him in a concentration camp for 19 months.

"He suffered terribly and was tortured. He lost nearly half his weight. He managed to lead a daring massive escape of 24 men. Once out of camp, they split up and made their various ways across Germany to France. The underground got them to the coast and they hid in a French fishing boat that sneaked them across the Channel to England. Not all of them made it, though. Three were found and shot. Five others were caught and returned to the camp. The rest, though, the rest made it back to England over a period of weeks. Never before had so many escaped to freedom from a single camp.

"It was in all of the papers and there was even a newsreel produced. When he got back to the States, they flew him to New York City where he got a ticker tape parade. Later, he met President Roosevelt at the White House. He was a real hometown hero.

"It was the proudest moment in the town's history when he finally came home. There were banners and bands and a parade and a town picnic. After we'd been married a couple of years, we were going through this box of clippings. He held up a picture of him at that town picnic, with the caption "Local Hero" underneath. He said that that was the second-most proud moment in his life.

"I was surprised at this and asked what his proudest moment was. He said his proudest moment was when –" she paused with deep emotion before she was able to finish, tearfully, "– when his boy was born." She looked over to Frank, who sat speechless, intently listening. "You were only a few weeks old at this time. We had wanted to have you sooner, but it seems the Good Lord wanted us to wait awhile."

She gave Frank a teary smile and patted his hand before continuing. Frank just looked down, still listening.

"Anyway, he was assigned to help solicit support for the War. 'His efforts helped bring an early end to the war in Germany,' President Truman wrote in a letter he sent after the war finally ended. Can you believe he actually took the time to write that?"

Grandma went silent, having told her tale. She looked at Joyce and the kids, and then at Frank. Frank was staggered by all of this news. The entire family sat speechless for awhile. The only sounds wafting into the living room were from the TV, where Kenny still sat watching a show.

"Why?" Frank finally asked in a subdued voice, "Why have you never told me any of this?"

"I had forgotten it all. Until now," she explained. "Really, I had. I had pushed it out of my mind, considering what he had done to us. I still can't understand why he would suddenly abandon us like he did." With a very bitter tone she hazarded the guess, "Perhaps the fame and attention was just too much for him. He had always been such a simple, humble man."

The kids had a multitude of questions, but Joyce cast them a gentle look that let them know that now was not the time to ask. Frank was beside himself with shock and amazement. They had never seen him in such a state. It was Luke who suggested to Emma that perhaps it would be best if they went to bed. She wisely and generously agreed.

* * * * *

Louis entered through the front door with a grocery bag and a huge smile. The room was ablaze with a beautiful orange hue of the sunset. He hummed to himself as he used his heel to kick the door closed behind him. He walked over to the kitchen, guiding himself by the dimming light that shone through the curtainless windows. There still wasn't power or water in the house.

He put the bag down on the counter and began to pull out its contents. He had bought a cheap pot, frying pan, large spoon, a couple of dish cloths, dish soap, bread, peanut butter, jam, a knife, some fruit, and even some napkins. He pulled out some shaving cream and remarked, "This will be so nice!"

He was nearly giddy as he started putting everything away.

"Did you remember the jam?" a woman's voice asked from behind him.

In his mirthful state, he responded, "Yes, yes, I got the jam!"

He turned and saw the room lit as brightly as a summer afternoon. The pretty lady from his flashbacks was looking through grocery bags that were placed on the dining room table, with her back to him.

She pulled out a pint jar of strawberry jam from one of the bags, and said, "Good! You usually forget the jam!"

"How could I ever forget your favorite - ?" he began to reply, but his words cut off in mid-sentence.

The room was dark again. The light, the lady, the table, the bags, all were gone. He was alone with his solitary bag of groceries. A tremendous sense of loss and melancholy hit him for a moment, as he still faced where the lady had stood.

He finished his sentence in a meager voice, "- kind?" He shook his head, and added, "How could I ever forget - you?" He turned back to his sack and added, "Whoever you are."

* * * * *

Later that night, Frank could hear weeping and went into the living room. He found his mother sitting in her chair softly crying.

"Mother," he asked, "what's the matter?"

"Oh, Frank," she said, "I really did love him."

"Love him?" Frank was shocked. "Is this true?"

"Oh, yes I truly did," she looked at him through teary eyes. "My happiest days were the ones I spent with him."

"I have always hated him," Frank admitted bitterly.

She reached out to him and gently touched his cheek.

"That isn't true," she said in a tone that almost sounded pleading. "There was a time that you loved him dearly." She ignored his shocked expression as he started to pull away. "And, your father loved you very much. I don't believe any father ever doted on a son more completely. Your father could barely come inside the house before you would run up to him and jump into his arms. And, he never looked happier than when he was holding you. In fact, it got so that it was difficult to picture him without seeing him holding 'his boy'.

"He would usually hold you as he walked across the kitchen to give me a welcoming kiss, then we'd have a family hug between the three of us, and he would take you into the other room and read to you, or play little games until it was time for supper.

"After supper, he and you would be together playing, or we'd all go on a walk, or tell stories until bedtime. Then, once you were in bed, he and I would sit up and talk for hours. I had never known a happier home. That's why it hurt so badly when he suddenly left. I never understood it. I never saw it coming. I never dreamed it possible."

At this, she broke down and sobbed. Frank was flabbergasted, stunned, and silent – even though a thousand questions were pummeling his mind. His eyes searched her face and fought back tears. His lips moved, but no words escaped them. Finally, he managed only the words "What?" and "Why?"

His mother's sobbing subsided and she looked up at him with a tear-streaked face.

"It broke my heart," she said. "It tore me apart. It ruined my world. I couldn't possibly let that happen to you, too. I simply stopped talking about your father. You would sit by the door for hours waiting, sometimes whimpering, but I would tell you no one was coming and that you should step away from the door.

"I tried to make up for your absent father by spending my life with my son, reading to you, playing with you, walking with you – the way your father used to. Whenever you asked about your father, I would simply tell you that you had no father, and that you shouldn't ask such things." She paused, then continued in a melancholy tone, "Eventually, the questions stopped coming and we were both able to live our lives as if he had never existed. It was hard at first – extremely difficult – but, we managed because we loved each other so much."

Tears were now streaming down Frank's cheeks, too. He asked the word "Why?" twice, but was unable to say more.

"Why did he leave?" she asked. "I wondered that myself, and when I found out the reason, I was even more hurt, angry, and betrayed than I thought I could ever feel."

"Someone else?" was all Frank managed to ask.

"Yes!" she nodded. Her answer was defiant and curt.

He sat back on the floor, even more devastated.

"I didn't think it possible," she said. "He always spent so much time with us. From the moment he got home from work, every waking hour was with us. But, I found out that he was seeing her before he would come home. He would get up extra early to go to work. I thought he just wanted to work overtime, to make money to build a better life for us, but he was just trying to put in his hours so he could go and see her before coming home. I never dreamed. I never dreamed..."

She sobbed.

"How did you find out?" he asked.

"Steve," she answered. "They worked together. It was a few weeks after he left that Steve, who saw my misery, wanted to try to ease my mind by at least letting me know what had happened. I was afraid there had been an accident. I was working with the police to see if they could find him. I was worrying myself sick. Steve saw this and didn't want me to fret so.

"He decided I needed to know the truth. He came to me and told me all that he could. He said that he had become suspicious of my husband's behavior, weeks before he left. He had stopped eating lunch with the other men. They used to love to sit together and joke around. Your father could spin wonderful yarns. But, one day, he stopped joining the men for lunch, and was sorely missed.

"He would leave for long lunches before returning to work. He would also leave before others finished their work and head off alone. Steve grew suspicious, and one day followed him. He saw him head down the street, cross it, cut through an alley and then come to a house. Steve said he saw your father quickly dash up the porch and enter without even knocking.

"Steve thought this was extremely peculiar, so he walked over to the house and searched for a window that he could peer through. He felt terrible doing such a thing, but needed to know what was happening. It was a very hot summer day, and one window was open to let the breeze enter. He heard your father's voice – and the voice of a woman. He peeked in, trying to keep from being seen. He saw them in there. He didn't recognize her, but she had flaming red hair."

"Red hair?" the disillusioned son asked.

"Yes. Steve said he couldn't believe what was happening, but it didn't take long before he couldn't deny it. The two were definitely lovers. He couldn't stand it. He had to leave. He felt shocked and betrayed himself as he went home that night.

"He didn't speak to your father for several days. And, each time that man left for his long lunches, or an early day's end, Steve would look at him and anger would fill his breast. He couldn't believe what your father was doing to me and you. He was fully indignant. He didn't know how long he could hold it in.

"One day, while your father was off to one of his long lunches, Steve decided to confront him and put a stop to it. He waited for your father to return to work, but he didn't. When the normal time came and passed, he suspected something was up. He went to that – that person's house and arrived just in time to see your father put the last suitcase into a car, climb in, and speed off. He ran after the car, but it didn't stop. He – we – never saw him again."

"He just drove off?"

"Yes. Steve said he was – he was – smiling," she sobbed. "He broke my heart – he ruined my life – he tore apart my world – and, he was smiling. It just hurts so. Even today it hurts as I think of it."

Frank put his arms around his mother and held her for awhile.

"I don't know what I would have done without Steve," she said at last.

"Steve?"

"Yes, he was my greatest comfort," she said. "He even moved in next door, so that he could be near me. He saw after our every need. You may not have had a father, but he saw to it that you had a good, decent man in your life to teach you right from wrong and to help guide you by example."

"Yes, I've always looked to Steve as somewhat of a father to me."

She smiled and patted his hand and said, "Oh, that would please him so to hear that!"

"You never remarried, though." He had always puzzled over this, but had never dared to ask it until now.

"Oh, I couldn't! I could NEVER!" she said in a very serious tone. "I had what I believed to be the world's most glorious marriage. I was truly in love and I sincerely believe that I was loved back. To have the man that I respected and trusted so much just walk out on me without so much as a 'good bye'. Well, it just hurt so badly. I could never put myself into such a situation again. I believe it would truly kill me. I could never love another as I loved your father. I – I still love him so."

"You do?? After what he did?"

"Yes, I still love him deeply. I still miss him terribly. That is part of why I can't ever talk about him."

Frank thought that he could not be more stunned than he had already been. Upon hearing this, though, he discovered that he was wrong. A thick silence filled the room.

"I could never love another," she whispered.

Without looking up, Frank asked, "What about Steve?"

"Steve?" she smiled behind tear-streaked eyes. "Oh, he IS sweet. He truly helped me in my time of most dire need. He has been faithful and true for many, many years. A woman could not ask for a dearer friend. But – but, I've just never seen him in THAT way. He has always just been a terribly dear friend. Although, I suspect he wanted it to be more. Actually, I know he has. He's said as much, but – "

"But, what?" Frank pursued.

"But, I always let him know that I dearly appreciate his concern and care, but that I just don't feel THAT way towards him."

"And, what does he say to that?"

She smiled and patted his hand and said, "He usually says, 'Well, maybe you don't right now. But, someday you might'."

"Has he spent all of these years hovering by, hoping that you'd - you'd - fall in love with him?"

"Oh, no, no," she said. "Or, - maybe..." She smiled in a flattered way and would say no more about it.

Chapter 26
A New Neighbor

$\mathcal{L}$ouis arose with the dawn in his new home. He changed into one of the two spare sets of clothes the family had given him, shaved with a straight edge - particularly enjoying his new shaving cream - and stepped out the front door.

As he pulled the door shut behind him, a young couple strolling past saw him and lingered with a bit of an astonished look on their faces. Louis waved to them in a friendly way.

He walked to the end of "his" path and opened the gate. They were still there, so he gave them a warm, "Hello."

"Um, hello," the husband said. "Forgive us, we don't mean to stare. It's just that this house has been vacant for so long. We had no idea anyone had moved in."

"That must be why I got it for such a good price," Louis smiled as he extended his hand. "I'm Louis."

"Well, uh, I'm Tom," the man said, as he shook his hand slowly at first, and then more vigorous and warmly. "This is my wife, Brynn."

"Well, hello," Louis said, bowing his head slightly as he shook her hand. "It's a pleasure to meet you."

"Thank you," she blushed. "It's good to meet you, too."

"We live just over there," Tom said, pointing two houses down. "Welcome to the neighborhood!"

"Do you have any family?" Brynn asked.

"Thank you," he said to Tom. Turning to Brynn he replied, "I'm sorry, but I do not."

"Will you be moving your things in soon?" Tom asked. "We'd be happy to lend a hand."

"I'm afraid I'm still waiting for my belongings to catch up to me. Frankly, I'm worried that I've been 'taken', as I haven't been able to get in touch with the moving company I've used. I'm unable to reach them by phone, either. I'm afraid that at this point, I am resolved to believe that I can't expect to ever see my belongings again."

These statements were technically true. As with seemingly every other detail of his life, he had no memory of moving from Oklahoma to the west. He assumed someone must have assisted him in some way. He had absolutely no way of knowing who they were, or, what their telephone number was.

"You mean they've taken everything you own?" Brynn said with a shocked expression.

"Are you going to sue?" Tom asked.

"I doubt it," Louis said calmly. "It really wasn't much, and it's not worth becoming bitter over. Besides, I now have a good job at the rail yard. I'm just anxious to just put the past behind me and start over."

"I must say, I admire your spirit," Tom said with genuine admiration. "If there's anything you need, just ask."

"I sincerely appreciate that," Louis said, shaking his hand again. "I should be fine, though. Just fine. You must come and visit me – once I've settled in."

"Yes, certainly," Tom said. "We'd love to."

The couple continued on their way talking quickly to themselves in shocked amazement. What little Louis could glean from their tone, was all positive. He smiled and headed down the street toward his work. He began humming to himself again. It was the same old '40s tune that he had hummed the night before.

* * * * *

The kids were just buzzing all through breakfast, repeating "Grandpa was a hero!" and such. Frank tried to quiet them down, but they couldn't be quieted. They were too amazed, excited, and proud. Here a man they never knew existed was not just related to them, but was a hero. A HERO!

"I wonder if I should have said so much?" Grandma commented when the kids finally cleared their places and ran out the back door to play.

"It's only right that the kids know something of their grandfather," Joyce reassured her. "And, it's good for Frank to know, too."

Frank looked at his wife in surprise.

"I suppose you're right," Grandma conceded.

Frank looked at her now. Just then Luke burst in through the door, with Emma and Kenny at his heals.

"Hey, Grandma!" he exclaimed. "Can we bring the box down?"

"Bring it down?" she replied. "Oh, dear. Well, yes, I suppose it should be brought down."

Before they knew it, Emma and Luke were pulling down the ladder to the attic and clambering up it. Frank caught up with them. When he got to the top, he looked around.

"You know," Frank said, "I don't think I ever came up here."

"You weren't allowed!" Grandma said from behind. "I guess I was afraid you'd find the trunk."

"It's right here!" Luke said, slapping it.

Frank went over to it and opened the lid. He saw the uniform on top of the papers and such. Apprehensively, he picked up the army hat on top and examined it. He tossed it back down and closed the lid.

"We should take it down where it's cleaner and there's more light," he said. "Let's brush off some of this dust first, though. Then we can take it to the living room."

*****

"Well, you look mighty pleased with yourself," Charlie noticed with a smile.

"I guess I am," Louis said with a touch of pride.

"Why's that?"

"I just closed on a house."

"A HOUSE!" Charlie exclaimed, agape. He took a staggering step back and nearly lost his balance. "How in the world were you able to do that so quickly? What did you do for a down payment?"

"I've been working on getting the house for quite some time," Louis somewhat truthfully explained. "What homeless person hasn't wished for a home?" he asked himself. "It took my entire life's savings," he added a BIT more truthfully, but still very liberal with the truth. "I only have $10 left to my name."

"Well, that won't get you very far! How will you make it to payday?"

"Oh, I'll manage."

"Do you have electricity? Water? You know, have you turned on the utilities?"

"No. I'll manage."

"Like heck you will. You have to have electricity, man. What are you thinking?"

"I'm thinking I'll wait for payday."

"Well, then this is payday. Come with me."

Charlie took him into the office and wrote him a check. Louis looked at it in awe.

"This is far too much," he said, handing it back. "It's much more than we had agreed to."

"It's not for time earned," Charlie explained. "It's an advance for the whole first two weeks of the job. I figure you can use this now."

"But, I haven't earned it all yet!"

"You ain't plannin' on runnin' out on me 'fore the two weeks is up are ya?" Charlie asked, purposely using a thick, accusatory drawl.

"No, sir, I ain't," he said, imitating Charlie with an admiring smile.

"Well, then take it!" Charlie slapped his shoulder and smiled back.

Louis looked at the check again, holding it with both hands. He couldn't remember ever having a check before. Suddenly, a concerned look came across his face.

"What's the matter, Louis?" Charlie asked.

"I - I don't have a bank account," he said.

"Well, then get one!"

"I - I don't know how," Louis admitted sheepishly.

"You don't know how?"

"I don't think I've ever had one..."

"What?? How can you never have had a bank account?"

"I always worked for cash."

"But, how did you pay for your home?"

"Cash and credit."

"No, I mean your other home."

"I've never had a home before."

"This is your first home?"

"Yes."

"Then it's high time you step up and open up an account - and, I think you ought to do it this instant!"

"Now?"

"Yes, let's get started."

"Huh?"

"I'm taking you to the bank, and we're going to open up an account for you and cash that there check. And, after we cash the check, we should call the city to get the utilities hooked up. You can't live without power and water, man!"

As they headed out, Louis commented, "You know, for working here, I don't seem to spend much time here."

"It's OK," Charlie reassured him. "I'll just dock your next check."

They both had a good laugh.

* * * * *

The family at Grandma's house was busily going through the trunk, item by item. Grandma explained each and every piece. Frank was overwhelmed. He wasn't sure what to think. Pride? Anger? Longing? Desertion?

The kids all stayed intrigued and Grandma was very proud of each item. She commented on how she hadn't seen these things for some 30 years.

* * * * *

Louis rounded the corner to his new home. The first things that caught his eye were several cars parked along the sidewalk. His face flushed. His heart pounded heavily in his ears. Had he been found out?

He could barely swallow. He considered running, but decided that he was tired of running – if that was what he had been doing. He stood up straight and tall and walked toward his house.

He was shocked as he came up to the fence and could see that the yellow lawn had been mowed. The trash and debris had also been gathered and removed.

His face was still flushing and his heart pounding even harder as he neared his front gate. A uniformed man saw him and went to him before he could go through the gate. The man did not look pleased and asked if he was Louis Smythe.

"Yes, yes I am," Louis admitted.

"Good," the man replied gruffly. "I've been waiting overtime for you to arrive." He stuck a clipboard into Louis' chest. "Sign this!"

"What is it?" Louis asked.

"It's the authorization for power," the man said with exasperation.

Louis signed it, bewildered, looking toward the house and sensing there were many people inside. The man disappeared into one of the cars and drove off. Louis walked up the steps to the front porch and prepared to enter the building.

He opened the door with a trembling hand. Suddenly, he was overwhelmed by shouts of "SURPRISE!"

He stumbled backward and asked, "Who – who are all you people? What is this?"

Tom and Brynn, the couple he had met in the morning stepped forward, smiling, and handed him a pie.

"We're your new neighbors!" they announced.

"My new neighbors?"

Everyone laughed and nodded, then came up to him in pairs and introduced themselves. Each one dropped a welcoming gift at his feet: a bag of potatoes, canned goods, a rolling pin, dishes, milk, and so forth.

"Who?" he began with tears welling up in his eyes, "Who are all of you lovely people?" he asked again, overwhelmed.

"We're your neighbors!" Tom announced. "We just wanted to make you feel welcomed. Welcome to Oklahoma!"

"Three cheers for Louis!" someone shouted. Soon, walls resounded with the sound of "Hip-hip-hoorays."

"But, I don't understand," Louis said. "I don't know any of you."

"You do now!" someone shouted, "And, you really ought to lock your back door!" They all laughed some more.

It was only then that Louis noticed that some of them were sitting on a couch and a couple others were on chairs.

"What – what is this?" he asked staggering up to the furniture.

"We heard of your loss and all chipped in," Tom announced. "It's mostly used stuff that we each needed to get rid of anyway," he added, trying to dismiss the gesture.

In one corner, stood a smartly-decorated Christmas Tree. Louis saw it and walked up to it slowly.

"A Christmas tree!" he said through misty eyes. "I don't believe I've EVER had a Christmas tree before. You people are just too much!" He reached out and delicately touched some of the ornaments and needles.

"Wait till you see the kitchen!" someone shouted.

"What?" and he wandered in, followed by a wake of eager faces.

He got to the entry way and saw a small, oval table with four chairs around it, a clock on the wall, a dish rack in the sink, and a tall, white refrigerator plugged in place.

Just then, the lights flicked on and the refrigerator began to whir. He was overcome and fell to his knees, sobbing into his hands. The uniformed man, who had slyly driven around the corner and then returned, poked his head in the kitchen door and announced, "Well, your power's on! Sorry for giving you a scare out there. Didn't want to spoil the surprise," he winked.

There was cheering at first, and then everyone was moved by Louis' emotions and got choked up. Husbands put their arms around their wives' shoulders, while the women tried to dry their eyes.

"This was a very good thing," one neighbor whispered to another. "Thanks for giving us a call and letting us be a part of this, Tom."

"There's more," Tom said, as he touched Louis on the shoulder.

"What?" Louis looked up through moist eyes. He was just noticing that the room was clean, really clean. His good neighbors had apparently scrubbed his house from top to bottom. Even the grime on the windows was gone. "What? MORE? What more?"

"Come upstairs," Tom requested.

The crowd parted and allowed him to make his way to the stairway. He saw a couple of pictures hung along the stairs. As he went along, he touched them gingerly.

"You can always swap these out with something else," a voice called up from behind him.

"No, I wouldn't change a thing. It's all too beautiful!" he said, looking around in amazement as he went.

They took him to the bedroom. He pushed the door open. There was a fine looking curtain in the window, a wooden dresser in one corner, and a bed made up with sheets, comforter, and overstuffed pillows, right where such a bed ought to be.

"A bed!" he said in a hushed voice. "A bed – for me!"

He went to it and pushed on the mattress and adjusted a pillow, proving to his senses that they were real.

"I don't know what to say!" as his knees gave way again and he sat down on the bed. "You people! You fine people! I don't even know you! You don't know me! Why would you do this?" Tears were streaming down his cheeks.

"We're just trying to be neighborly," a voice from the crowd said, thick with emotion.

"Think of us as Good Samaritans," another voice in the back announced.

"Good Samaritans??" Louis started at this.

"Yes, you know, from the Bible story."

"Yes, yes, I know! I've heard that story recently!"

"Well, you seemed in need, so we all pitched in."

"You wonderful, beautiful people! I don't know if I can ever repay you. You don't know what this means to me. What you've done for me! Thank you! Thank you! Thank you, so very much!"

There was a silence that was finally broken by someone in the hall shouting out, "Isn't it time for the food?"

Everyone laughed.

Louis asked what was going on.

"This is Oklahoma, sir!" someone said. "You can't get this many people together without having food!"

Soon, everyone was downstairs eating a steaming ham that had been brought over, with potatoes, vegetables, rolls and salad and other items, and having a grand time. Afterward, Louis wandered about, still finding new things in his house. Peering out a window, he could dimly make out several yard tools leaning against the shed.

He then went from one couple to another, formally introducing himself and asking for their names again. Everyone was impressed with him and his heartfelt gratitude. Someone broke into a rousing strain of, "We Wish You a Merry Christmas," and everyone spontaneously joined in.

Chapter 27
The Truth Unfolds

𝒯rank puttered around in the backyard. He appeared to be trying to adjust the Christmas lights, but a close observation would show that he was just puttering. Steve came out from his house with a bag of trash and headed for his trash cans. He couldn't help but see Frank, who seemed immersed in doing nothing of any significant consequence.

"Hello, Frank," he called out cheerily. Getting no reply, he repeated, "HELLO, Frank!"

"Huh? Oh, uh, hi, Uncle, uh, I mean Steve," he said distractedly.

"If you don't mind my saying so," Steve replied. "It looks like you have something on your mind. Or else you're trying to take down your Christmas lights a bit early."

"Huh?" Frank replied absently, and then noticed that he had just pulled a strip of lights from the side of the house and was balling them up. "Oh, uh, yeah, I guess I just have something on my mind."

"Oh?" Steve smiled, "I couldn't have guessed it. I don't want to pry, but if there's anything you want to talk about, I'd be happy to listen."

"No, no," Frank said, then changed his mind, "actually, there is." Steve deposited his bag of trash and gave Frank his full attention.

"My kids found this old trunk in my mother's attic," Frank explained.

"Yes, the kids told me about it yesterday," Steve confided.

"They did?" Frank asked in surprise. "What did they tell you about it?"

"Nothing much, really," Steve said. "Not much other than that it had some old WWII things in it. I assumed it was your father's. They asked about it, but I told them they should ask their grandmother about it."

"You – ? That's right. My mother said you knew my father."

"Certainly! I owe my life to him!"

"What?"

"Yes, he was a very brave man. A selfless leader. I was one of the men he saved. I assume your mother has told you the story now?"

"Yes, she did."

"She probably didn't tell you of all the times he shared his rations with us. How many times he went hungry, so that weaker or sick men could get just a little more."

"No, she didn't," Frank said, momentarily glancing sheepishly toward the house.

"That's probably because he never told her," he nodded to the kitchen window where Grandma was doing the dishes.

She saw them and smiled and waved. Steve and Frank waved back as innocently as if they had merely been talking about the weather.

"That was his way," Steve continued. "He never wanted attention. All that hero hoopla probably nearly killed him.

"He probably didn't tell her of all the times he risked his neck getting us to France, either. Even after twisting his ankle terribly, he insisted on taking point whenever we came to an open field, or a road that needed crossing. He wouldn't let any of us come across until he made sure it would be safe. We all owe our lives to him. He was a great man."

"Not totally great," Frank said bitterly.

"Oh, so she told you about the lady too, eh?"

"Yes. I can't believe it. It figures, though. I guess that hero hoopla didn't kill him, it must have gone to his head instead."

"I still can't believe it myself. When I saw him ride off with that blonde girl, I was shocked and hurt."

"Blonde? Mother said she was a redhead."

"What? Oh, yes! Well, when you get to be my age, you'll be mixing up your colors, too! Next time, it will be a gal with purple hair!" he laughed uncomfortably. "Yes," he continued, "your father did some great things, both great and terrible."

*****

Louis was already hard at work when Charlie showed up. Charlie saw him tossing old boards into a dumpster, hollered to him and called him over.

"Well, did they get the power on at your place yet?"

"Huh? Oh, yes, yes they did," Louis responded.

"I bet that was better than eating in the dark!"

"Yeah, uh –" Louis started to respond, but choked up.

"What's wrong, Louis?" Charlie asked.

It took a bit, but Louis explained to Charlie what had happened. Charlie listened to the entire tale without interrupting. He watched Louis' eyes as he spoke, admiring his new friend.

"Good Samaritans, eh?" Charlie said, impressed. "You've found yourself some powerfully good neighbors, Louis. Or, maybe you just bring out the best in people."

"Me? What do you mean?"

"I mean exactly what I said. You're a good man. I could tell the moment I laid eyes on you. There's a good spirit about you. You're honest. And hardworking. What did you do before you came out here, anyway? You never have told me."

"Nothing," Louis confessed.

"Nothing? So you were retired, eh?"

"No, I didn't do anything," Louis said.

"What do you mean you didn't do anything?"

"I was a shopping cart man, OK? I didn't do anything but live off the street and bum money off of people!" Louis said with bitter honesty.

"What? I find that hard to believe."

"So do I, now," Louis added. "It's as if I was living in a fog. Nothing seemed real. Nothing was right. But, ever since I came back here, that fog has started to lift. I'm starting to see clearly, but I'm not sure what it is I'm seeing."

"Maybe you're finally seeing the good in yourself."

"Maybe, but I sense there's something more," Louis inadvertently fingered the ring on his finger.

Charlie noticed too, and added, "Maybe you still need to learn that ring's story."

* * * * *

"Pass the sandwiches, Emma, please," Luke said, reaching hungrily for the plate that sat to Emma's left.

"I can't believe it's almost CHRISTMAS," Emma exclaimed as she handed the plate to Luke.

"Yeah I know, I can't WAIT," he said, as he grabbed a ham sandwich and passed the plate to Kenny, who did the same before passing the plate along.

"Wouldn't it be fun to have Sam over for Christmas?" Emma suggested. "He's practically like FAMILY. We could even get him presents."

"If not Christmas," Luke added enthusiastically, "how about for Christmas Eve? We could at least have him over for dinner, couldn't we?"

Everyone agreed that it was a splendid idea.

Kenny tugged at Luke's sleeve and then held up his hands questioningly.

"Oh, you're right, Kenny," Luke acknowledged, "we don't even know where he is."

The room was filled with disappointed sighs and "if only's."

"Wait a moment," Joyce said. "Didn't he say he got a job somewhere?"

"That's right!" Frank agreed, "But, where was it again?"

No one could think of it. The revelations about their grandfather seemed to have blocked out other issues. They made a few guesses, but none seemed right. Kenny started playing with his knife and fork, placing them end to end and then moving them across the tablecloth, blowing as he did so. No one paid him any mind, so he had them travel over Luke's plate.

At first, Luke was annoyed, but when Kenny tapped him, pointed and repeated the motions, Luke said, "Hey, I think Kenny's trying to tell us something."

Kenny nodded and continued while everyone watched.

"Oh, yeah!" Luke said, "TRAINS! He's working with trains!"

"What?" Joyce asked.

He repeated it and Frank said, "That's right, he said he was working at the rail yard! Good job Kenny!" Kenny smiled, then took a big bite from his sandwich.

"Can we go look for him after lunch?" Emma asked.

"I see no reason not to," both parents agreed.

* * * * *

Upon hearing a knock, Charlie opened his office door and met a family of five.

"My sakes!" he exclaimed. "What can I do for all of you?"

"We're looking for a man who said he got hired on here recently," Frank explained.

"You mean Louis?" Charlie asked.

"Louis?" Joyce asked. "That's right, that's right. He told us that was his real name. Did he start here recently?"

"Yes, just this week," Charlie said. "He's a mighty fine worker, too. Say, you wouldn't be the family he told me about would you? The Good Samaritans?"

Frank and Joyce blushed.

"That's us!" Emma admitted, with cheery pride.

Charlie held out his hand to Frank, "I ain't never shook the hand of a Good Samaritan before! I'm mighty glad you brought Louis my way. He's just the man I needed, and is already a good friend, too."

"That sounds like our Louis," Joyce smiled. "We're so glad he found a good man like you who would hire him."

"I'm the lucky one!" Charlie said.

As the adults talked, Kenny grew distracted by all of the pictures on the wall. They were so abundant that many of the frames touched. It was like a mural of history dating back decades. Several types of trains were pictured. Most of the pictures were old. To Kenny, they were ancient. They were black and white photos tucked behind the glass of old wooden frames. Many of the photos were of engines with the engineer and his crew standing proudly beside them.

Boxes, stacks of papers, and even file cabinets blocked many of the pictures. Kenny was so engrossed with the photos, that he grew bold enough to move a box that sat on top of a short file cabinet in the corner. The box was mostly empty and was sitting on stacks of papers that nearly fell off the cabinet when Kenny lifted the box. When he set the box down on top of a pile of magazines on a chair in the corner, a cloud of dust billowed up and then trickled down to the floor.

He had been looking at the newly revealed photos when his eye caught hold of something that drew his attention to it. One of the faces peering back from the wall seemed somehow familiar. When he realized why, he grew very excited and began tugging on Luke's sleeve.

Luke saw that Kenny was pointing at a photo of the very building in which they were now standing. They could clearly make out "Bartlesville, OK" above the door. Standing in front of the door were three men wearing overalls and flannel shirts. Each had on a hat. The guy on the far right was the only one smiling. He was the one that Kenny was pointing to.

"What is it, Kenny?" Luke asked his brother. "What do you see?"

Kenny simply pointed more emphatically and Luke looked at him and then back at the photo. He leaned in close to get a better view. Suddenly, he jerked his head in surprise and turned to Kenny.

"Hey! I think you're right, Kenny!" Turning to his family he said, "Hey! Come and see what Kenny's found! He's found Sam!"

"What?" Frank asked with surprise. "What do you mean he's found Sam?"

"He's here in this picture!" Luke said, pointing enthusiastically.

The family hurried over to the corner, followed by Charlie. Soon, they were all bending over the cabinet trying to get a good look. Charlie reached out and pulled it from the wall. The area of wall where it had hung was decidedly darker than the surrounding wall, attesting to how long it had remained unmoved.

"Well, I'll be!" Charlie exclaimed. "Would you look at that?"

"It sure looks like him," Frank agreed.

"My goodness," Joyce said, "do you think it's really him?"

"Look at the eyes," Emma pointed, "you can see it in his eyes. That's him all right."

"Sure enough!" Charlie confirmed. "That's Louis all right!"

"Way to go, Kenny!" Luke said, giving his brother a punch on the shoulder. Kenny beamed.

"I'll have to show this to Louis when he gets back up here. He'll get a real kick out of it," Charlie smiled. "He should be down by the tracks. I asked him to clear out an old shed down there. You go on, just watch your step.

There's still plenty of junk around to trip on. This old rail yard has seen much better days."

The family headed out to find Louis. They saw him in the distance, stooping, with his back turned to them. He was trying to lift something heavy.

"Louis! Louis!" the family all called out his name.

He heard unexpected, but familiar voices, and was startled. He turned to see who had come. As he turned, the sky went black. Wind and rain forced themselves brutally upon him. He could see a malicious group of men with rain-drenched, wilted, wide-brimmed hats gathering around him. One called him by name. They all looked menacing.

Lightning flashed eerily and the thunderclap drowned out their leader's final shout of "Louis!" The man looked familiar and even in the midst of the turmoil, Louis tried to place the man's face.

The familiar man stepped forward and demanded, "Where is it, Louis? What'd you go and do that for?"

"It wasn't yours!" Louis responded defiantly. "You've no right." Even as he shouted these words, the present-day Louis wondered what they were after.

"No, YOU'VE no right," the ringleader retorted.

The men gathered closely around him and grabbed his arms. He struggled and saw one man raise a metal pipe high above him, ready to crash it down on him. As the arm came swinging down, there was a blinding flash of light.

Louis found himself standing awkwardly in the daylight. He saw a group of people coming toward him, calling his name, "Louis, are you all right?" a male voice asked.

"What? Yes, who's there?" he said, rattled.

"It's us," Joyce said.

"Your Good Samaritans!" Emma added with a sorrowful look of concern.

Louis shook his head and was finally able to see clearly.

"Why it is! My Good Samaritans! How blessed it is to see you again!"

He opened his arms and hugged Emma as she rushed up to him. He hugged Joyce as well. Frank reached out his hand, but Louis gave him a hug instead. His eyes were filling with tears as he embraced Luke and Kenny.

"I can't tell you how absolutely thankful I am for what you've done for me!" he proclaimed. "You've changed my life. No, you've given me back my life! Thank you, THANK YOU!"

Charlie had been watching from the office. He wiped a tear from his eye as he puffed at his pipe. As he turned to go back inside, he mumbled, "Good people..."

"Louis," Frank said, "tomorrow is Christmas Eve. Would you be willing to come for dinner and celebrate with us?"

"Your home, for dinner?" Louis asked. "No, I couldn't possibly."

The family was shocked and devastated.

"But, why not?" Emma said, on the verge of tears.

"Because I'll be busy," he replied.

"Busy?" Luke asked. "How can you be busy on Christmas Eve?"

"I'll be busy feeding YOU all Christmas Eve dinner at MY home!" Louis announced.

"YOUR home?!" the family all said at once.

"Yes, MY home!" Louis said, with a broad smile. "And, I insist that you must all come see it."

"We wouldn't miss it," Frank said. "But, how is this possible? How does a man off the streets suddenly become a home owner in a week's time?"

"Good Samaritans!" Louis smiled with his arms open widely.

"Well, where is this Good Samaritan home?" Joyce asked.

"The corner of Locust and Arbor, just like I told you!"

"Locust and Arbor??" Frank repeated, "This is incredible!"

"Isn't it though?" Louis replied. "If you come around 6:30, I should have a wonderful Christmas Eve feast waiting for you!"

"We'll be there!"

"Oh, and be sure to bring your grandmother," Louis requested. "I have to meet the mother of such a wonderful family!"

Chapter 28
Dinner With Louis

"This is all so extraordinary," Grandma said, sitting in the front seat next to Frank. Joyce and Emma were in the second seat. The boys were in the back, getting their cards ready for a few tricks along the way. "You befriend some homeless man and now he owns a house? Is he some sort of con artist?"

"No, no, no," Frank laughed. "You'll see. He's a wonderful man. I don't know how he did it, but I'm very happy for him."

"You'll like him at once," Joyce added.

"Well, we'll see about that," Grandmother added apprehensively. "He did mention it was all right for you to bring me along, now didn't he? You know that I'm not one of his 'Good Samaritans' like all of you seem to be."

"Yes, Grandma," Emma shouted, "he especially wanted to meet you because you're the mother of the Good Samaritans!"

"My goodness!" Grandma replied.

As they neared the location, Grandma seemed to grow uncomfortable and mumbled something that no one understood.

"What is it, Mother?" Frank asked. "Are you feeling all right?"

"It's just that - just that I haven't been in this part of town for many years," she said.

"You haven't been in this part of town??" her son asked, doubting this news. "But, it's not that big a town. How could you not have been here?"

"I've just sort of avoided it," she said flatly.

"Avoided it?! Why, is it dangerous?" Joyce asked.

"No, I just don't like it," she said, and would say no more.

As they drove down Locust Avenue, Grandma became even more agitated. She kept repeating "Oh my," over and over.

"What is it, Mother?" her son asked again.

"I used to live on this street," she said at last.

"You used to live here? When?" he asked in surprise. "When you were a girl?"

"No, when you were born," she replied succinctly.

Frank almost screeched to a halt, "What? I thought you've only lived in one home - the only home I've ever known."

"No," she corrected, "no, we didn't move there until you were about four. I moved there shortly after 'he' left me. I couldn't bear to stay in that house any longer. Too many memories."

"And, that's why you've not been back?" Joyce asked.

"Yes."

"Well, I'm sure a lot has changed in 30 years," Frank said, as he continued down the road.

"Yes, I'm sure it has – at least on the outside."

They pulled up to the house and Grandma was completely beside herself.

"Why – why, this is the very house!" she gasped. "The very house!"

"What house?" Joyce asked.

"The house I used to live in!" she replied looking down as if shielding her eyes from haunting memories.

"What?" Frank asked. "How could it be? Surely you're mistaken. You've already said you haven't been back here for thirty years."

"It is. It IS, I tell you!" Grandma insisted.

"Well, we're here," Frank said, seeing no other alternative and hoping to quell his mother's anguished feelings. "Let's go meet our host."

"Sure could use a paint job," Luke observed. "And some water on what's left of that lawn. But, hey, it looks like it's been cut recently."

They piled out of the car. Louis heard a knock on the door and opened it. The first one inside was Emma who "oohed" and "ahhed" at his home. She was followed by the two boys and their mother, who thanked him for having them over. Joyce looked around curiously.

"Where's your husband, and his mother?" Louis asked, standing, holding the door open.

"He's helping her up the steps," Joyce replied.

"Oh, sorry for the darkness," he apologized. "I haven't had a chance to replace the porch light yet."

"Hey, where'd you get all this stuff?" Luke asked.

Emma began pummeling him with questions, as well. Louis stepped away from the door to answer them. He stood in the living room responding to questions from the kids, especially Emma, about what he'd been doing and such. Frank helped his mother into the room.

Louis was turning to greet them when he was hit by the intense sensation of a bright, summer day. His beautiful wife was entering the front door. He saw her face clearly for the first time. His heart throbbed in his chest. With shocked pleasure he cried out a name he hadn't remembered in thirty years.

"Grace?! Is that you?" he asked with anticipation.

The old grandmother looked in the room and saw the man standing there. She had heard him call her name and looked at him. She paused and squinted, looking at his face carefully.

"Louis?!" she asked. "Louis? Is that you?"

Still seeing the young beauty, Louis replied, "Yes, my love, it's me!" and he held out his arms, while the family stood flabbergasted.

She stumbled toward him, repeating her questions. She stood right before him looking up, "Louis? It IS you!" she said at last.

Louis' view of the room suddenly twisted. It was that terrible night by the tracks. The pipe came down and landed him a powerful blow on the head. He heard a sinister voice say, "He'd never tell US, now he won't tell ANYONE!"

At this moment, Grandma reached out her tiny right hand, as if to embrace the man. The family was shocked to see her raise her hand and let it fly at the man's face. She landed what for her was a powerful slap.

In spite of all the good she had heard of this stranger, the shock of seeing her faithless husband was just too much. Three decades of anger, hurt and betrayal unleashed itself in that one slap. It was at that very moment that Louis saw – and felt – the pipe hit him. He tumbled to the floor, unconscious.

"MOTHER!" both parents shouted. "What have you done?!"

She was trembling, standing over his crumpled body. "Something I've wanted to do for three decades."

Louis didn't move.

"I – I didn't think I hit him THAT hard, though!" Grandma said, looking at her hand.

Frank ran forward and crouched over him. "He's out cold!"

Louis' flashback continued. All was black. He was completely blind. But, he was still aware of his surroundings. He felt strong arms grabbing at him. He felt them jostle him. He felt another terrible blow on the head from the pipe and his body jerked, then lay motionless.

He heard someone shout, "You've killed him!"

He felt hands pull at his fingers. He felt his rings begin to slide – his high school ring and his wedding ring – until they slipped from his fingers. He heard someone shout "Gimme that!" followed by the sound of the larger ring tumbling on rocks. He heard an angry voice shout, "Where'd it go? Ah! You've lost it, you fool!"

"At least I got this one!" another voice declared, and he knew it had to be his wedding ring.

He heard a railcar's door slide open. He felt the door slide and then slam closed. He heard muffled voices shouting many things.

He felt a sudden jostling as the train began to move. He tried to rise, but was in too much pain. He could feel the warmth of his own blood trickling down his back. He fell back and collapsed for countless hours as the train rolled on.

*****

The family was gathered in the hospital waiting room – waiting. They were each very anxious. Grandma was sobbing. Joyce sat beside her trying to console her. Frank paced and occasionally bent down to tell his mother that it wasn't her fault. The kids were silent and sullen.

"You know," Frank bent over and whispered to his wife, "we really ought to call Steve to see if he can help."

"I agree," Joyce said. "Maybe his presence will help calm your mother."

"Mom, uh, Mother," Frank asked cautiously, "can you tell me Steve's number?"

Getting no reply, he repeated his question. His mother finally looked up with a blank stare. He repeated it again. She at least heard the question this time, but it seemed like too much information for her to process.

"I can't remember it," she lamented. "Maybe I have it here in my purse." She began fumbling through her purse pulling out pens, papers, coupons, a brush, lipstick, and such. She stopped her pursuit suddenly and declared, "Oh! I know his number perfectly well. It's 555-9640. No, wait! I mean 555-9460!"

"Are you certain?" Frank asked.

"Yes, I'm certain," she said with confidence. "I know I am. 9460."

Frank walked to a phone. He pulled out a dime from his pocket, slid it in the slot, and dialed the number. Steve answered. Frank was a bit flustered and explained everything much too quickly.

"Steve, Steve!" Frank replied. "We're in the hospital. Mom found my Dad. But, he's out cold. We don't know why. He just went down. He's the guy we were Samaritans to. It's amazing. I'm so confused. Mom is a mess. Can you come here right away?"

"Wait, wait," the voice on the other end pled, "what's this you're saying, Frank? You found your father? What do you mean? Where was he? Where are you? What is all this?"

"I'm sorry, I'll slow down," Frank said. "We've found my father, Louis. It turns out that the man we gave a ride to, you know, that one Emma said we were Good Samaritans to? It turns out that HE was Louis, my father. When we went to his place for dinner tonight, and my mom saw him, she recognized him. Well, we no sooner came in, then he tumbled down. He just went down. He's been unconscious ever since. We're at Jane Phillips Hospital. Can you come? Mom's pretty upset."

"You've found Louis?" Steve asked, astounded. "Is he ALIVE, then? Is this really possible?"

"Yes, yes," Frank said. "He's alive, but unconscious. Something's happened to him. They've taken him into surgery. We're worried sick. Can you come down here, please?"

"What do you think has happened to him?" Steve asked.

"We don't know," Frank said. "We think it might have had something to do with the shock of seeing his wife so unexpectedly. Please, if you just come, we can explain it all once you get here."

"Yes, yes," Steve said, with a sense of urgency, "I'll come."

"Thanks," Frank said, "she's very distraught. Nearly inconsolable. Perhaps an old friend at her side will help her."

"Of course, of course," Steve assured him. "I'll leave right away."

Returning to his family, Frank reported that Steve should be there in a few minutes. Everyone was relieved. Even Grandma calmed down a little.

*****

The doctors deemed Louis' condition to be serious enough to require immediate surgery. He was whisked into the operating room. His body may have been on the operating table, but his mind was far away. The bitter flashback had not stopped. He continued to lie helpless on the floor of the railcar for days. It stopped occasionally for hours at a time, then rolled on ahead day and night. He knew he must have crossed several states. It dawned on him, that this was how he found himself so far west.

One day, the train stopped and the door to his car was opened. He heard angry voices shouting about a stowaway. They shouted for him to clear out, but he couldn't move. Two men climbed aboard to force him out. They noticed dried blood all over the floor of the car and commented on what a mess he looked. They took him by the shoulders and dragged him out of the car.

They continued to call to him, but he was still only partially conscious and unable to respond to their queries. He heard them ask someone what they should do with him. A commanding voice told them to take him down by the river and let him rest in the shade of the bushes, then laughed.

He was deposited very roughly on the riverbank, as had been prescribed.

Chapter 29
Old Friends

$\mathcal{F}$rank was still pacing as Steve came into the area. All eyes turned toward him. Frank rushed to him, thanking him for coming. He went right up to Grace, the grandmother, and asked if she was all right.

"Oh, Steve, it's so awful that he's hurt!" she lamented. "It's so hard to believe that it's Louis – after all these years – but, I'm certain of it. It's him! It just HAS to be him! Oh, my!"

"Has he said anything yet?" Steve asked.

"No, he hasn't," Frank replied. "We just showed up at his home and he collapsed. He's been unconscious ever since."

"That was all?" Steve asked.

"Well, not quite," Grandma conceded. "I hit him."

"You hit him?" Steve asked incredulously.

"Yes, then he fell," she said, and burst into tears again.

"You knocked him out with one blow?" he asked.

"Yes, she SLAPPED him," Frank emphasized. "But, this seems to be something more than just that. I don't know if it was the shock of seeing her, or something else. All we know is that he collapsed. I doubt it was her slap that did all this to him."

"I agree," a voice from behind them declared.

They turned and saw a doctor approaching, with his mask pulled down.

"It wasn't your blow, dear lady," the doctor said, "and it wasn't the shock of seeing you, either. Although those probably contributed."

"Then what was it?" Frank asked.

"Will Sam, I mean Louis, be all right?" Emma asked urgently.

"I don't know yet," the doctor told Emma. Turning to Grace he added, "It was a massive blow to his head that has caused the problem."

"A massive blow to the head, but when? What – ?" Frank asked.

"As far as I can tell, it happened many, many years ago. It's a wonder he's lived this long at all," the doctor revealed.

"But, what do you mean?" Joyce asked.

"Did you know he had a metal plate in his head?" he asked Grace.

"Yes, it was put in by the Germans," she replied. "When they captured him during the war."

"My goodness, that long ago," the doctor commented. "Well, we found a large dent in the plate, it must be at least half an inch deep. It is a perfect groove as if he was hit with something round and hard, like a metal pipe or some such. But, the skin has long since healed. This had to have been many years ago."

The family was aghast.

"It's a wonder he is sane at all," the doctor commented. "I can only imagine the pain it must have caused. How is his memory?"

Frank sat down, nodding his head comprehendingly. The doctor had to repeat his question.

"Actually, it's not good at all," Frank said at last. "He remembers almost nothing of his past. He also said that he has been suffering from some very violent dreams lately."

Steve looked at Frank and furrowed his brow.

"He said they seemed so real. They really disturbed him," Frank said. "They seemed pretty intense."

"What sorts of dreams?" Steve questioned with great curiosity. "Did he see anyone in them?"

"Yes and no," Frank continued. "They were like flashes. They would always be on a dark, rainy night. He'd see flashes of faces, but couldn't make them out."

"That was it?" Steve asked.

"He also said something about trains in them," Frank added.

"Trains?"

"Yes, trains."

"He works in the rail yard!" Emma piped up.

"Louis seemed to think the dreams were pieces of his memory coming back," Frank added.

"How upsetting," Steve frowned.

"Well, we've managed to remove the plate," the doctor announced.

"Removed it?" Joyce cried out. "But, what – ?"

"And, we've replaced it with more modern material," the doctor reassured her. "He should be good as new. Actually, he should be better. I suspect that the pressure on his brain, caused by that dent in the plate, wreaked havoc on his mind and memory. I believe that – gradually – he should be able to regain his memory and function as normally as possible."

"He'll be good as new?" Steve confirmed.

"Yes," the doctor replied, "although he's not out of the woods yet. He'll be touch and go for a few weeks. We had to remove nearly a third of his skull – or rather, the plate that had been his skull. He mustn't be moved for several days, just to be certain. It's nothing short of a miracle that he's lived so long this way. He must be a very special man."

"He is, doctor," Frank said. "He is."

*****

Louis' body lay in a hospital bed, bandaged and unconscious to the world, but his mind continued to leap through the flashbacks mingled with nightmares. He saw the entire ordeal from start to finish. He saw the faces of the men more clearly. He saw his friend's face in particular. His friend's face kept coming at him, over and over, brandishing a pipe, ready to swing it.

Having made sense of the flashbacks, his mind raced onward making leaps into Louis' deepest, darkest fears and worries. He saw glimpses of his home, his wife, his beloved son, being torn from him. He saw his friend swinging the pipe - his friend - striking his wife and child. He sat helpless, unable to stop it. He screamed and opened his eyes.

He was groggy and barely able to keep his eyes open. He saw lights, machines, and tubes. He saw the silhouette of a head approaching him. He couldn't make out the face, because of the bright lights behind it.

"Hello, Louis," he heard the shadow call his name. He recognized the voice. He tried to name the voice, but his lips could barely move.

"You shouldn't have come back here, Louis," the voice warned. "You should have stayed wherever you've been hiding all these years."

He could only make out what seemed like the shadow of an arm reach over to one of the tubes. Its hand reached for the tube and the fingers pinched it.

Louis felt a piercing pain shoot through his body. He was being deprived of something he realized he desperately needed, but didn't even know what it was. He couldn't cry out. He couldn't move. He couldn't even close his eyes. He was powerless to free his body from the pain.

He could see a flashback of the face again. The voice matched the face, and he suddenly realized who it was. The voice again taunted him.

The machines stopped their regular beeping and produced a long, shrill whine instead. He realized he was dying. He had come so close, and now he was dying. The voice told him goodbye.

Suddenly, the shadowy face was pushed aside. Lights were struck and moved erratically. The tubes were jerked and swung about. He could hear scuffling. He could make out the words, "What do you think you're doing?"

The pain subsided. The liquid was flowing. The machines returned to their steady beeping, although the pace was faster than before. Louis began to regain his senses, but remained groggy.

Two men grabbed the shadow and brought him to his feet. Louis could see the flashback face again, only it was older now, much older. It dawned on him that this was not the flashback. It was now the present, and the face he had seen in the flashbacks - and the yearbook - had aged.

He was barely able to move, but uttered two words, "Steve – why?"
All went black before he could hear an answer.

* * * * *

Louis opened his eyes. It was several days later. He had barely opened them, when he heard his name called out. He then heard shouts around the hospital room and out into the hallway.

"What?" is all he could manage to say.

He then saw a beautiful, aged woman step up to his bedside and lean over him with the most angelic smile he could ever recall seeing.

"Grace!" he said at last through parched lips. "My Grace! Is that you?"

"Yes, Louis," she said, smiling. "You've come back to me! You've come back to us all!"

Louis felt a powerful hand on his left arm and turned to look. The man who had picked him up at a gas station so far away and had driven him to his old hometown stood looking down at him.

"Welcome home, Father!" the man smiled. "I've missed you!"

Louis smiled and managed the word, "Home!" before he faded to sleep again.

Chapter - The Last
It Happened at Night

The family arrived at Louis' home, pulling up in their car. As Frank got out and walked around to help a still-bandaged Louis out of the car, one of the neighbors saw them.

A neighbor hurried over with a look of genuine concern. It was Tom. After two weeks of watching, he was relieved to finally see Louis returning home.

"Everyone has been praying for you," Tom said. "We hope you'll be all right."

"I'm surprised you even knew anything had happened," Louis said in amazement. "How did you know?"

"There had been an ambulance," Frank pointed out. "It created quite a stir in the neighborhood. I've never seen so many people show up so quickly and show so much concern for what I had thought was a stranger to them. But, I quickly learned that these 'strangers' had already taken quite a liking to you. You seem to have quite an impact on people."

Tom helped Frank get Louis up the walk and steps to the house. By the time they made it to the door, several others had already come by to wish him well. Once inside, Louis turned to wave thank you, but got dizzy, so Frank and Tom sat him down.

He rested for a bit before they helped him up to his bed.

* * * * *

Louis slept clear until the next evening, when he slowly awoke. As he slipped back into consciousness, memory of recent events drifted before his mind. He grew fearful that he was back in one of his flashbacks. He was particularly unnerved when he saw the same smiling lady he had been seeing, standing over him.

"Louis," she said. "Louis, are you all right, you sleepy man?"

"Grace?" he replied. "Grace, is that really you, or am I dreaming?"

"It's really me," she said soothingly. "You're back home again, with me."

She helped Louis sit up and called to her son, who came up.

"I'd like to go downstairs," Louis said.

"I don't know, Dad, it might be too soon," Frank said with concern.

"Why do you keep calling me that?" Louis asked Frank.

"Calling you what?" Frank asked.

"'Dad'," Louis said.

"Don't you know?" Frank said with a lump in his throat.

"Louis," Grace spoke up, "this is Frank. This is our boy, Frank. He's your son, Louis."

"Little Frankie?" Louis gasped. "Is it really you? Oh, SON! How I've missed you!"

Frank bent down and hugged Louis – hugged his father – for the first time in his memory. It was a long, tearful, heartwarming embrace. Grace's eyes streamed tears as well.

Finally, Frank stood up, cleared his throat a couple of times and then said, "Well, uh, – Dad – what were you saying about going downstairs? I think it just might be a little soon for that."

"I'll be fine – Son," Louis assured him. "I'd really like to go downstairs."

They helped him down the stairs and sat him on the couch. He ate a bowl of soup while sitting in the living room. The family sat around him staring and smiling. The kids remained quiet and attentive.

As he sipped, he suddenly remembered something and asked, "Say, shouldn't you all be heading out West again? Won't you be missed?"

"I was supposed to be there over three weeks ago," Frank said. "But, don't you worry. I called my boss and let him know what had happened. He told me to stay here for however long I'm needed. I'll be just fine, so long as you're fine. That's all that matters right now."

"By the way," Frank continued, "speaking of bosses, yours dropped this off."

He handed Louis a jar of homemade strawberry jam with a note attached. Louis read the note, "Louis, I'm terribly sorry about what's happened. Your son told me. I'm glad you found your son! I hope you like strawberry. This is my wife's favorite. Your job will hold until you're well. Take care and thank God for Good Samaritans!"

"I do! I do!" Louis said in response to the last comment on the note.

"How do you feel?" Joyce asked.

"Actually, I'm feeling very good. My mind is clear. The flashbacks have stopped."

"They have?" Frank interrupted.

"Yes," Louis said. "They started shortly after you picked me up. They're what I called 'dreams' when I told you about them. But now I see they were more some sort of flashbacks. They were growing more and more intense the longer I was here. None of them made much sense, until that day I collapsed. While I was unconscious, they all sort of wound together and told me my story. I now know who I am, and what happened to me."

"Can you tell us?" Frank asked.

"I believe I have to," Louis said. "I have to tell somebody. Who would it be better to tell than my dear family?"

"Years ago, I worked at the rail yard," Louis explained.

"The SAME rail yard?" Emma asked.

"Yes, the same rail yard I work at now," Louis confirmed. "Steve, a good friend of mine, also worked there."

Family members exchanged concerned looks at each other, but no one interrupted.

"One day, there was some big museum exhibit coming through town," Louis continued. "There was art and artifacts from some big dig somewhere. I don't remember where it was from. I wasn't really interested. Some of the stuff was real valuable, especially a large necklace made of pure gold."

"Gold?" Luke's eyes went wide.

"Yes, gold," Louis confirmed. "It was worth more than anyone could guess. Steve just went on and on about it. He was very interested. Well, it turned out the museum people needed extra hands to work security, especially at night. Steve found out about it and said we ought to sign up. I didn't want to. Sure, we could have used the money, but I didn't like spending my nights away from my family."

Grace was sitting next to Louis as he told his tale. Louis was holding her hand. He gave it a squeeze as he looked at her with love in his eyes.

"Steve was one to always want another dollar, so he went and signed up for night duty. He'd go down there about 9 every night to guard the exhibit and work until about three in the morning. Then, he'd come back to the rail yard and put in a day's work there. I don't know when he'd sleep. Maybe that was his undoing.

"It turned out that Steve had some unsavory friends. He got drunk with them over the weekend and told them about the exhibit, and his being a security guard for it. One thing led to another and they somehow convinced him to swipe that gold necklace.

"On the day of the heist, he got awful quiet. During lunch, I asked him what was up. He said it wasn't anything, but I could tell he was lying. I pestered him all day. He finally got mad and told me to leave him be.

"Well, he was my friend. I couldn't just leave him be. I stopped pestering him, but I decided I had to find out what was ailing him. I suspected he was in some sort of trouble. I didn't want to see my good friend get in trouble, so I followed him that night.

"Sure enough, he headed over to the museum, but didn't go in. Instead, he met a bunch of these bad characters he knew, around back. I hid myself in the bushes across the street and could see these guys were up to no good. I thought about running over and saying something - anything - to pull Steve away from them, but before I could make my mind up on what to say, Steve had unlocked the door and they all slipped inside like so many black cats.

"I stayed hidden and was just beside myself trying to think of what to do. If I ran for the cops, they might come out long before I got back. Besides, then Steve would be caught. I thought maybe somehow I could pull Steve aside after they came out, but realized that wasn't practical.

"Before I knew it, they were coming out with a big bag. I knew what was in it without even seeing. It had to be that big gold necklace. The one all the papers had written about. The one Steve kept telling me about.

"Well, they carried it out in this black bag and stuck it in their car. Steve was all ready to go, but some of the others got extra greedy and wanted to go back in for more.

"They got into an argument. They started beating each other and stuff. I saw my chance and snuck up and took the bag, right out through the open car window. I figured I could hide it until morning and then return it. If it showed up again, then I figured Steve wouldn't be in so much trouble.

"I was almost clean away when someone noticed the bag was missing. He stopped the others from fighting and they saw me heading through a fence. They were hot on my trail. I was near the rail yard, so I made my way there. I knew they'd catch up, so I had to think fast.

"I knew that if they caught me with the bag, they'd get it back and Steve would be in an awful fix. I decided to stash the ill-gotten booty. I knew the yard well, so I already had a good place in mind. I dumped it off and ran. I was hoping to get through to the other end of the yard, without getting caught, but I tripped on something. Don't know what, but it slowed me down. I was just getting ready to cross the tracks, when they came into the yard and saw me."

Louis now knew that his traitorous friend, Steve, had been the one wielding the pipe, intent on killing him. Something in his heart had told him to omit that detail in this telling. "Forgive the past and move on. Focus on the future," he thought. There had been enough pain and suffering already. Steve was in enough trouble now, as well. He didn't see value in heaping further accusations. He purposely kept his tale brief and general with regards to assigning blame.

"It started to rain and thunder something awful. They were as angry as hornets when they cornered me. They tried to get the bag back, but when they saw I didn't have it, I lied and said I'd dropped it. They roughed me up a bit, trying to get me to talk. They finally gave up the hope of getting it from me. That's when they were so mad they hit me with a pipe. They hit me so hard, my skull should have splintered. Thinking they'd killed me, they stashed me in an empty railcar, and let the rail company get rid of the evidence.

"I would have died, too, if it weren't for that metal plate the Krauts stuck in my head. By the time I woke up, I was clear out in Nevada. Worse still, I had no memory of anything. I didn't know who I was, where I was, how I got there, or anything. I just wandered around until you people found me there – and rescued me."

"Frank," Joyce said with a look of sudden realization.

"What?" Frank asked, concerned.

"Do you remember what that attendant at the service station said?" she asked.

"What attendant?" Frank asked.

"The one where we picked up Sam, I mean Louis, I mean – your father," she clarified.

"Yeah, well, he said a lot of things," Frank said. "Most of them made me feel uncomfortable."

"Yes, yes," Joyce said, "but what he said about Louis. He said he always came and sat down on the curb there every day."

"Yeah, that's right!" Frank remembered. "He said that he looked like he was 'waiting for someone' or something like that."

A chill went down several people's spines at this revelation.

"I wonder," Joyce said, turning to look at Louis, "I wonder if he was waiting for us to find him?"

"Huh!" Louis remarked. "It's funny, but that part of my memory is starting to get a bit fuzzy now. I really can't say. All I do know is I can recall feeling that it was somehow important to hang around that area."

"Maybe God was inspiring you!" Emma suggested.

"Maybe!" Louis smiled. "He certainly seems to have inspired you!"

"Hey!" Luke called out wide-eyed. Everyone turned to find out what he wanted. "All I want to know is – WHAT HAPPENED TO THE TREASURE??"

"Treasure? You mean the golden necklace?" Louis asked. "I don't know. It's either been found, or it's still there. It doesn't really matter. To me, my family – my long lost family – is my treasure."

"Oh, that's so sweet!" Joyce said as she wiped a tear from her eye.

"That's why I love him!" Grace beamed.

"Yeah, but, where is it?" Luke persisted.

"Do you remember where you put it?" Frank asked.

"Of course I do!" Louis announced. "In a safe place!"

"So, you know where the gold is?" Luke asked with great anticipation.

"Yes," Louis repeated. "Or, at least I know where I put it. Who knows if it's remained hidden after all these years?"

"Well, where is it?" Luke asked.

"There used to be a couple of tool sheds down at the rail yard," Louis explained. "One of them had a loose floor board. I ran over to it and stashed it under the board, then pulled some big box over the board. Say – come to think of it, that shed's not there anymore."

"It's NOT?" Luke was disappointed.

"No," Louis confirmed. "I've been working there, remember? I just realized that the shed I hid it in is gone. But, it's not like it was removed. It's more like it's all fallen over. There's just a heap where it was. I've been working my way towards it as I cleaned up the yard all this time. Huh! Imagine that! I've been working my way toward it without even realizing it. I'm sure it must still be there buried under a bunch of wood and such."

"Then we can go get it?" Luke asked, excited.

"It isn't mine," Louis pointed out. "It should go back to those whoever own it."

"But, there might be a reward!" Luke suggested.

"If there is," Louis noted, "it should probably be used to pay all those fine doctors and nurses who took such good care of me."

"Oh, and I thought this was going to be good," Luke said, as he dropped his chin to his palm.

"By the way," Frank asked, "tell me, just how did you come about owning this house?"

"This house?" Louis repeated with a smile. "Funny you should ask. I could tell it had been abandoned for years. I figured if no one bothered to do anything with it uninhabited for all those many years, then no one would bother doing anything with it once it got inhabited. I went and found me a 'Sold' sign, and planted it in the front yard, and let nature take its course."

"You just stuck the sign in the yard?" Joyce laughed.

"Yes, and before you could say 'Cock robin' I had people coming over to congratulate the new home owner!"

There was a tremendous deal of laughter. Louis added with sincerity, "What I didn't count on was how benevolent everyone would be. There are some mighty fine people living in this neighborhood! I'll dearly miss them when I have to leave."

"Who says you have to leave?" Grace asked.

"Well, eventually word is bound to get out," Louis said, "and I'll have to leave."

"Not if the rightful owner lets you stay," she responded. "And certainly not if the rightful owner moves in with you – that is, if you'll have her."

"If I'll have her?" Louis asked, "Who? You? How? You'd move in with me?"

"You're my husband, are you not?" she asked. "The last time I checked, I was still your wife!"

"But, you said the rightful owner," Frank said. "Are you - ? "

"I may have moved," she said, "but I never sold the house. I just couldn't bring myself to do it. Why do you think no one ever moved in?"

"You never sold the house?!" Frank exclaimed. "How on earth could you have afforded TWO houses?"

"Oh," Grace smiled. "We got this one for a song after the War. And, with the money from Louis' GI bill, it was nearly paid for. When Louis - uh, left - we moved into my mother's home."

"Your mother's home?" Frank questioned. "You mean...?"

"That's right," Grace confirmed. "You don't remember her, do you? When we moved in with her, you were only three. She died before you were four. I inherited the house from her. And, I never set foot back here again until that night you brought me.

"Steve moved in next door, not long after mother passed," she added. "He claimed he wanted to be nearby in case I needed a man around the house - what with Louis gone. What if he was merely keeping a lookout for Louis? I can only imagine! I could never keep living by that cad now. I can't believe what he's done. What he continued to do for all these years! It makes me shudder!"

"I guess it's safe to say there wasn't a redhead involved," Frank whispered.

"A what?" Louis asked.

"Nothing, nothing at all," Frank said. "Say, will you press charges against Steve?"

"I don't believe the Law gives you any choice on attempted murder," Louis said. "Either way, I'm not going to spend my days concerned with it. I figure he stole my family from me. He stole my life from me. That is something so precious that it can never be replaced. Not for all the gold in the world, and not by all the time served in prison. I figure I can either be bitter and spend the rest of my days angry, or I can move on. I want to put the past behind me, and enjoy what time I have left. If I have any chance of being a Good Samaritan - like everyone else around here seems to be - then perhaps my best chance is to drop any anger towards Steve and anyone else and just try to be happy with what I've got and spend my days loving my family."

Louis looked out the front window as the sun began to set. He saw his favorite new neighbor couple, Tom and Brynn, walking past his yard. He smiled and waved, and they did the same. He looked down and it seemed to him that the yellow lawn was taking on a shade of green.

"Hey, Dad," Luke said. "Can we give Sam, I mean Louis, I mean Grandpa, his Christmas presents?"

"Oh?" Frank smiled, "I don't see why not!"

"'Grandpa'?" Louis asked, turning back from the window.

"Yeah," Luke said, "you're our grandfather, so we want to call you 'Grandpa'."

"That's all right, isn't it?" Emma asked.

"That would be WONDERFUL! As long as it means I also get hugs!" he replied, leaning over with his arms opened widely.

Luke and Emma rushed to him and they embraced. Joyce quickly reminded them to "Be careful! He's still recovering!"

Kenny stood back a moment, then approached more cautiously. Luke and Emma were all smiles.

"Come on, Kenny," Luke coaxed, "give Grandpa a hug!"

Kenny walked up to the old man, held out his arms, and then gave him a warm embrace. Then, clearly enough for all to hear, he said, "Grandpa, I love you!"

Louis stayed where he was, with Kenny's arms wrapped around him, and patted Kenny on the shoulder. He was speechless. Grace gasped and put her hand to her heart. Luke did a double take. Frank just stared, as Emma's eyes went wide.

With tears of love and gratitude in her eyes, Joyce walked up to Louis, wrapped her arm around his and in a shaky, sweet voice said, "I guess you were right. Kenny WOULD finally say something – when it was important enough to be said."

"Well, FINALLY, all is as it should be!" Emma declared, with a satisfied smile.

"What? What was that you said?" Louis asked, turning toward her with a look of disbelief.

"I just said everything's finally all fixed," Emma said.

"No, you said, 'all is as it should be,'" he corrected.

"Yeah, well, that's what I meant by it," Emma said, looking a little concerned now.

"Oh, there's nothing wrong, Sweetheart," Louis consoled her, as he left Kenny and reached out for her. "It's just that that's what a little girl said to me in that first dream I had."

"You dreamed about me?" Emma asked.

"No, not you," Louis shook his head. "But, yet, maybe. It's hard to say. You did pick me up out of the gutter, so to speak. That's what this little girl was doing. You never know. It's quite a puzzlement, isn't it?"

"Puzzlement?" Grace asked with a start.

"Yes, it means it's a bit of a mystery," Louis explained.

"I realize that," Grace agreed. "But, don't you know where that word comes from?"

"Comes from?" Louis questioned. "It just came to me one morning on the trip."

"Yes, but, it comes from 'The King and I'," Grace explained. "That was the film you and I saw on our last anniversary together! We both loved it so much, we went back to see it two more times."

"Well, what do you know?" Louis replied. "Now, that IS a puzzlement!"

"It seems things really are as they should be," Joyce observed.

"*Silent night, holy night*," Emma started to sing. Her voice sounded angelic.

"*All is calm, all is bright*," Frank and Grace joined in.

One by one the family moved closer together until they were standing in a circle, holding hands.

"*Round yon Virgin, Mother and Child*," Luke blended his voice with the others as they gathered around Louis and Joyce.

"*Holy infant so tender and mild*," Joyce and Louis smiled as they added to the harmony. Louis reached out and put his arm around Grace. The others all held hands in a blissful circle of unity.

"*Sleep in heavenly peace*," The family all smiled broadly as Kenny contributed his voice to the family's favorite Christmas carol for the first time in far too long.

"*Sleep in heavenly peace.*"

True, it was no longer Christmas, but it certainly felt like it.

The End